OLD SCHOOL TIES

By Daisy Waugh

The Todes of Tode Hall:

In the Crypt with a Candlestick
Phone for the Fish Knives
Old School Ties

The Desperate Diary of a Country Housewife
Last Dance with Valentino
Melting the Snow on Hester Street
Honeyville

WRITTEN UNDER E.V. HARTE:

The Prime of Ms Dolly Greene
The Case of the Fool

DAISY WAUGH

OLD SCHOOL TIES

PIATKUS

PIATKUS

First published in Great Britain in 2023 by Piatkus

1 3 5 7 9 10 8 6 4 2

A CIP catalogue record for this book
is available from the British Library.

ISBN 978-0-349-43117-8

Typeset in Galliard by M Rules
Printed and bound in Great Britain by
Clays Ltd, Elcograf S.p.A.

Papers used by Piatkus are from well-managed forests
and other responsible sources.

MIX
Supporting
responsible forestry
FSC® C104740

Piatkus
An imprint of
Little, Brown Book Group
Carmelite House
50 Victoria Embankment
London EC4Y 0DZ

An Hachette UK Company
www.hachette.co.uk

www.littlebrown.co.uk

For Peter

with my love

Alium Dime in Jukebox Pone

THE
TODE FAMILY TREE

Sir Ecgbert (10th Baronet) & Lady Tode (Geraldine)
1900–1943   1907–1971

Albert Tode   m.   Mrs Tode (Daphne)
1928–1985   1938–1997

Sir Ecgbert   m.   Lady Tode (Emma)
(11th Baronet)   1946–2018
1926–2017

Egbert(Mr)   m.   Mrs Tode (India)
1984–   1985–

Mad Sir Ecgbert m. Lady Tode (Alice)   Nicola (She/Her)   Esmé
(12th Baronet)   1967–   1970–   1973–
1967–

m.   Mrs Tode
(Chelsea-Reine)
Div. 2022

Piper Tode   Kyle Tode   Ludo Tode   Passion Tode
2010–   2013–   2014–   2015–

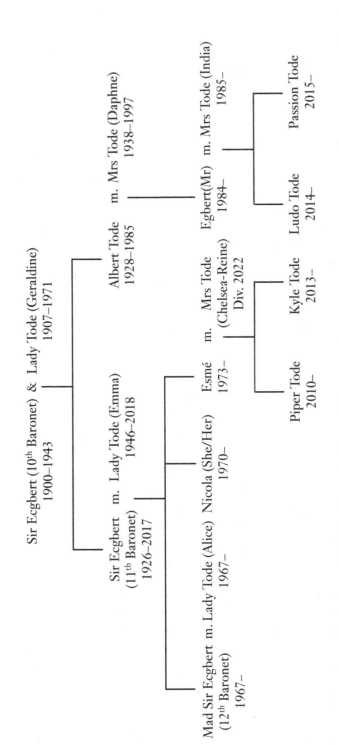

AUTHOR'S NOTE ON THE GARDENS OF NINFA
AND THE FICTIONAL GARDENS AT ROSPO NEL BUCO

The gardens at Rospo are geographically and historically based on the Gardens of Ninfa in Lazio, Italy, which are magical, open to the public and easily reached from Rome. I highly recommend a visit.

Built around clear-water springs and the ruins of an ancient city, the city of Ninfa was sacked in 1369 and never quite recovered. At the turn of the twentieth century, Ninfa was transformed into a pleasure garden by English aristocrats. Gardeners working there today still occasionally dig up human bones.

Leonardo da Vinci, of many talents, was sent to the crumbling city of Ninfa by the Duke of Milan to do something about the drainage. It was one of the many tasks he never saw through to the end.

I should add that although the gardens at Rospo are very much inspired by the Gardens of Ninfa, all the characters in my novel and the events that take place are, of course, a product of my imagination.

OLD SCHOOL TIES

TODE HALL

YORKSHIRE
ENGLAND

A NICE DAY IN OCTOBER

INDIA TODE'S BEDROOM

8.41 A.M.

'Well, I must say, Munchie – one thing I will say. We're jolly lucky with the weather. *What a day!*' Egbert Tode(Mr), handsome, fit and dressed for sport, gazed in gratitude and wonder over the landscaped parklands of Tode Hall, recently voted 'Britain's Eleventh Most Interesting Stately Home' by the Chinese travel website Wanakhe Zen-Hao! (spelt here phonetically). Egbert's beautiful wife, India, was sitting up in bed, drinking coffee, and Egbert spoke to her from their adjoining dressing room. His was very much the sort of voice that carried.

'Amazing for October,' she replied.

Egbert confirmed this.

'A perfect autumn day,' added India.

'A perfectly perfect autumn day! Crisp and bright. Amazing stuff! We really are lucky. Don't you think, Munch?'

'It could almost be Italy,' India declared obligingly.

'Yet here we are, in boring old "rainy" Yorkshire ... Lucky us!'

A similar conversation took place between Egbert(Mr) and his wife every morning that it wasn't raining: so at least one morning a week in the summer. Egbert was conscious that life in a massive house in the middle of boring old Yorkshire could be dull for a vivacious woman like India. She was the sort of girl who liked parties and suntans, and Tode Hall, though grand and very spacious, offered neither. With its three restaurants, two cafes, two tourist shops, its twenty-five holiday cottages and forty-six other cottages, its 15,000 acres of fertile farmland, its grouse shoot, pheasant shoot, its archery school, its slowly dilapidating Grade-1-listed mausoleum, its twelve reception rooms (not counting the Great Hall or the Long Gallery) and twenty-seven bedrooms, its pottery arcade, its 'Keep off the Grass' signs, its burglar alarm systems, its 138 pasty-faced estate staff – not to mention its recent influx of tourists from the Orient . . . life as the mistress of Tode Hall offered money and status. And politeness and duty. Egbert(Mr) worried his wife was bored.

She was, a little, too – despite the occasional dramas: two unrelated murders since she and her husband took up residence four years ago; and yet another murder only four months back, which was still to be solved – '*If,*' as Egbert(Mr) like to remind India, or anyone else who was listening, '*if,* indeed, it actually *was* murder.'

Which it was, by the way. Even *if* there was still no evidence to prove it. No obvious bruises. Not a trace of chemicals in the body. Nothing. Egbert(Mr) was relieved that the June murder, though it had taken place on important Tode property, did not, at least, take place at Tode Hall – or even in Yorkshire. The victim's body was found in the famous garden of the Villa Rospo at Rospo nel Buco, about a half-hour south of Rome (added to the Tode portfolio, via marriage, in 1906), and its discovery had wrecked everyone's holiday. They'd all had to pack up and come home.

But Egbert(Mr) worried too much. Yes, his wife was a little bored, hidden away in boring old rainy Yorkshire. For example – last week – she'd been obliged to host a tea party in the Yellow Drawing Room for seventeen road safety compliance officers from Yorks-Central County Council, to thank them for not obstructing a project involving the Todeister by-pass, and a small turning which would better facilitate coach access to the Hall via the East drive . . . *Wow*, that was boring.

On the other hand, four and a half years ago she and her husband had been living a fairly ordinary, upper-middle-class life in a terraced house in Wandsworth, London.

The Surprise Elevation – the call from Egbert(Mr)'s recently widowed aunt to take over the reins at Tode Hall – had not been 100 per cent quarrel-free. For example, there had been a murder. But luckily that was now in the past. Today, on the whole, with one or two exceptions, people seemed to accept the situation for what it was. Egbert(Mr), who was a decent man and did a good job running Hall and estate, never stopped thanking his lucky stars.

India might well have preferred a more urban existence. But she understood that in life, even in a life as blessed as her own, there needed to be trade-offs . . . and what with the ponies, rowing boats, mausoleums, attics, outhouses, etc., there could be no better playground for her and Egbert to raise their young children, Ludo (8) and Passion (7). Also (not that she'd ever been poor), she was *very* rich nowadays. With so much money and hired help on tap, suntans and parties were never terribly difficult to come by.

5

In the meantime, the weekend ahead offered potential for some intrigue, at least. Four months after the unsolved murder in the gardens at Rospo nel Buco there was to be a weekend house party: a party that Egbert(Mr)'s older cousin, Ecgbert(Sir), insisted on referring to as 'the Reunion of the Suspects'.

Staying at the Hall this morning and already making their way towards breakfast, was every one of the guests who had been present when the murdered body was discovered floating in the cool, clear waters of the Rospo on that fateful night in June.

Egbert(Mr)'s mind turned from the beauties of the morning to the duties of the day ahead, and for a moment his pleasure dimmed. There was a pheasant shoot scheduled, starting later in the morning than Egbert(Mr) thought appropriate, but there was nothing he could do. Control of this particular weekend house party had slipped from his grasp more or less since its inception – or before then, even, since he'd never wanted the weekend to happen in the first place. He blamed his cousin Esmé.

He left the dressing room and wandered across to the end of his wife's bed. A luxurious, modern divan: it was the only modern piece of furniture in the house. When they moved to Tode Hall India had insisted, amid much local-expert tutting, on dismantling the monumental eighteenth-century four-poster which had stood in the room since rain first fell in Yorkshire, and replacing it with her own bed from Wandsworth.

She lay on it now, propped up by pillows, sipping coffee delivered to the bedroom door by Mr Carfizzi, the butler, and by Egbert(Mr), the husband, from the door to the bed.

Egbert said: 'I'm still not sure quite how we got corralled into this ruddy weekend, Munchie. It's a bit ghoulish, isn't it? I'd much rather we just sort of *got on* with everything and forgot about the murder, like we normally do. It's going to be awfully tense.'

'Oh, come on, it'll be interesting!' replied India. 'Where's your sense of mystery, Eggzie?'

Egbert thought that was a silly question. He didn't reply.

'Alice says she thinks it was Piers who did it,' India continued. 'Alice doesn't like Piers *one bit*. Never has ... But that would be *too* obvious, wouldn't it? Seeing as Piers was married to her. And also shagging her sister—'

'We don't actually *know* that.'

'Oh my goodness, Eggzie, *yes we do!*'

'Not for sure. Also—'

'Anyway, personally, I think it was that creepy little kid with the funny name. There's definitely something weird about him.'

'Tippee,' said Egbert(Mr). 'Tippee Tysedale. Munchie, it's a bit much to go around accusing young children of murder, just because they've got funny names. It's not really on ...'

'You're telling me it's not really on,' India said. 'Anyway, *somebody* did it. We better hope it wasn't you-know-who ... She's got the track record, after all.'

'Nicola?'

'Your lovely cousin, Nicola Tode. Yep.'

'*Munchie!*'

'I don't know what they did to her in the Arizona Nut

House but whatever it was, it didn't work. I don't want to be horrid – but she's actually *more* bonkers than she was before she went in. Don't you think so?'

'Shhh!' Egbert(Mr) glanced at the door. 'Honestly, seriously, Munch. *Seriously* . . .'

'Maybe it wasn't her, anyway . . . It could've been any one of them, frankly,' India continued, unperturbed. 'That's the fun of it.' She stretched. It was time to get up. 'And I'm looking forward to getting to the bottom of it, even if you aren't.'

'Of course I'm looking forward, Munchie!'

'Even Alice is quite psyched, and she never gets psyched about anything. And Mad Ecgbert's been making *tons* of notes. It's going to be *fun*. For heaven's sake, Eggzie-Peggz, *live* a little! Stop worrying so much!'

Eggzie-Peggz(Mr) looked doubly forlorn. 'I don't mean to be a killjoy, Munch, I really don't. I'm just feeling a bit . . .' He was not well trained in putting words to his feelings. ' . . . It's not about the murder, Munch, honestly, it's . . . I suppose I just feel a bit *got at* . . . It just feels a bit like everyone wants a piece of one . . . Do you know what I mean?'

'Well,' replied India, who didn't really know what he meant, 'that's what happens when you have so many pieces.'

He didn't know what she meant by that. Neither did she. No one understood what anyone meant, and in any case, it was time to join the guests for breakfast.

Time to crack on. Egbert(Mr) wondered which of the guests he dreaded seeing most. His cousin Esmé, probably. Lately just the thought of Esmé made Egbert's heart sink.

Five years ago, shortly after the death of his father, the 11th Baronet Tode of Todeister – see The Tode Family Tree on page x, Esmé Tode had been asked by his mother, the 11th Baronet's widow, to abandon a successful life in Australia and take up the reins at Tode Hall. She wanted him to step in for his older brother, Mad Ecgbert(Sir), now the 12th Bart, who was assumed correctly by everyone not to be up to the job. Esmé had refused.

But how things can change! The bat/non-bat virus, whose name shall never darken these pages, had indirectly decimated a lot of things in Australia, among them Esmé's affection for the country, his thriving Sydney-based luxury gym business, and his marriage to the Australian former model, Chelsea-Reine. Esmé had returned to the UK just three months ago, leaving everything behind him, including two much-loved children. He was currently living alone in a borrowed flat in South Kensington, putting on a brave face and trying to rebuild his life.

Esmé was broke: or at any rate, broke for a Tode of Todeister. Since returning to England he had been sniffing around Tode Hall in a way that made his cousin Egbert(Mr) feel very edgy indeed. It wasn't that Egbert(Mr) didn't sympathise with Esmé's plight. There was no question Esmé had been hit with a run of extreme bad luck. *But even so* . . . somebody needed to make it clear to Esmé that as far as his inheritance was concerned, he really had, as Egbert(Mr) liked to put it when discussing the matter with his lawyers, '*missed the bus*'. As Egbert(Mr) often said to his lawyers, his wife, his biking friends: 'Obviously I want to do what I can for my dear coz. In the circumstances, one is duty-bound . . . But I mean – you know – *within reason* . . . '

The weekend house party had been organised on Esmé's insistence. He said it would be good to reunite the holiday guests so they could 'blow the cobwebs off the horrid Villa Rospo situation' altogether. This made no sense to anyone, except to his nonsensical older brother, Mad Ecgbert(Sir) 12th Bart, who for reasons unknown to himself, or to anyone else, had latched on to the idea and would not let it drop. Once the two brothers had joined forces – and between them persuaded India that the weekend might be fun – there wasn't much Egbert(Mr) could do to stop it.

And so here they were. Entertaining a houseful of possible murderers, yet again. Egbert(Mr) wasn't stupid. Esmé didn't give a damn about holiday cobwebs at Villa Rospo or anywhere else. He and Charlie Tysedale (Tippee's father) had a business proposition to make. The three of them had a meeting scheduled before dinner tonight. And Egbert(Mr) was dreading it. *Dreading* it.

It so happened that he and Charlie Tysedale had been in the same house at Eton together, briefly. Charlie had been four years above him, and better at sport, better looking, better at all academic subjects and better at making friends. Also, quite unkind. This did not help.

In fact, reflected Egbert, the Reunion of the Suspects was quite the school reunion too. Esmé had been at Eton, though admittedly long before Egbert(Mr) ever got there. He and Charlie Tysedale had overlapped, though thankfully only by a single year ... And bloody Piers Slayer-Wilson-Tite, who since the tragedy at Rospo had taken up residence in a cottage on the estate, had not only been in the same house at Eton, but the same year ... Sometimes, Egbert reflected, there was no escape. No respite. Not from anything.

10

He looked at his wife. She liked to have a bath in the morning. It would be at least another hour before she was ready for the day.

'Shall I wait?' he said. 'I think I'll head on down.'

It was a large bedroom. A beautiful room with high ceilings and mahogany doors. Egbert(Mr) padded the 25 feet, across ancient Aubusson, from mid room to exit, pulled back the door, which opened onto what was meant to be a private landing, and walked slap into—

The dreaded Adele.

Like many men before him, Egbert(Mr) had tried and failed to find Mrs Tysedale attractive. There was no doubt she was pretty. Icy blonde. Neat. *Symmetrical*. Not a skin pore out of place. Maybe that was part of the problem? Adele Tysedale could have been aged anything from twenty-five to 163 years old. She could have been a vampire. In fact, she was forty-one, and human, and dressed, on this crisp October morning, in many careful layers of breathable exercise clothing: loose and *tight*, tight and *loose*, each article, hair accessory included, in a complementing shade of fawn.

'Good morning, Adele!'

Adele looked put out. But not half as embarrassed as Egbert(Mr) did. He hoped she'd not overheard India accusing her young son Tippee of murder. That would have been pretty awful.

' . . . How lovely to see you up here!' he continued. 'Are you lost?'

She said not. She said she was looking for young Tippee.

'Ah, yes. Tippee Tysedale! The excellent Tippee!' exclaimed Egbert fatuously. 'I haven't seen him, I'm afraid. But not to worry, he can't have gone far. It's not nine o'clock yet, so if he'd tried to go outside, he would have set off one of the alarms. We'd have police crawling all over the place!'

'Scenario: unlikely,' replied Adele, with a symmetrical smile. 'Tippee doesn't like outside. I think he must have forgotten we have the yoga in a wee bit.'

'Right-oh,' said Egbert(Mr), not very interested.

Adele seemed to be expecting something more.

'Gosh. Well ... Poor little chap!' Egbert added obligingly. 'I suppose one could hardly blame him.'

Adele waited.

'I mean to say ... I don't suppose when I was twelve – is he twelve?'

'Eleven years and seven months, Egbert. He'll be twelve in April.'

'Well, I don't think, at eleven years and seven months, I would have been leaping with joy at the prospect of an early-morning yoga class with my ma! Perhaps he's hiding somewhere?'

Adele shook her head. 'Oh no, Tippee really enjoys his yoga. We do it together every morning. Usually online, for hygiene and safety reasons. But today we were excited because we had the gorgeous Frederica here in person, to lead us through our practice! She says she's not taught a single lesson since she left Rospo. So – as I said to Tippee, and Tippee said to me – we're feeling a teeny bit blessed.'

'Indeed ... The wonderful Frederica ...' Egbert nodded vaguely. Not wonderful. Awful. Beautiful, *yes*. But exhausting. The loudest, most argumentative woman he had ever met. She lived with Piers at Ludo Cottage (which needed its roof insulation looked at. He must remember to tell Mr Kirchsome), another refugee from the Rospo tragedy. They had to be

12

kind to her, because it was her sister who'd been murdered ...
Egbert secretly thought Frederica might have been the one who
did it, but he couldn't say so, for obvious reasons. *Not in the
current climate*, as he so rightly observed (to himself). *Being
of 'swarthy'/'Italian' appearance and also 'female' as it were –
yikes! – it'd be a bit off to suspect her of murder. And quite right,
too, no doubt! One couldn't be too careful.* His stomach rumbled.
It was breakfast time.

'Tippee finds his yoga very calming,' Adele was saying.
'Especially,' she added, and it sounded slightly reproving, as
if Egbert(Mr) might have forgotten, 'after everything that
happened.'

It was Tippee who found the body floating face-up in the
chilly, crystal waters of Rospo four months back. The water
was full of swollen grapefruits because of the citrus orchard
upstream. Tippee, under the light of the summer moon, had
been prodding the grapefruits with a stick. Apparently. That's
what he said.

Egbert(Mr) shuddered. It wasn't a pleasant memory. 'Oh yes,
of course,' he said. 'How's he doing? Poor little chap. It must
have been such a shock.'

'Well, he loves his yoga,' Adele said again.

'Oh, I'm sure ...!'

Egbert thought that perhaps, this morning, he might treat
himself to eggs and bacon for breakfast. It being a Saturday.

'But he's at that stage, Egbert, where he's dealing with his
trauma issues on a sort of "moment-by-moment" basis. So one
minute he's saying to his daddy, "Daddy, *you're* a killer!" Next
minute he's saying, "Mummy, *you're* a killer!"' She tittered.
'I'm afraid he'll be accusing us all by the end of today. He's
already had a little go at your butler chappie ...'

'At Mr *Carfizzi*?' The dreaded Adele certainly had his attention now. Egbert was aghast.

'Well, there was a chap on the stairs in a uniform, carrying coffee ... I don't know his name.'

'But Mr Carfizzi wasn't even at Rospo! He was here at Tode Hall the whole time!'

Adele didn't seem terribly concerned. 'The best thing to do is ignore him. That's what I tend to do. And it's what I said to your butler chappie. "Just ignore him," I said. Tippee's therapist says "shocking outbursts" are a very natural response and should be encouraged. And I agree with him. This weekend will be very helpful for Tippee. So ...' She crossed her fingers, symmetrically. 'With a bit of luck we'll be able to put it all behind us.'

Egbert(Mr) nodded glumly. 'Absolutely. Of course.'

She was still standing there, though, not moving on.

'By the way,' he added (changing the conversation), 'are you coming out with us this morning? I think Charlie said you were shooting? We've got a gun ready for you ...' He looked at the clothes. 'Only I worry you might get a bit cold.'

Adele was briefly flummoxed. She laughed. No, no – this wasn't her shooting gear! She was dressed for *yoga*, not for *shooting*! Frederica had postponed the yoga class until 10.30 a.m.

'What's that? I wasn't aware–' Egbert was confused. 'I thought we agreed yoga at seven thirty.'

'She changed it. Texted last night.'

'*Changed it? Texted?* Why didn't she text me?'

'I'm sure she meant to.'

'Honestly, Frederica is infuriating! Kick off's at ten, Adele. Frederica knows that perfectly well. It's already later than I would have liked. We really cannot put it back any further.'

14

'Not a problem!' Adele smiled brightly. 'Tippee's got tutoring in the p.m., anyway. So that actually works very well for me. I'll probably just join in after lunch.'

'What?' Egbert was quite put out. 'The thing is that's not really how we do it. It's sort of an *all or nothing* scenario. Our lovely gamekeeper goes to a lot of trouble—' He stopped. From among the shades of fawn, Adele had produced a phone. She clearly wasn't listening to him, and there was nothing to be gained from making things unpleasant, just for the sake of it. Egbert believed this quite passionately. 'Well, anyway,' he sighed, 'I'll see you down at breakfast then, shall I? Do you know the way?'

'I'll find it! Don't worry about me!' she replied. 'I just need to make a super-quick phone call.'

And at that moment the phone in her hand started to ring. It's how efficient she was. Her smile vanished. She nodded to Egbert(Mr), dismissing him, and stepped away.

Somewhere along her relentlessly self-improving, upwardly-mobile trudge, Adele Morely of Nuneaton had married Charlie Tysedale of many millions. It was an odd choice – for both of them. They didn't seem to have anything much in common – except, perhaps, their love of money. And perhaps that was enough.

Twenty years ago Charlie Tysedale, rich from birth, had made himself even richer by founding Mark of Marylebone, a clothes label that sold 'athleisure-to-workwear' (according to the Mark of Marylebone sales team) to the sort of middle-aged men who went to gyms. Adele, meanwhile, had been no less clever. Her book, *The Ape and the Unicorn, Squaring the Me–Him Circle*, was the fourth best-selling couples' therapy book in UK/US publishing history. She wrote it eleven years ago, according to press releases, while simultaneously breastfeeding and suffering from acute post-natal depression. Since then (so far) the book had been translated into 137 languages, and she had squeezed out a further five editions with updated subtitles.

And now, to coincide with the US publication of its long-awaited sequel: *The Ape, the Unicorn ... and then comes Baby Mouse*, Netflix wanted her to present a family therapy show from a US-based studio replica of her own beautiful Oxfordshire kitchen. This was big stuff.

Adele's ongoing search for Baby Mouse, now eleven years and seven months, was paused momentarily, as she stood on Egbert's bedroom landing and discussed with her Singapore agent percentages and terms.

Egbert watched her leave. He shuddered.

He wondered if he dared to duck breakfast with his guests. He thought perhaps he could sneak out and have it at the Gardener's House with Alice and Ecgbert(Sir) instead? Alice made the best scrambled eggs, and things were always a bit jollier over there ...

But no. Duty called. The guests would be expecting him. He mustn't be rude. Egbert(Mr) was never a man to duck out of a duty.

THE CHINESE DINING ROOM

9.03 A.M.

... has two Reynolds and a Stubbs on its walls, and seats twenty-five with comfort and ease. It is the smaller of the Hall's two dining rooms, if you don't include the Long Gallery, which is usually only used for banquets of over 100, and doesn't strictly classify as a dining room.

Hunched over his plate at one end of the long table, eating beadily, sat Adele's husband, Charlie Tysedale. His grey, shoulder-length locks were smoothed off his face with the help of rich-smelling hair oils, and he was dressed for shooting. Charlie was only four years older than Egbert(Mr), but looking at him now, no one could have guessed it. He'd been handsome as a schoolboy. Beautiful, even. At forty-three, after however many gallons of expensive wine, however many million cigarettes, however many kilograms of cocaine, he looked bloated and disreputable, like a man who spent a lot of time and money on hookers. As, indeed, he did.

17

Egbert(Mr) had a memory flash. Charlie Tysedale and a boy called Humbert Tarvish, whose father owned great swathes of Hong Kong, pinning him down on the snooker table, smearing his face with margarine and forcing him—

But never mind that.

'Here we are!' cried Egbert(Mr), rubbing his palms together, like all good hosts must. 'Jolly good! Did you sleep OK, Charlie?'

'Very well indeed,' lied Charlie, who never slept well, whose once-thriving athleisure-to-workwear clothing brand, Mark of Marylebone, was now *that close* to going under, and whose arteries were *that close* to—

But never mind that.

'Like a baby,' he said. 'Where the hell is everyone?'

As he spoke, the door swung open and in stomped Egbert's troubled cousin Nicola Tode. Egbert was trying his best to move her out of the Hall and into a cottage on the estate, but no matter which cottage he offered her, it didn't seem to satisfy. Nicola found life difficult. Life found *Nicola* difficult. (She had a bad track record. See previous adventures at Tode Hall.) In the meantime, she lived at the Hall, because that was where she grew up, and because—

Just, *because*. Egbert and India didn't have the heart to throw her out.

She was wearing PPE. As always. She tended to eat breakfast with a plastic visor on, to set a safety example to others (so she said). Egbert(Mr) thought that was all well and good, inasmuch as he thought about it at all. But she never seemed to wash it so it was quite hard, beneath the smears and splodges, to see her face. He wondered how she could ever see out. Perhaps she couldn't.

18

'Here we are!' cried Egbert(Mr), rubbing his palms together again. 'Jolly good! Did you sleep OK, Nicola?'

Nicola didn't reply.

QUEEN CHARLOTTE'S BEDROOM

9.05 A.M.

Bunny Rostovsky had an excellent eye for antiques. Somewhere in her mysterious youth she'd studied the value of small objects. Also, of equal importance, how to pick locks and steal things. While her husband, Putin Rostovsky, splashed about in the bathroom next door, she examined a golden coin from Caligula's Rome, spotted behind a display cabinet in the Long Gallery on her way down to dinner last night. Very nice indeed. She tucked it into her suitcase, beside the Zhou dynasty amber contemplation beads, found in a similar cabinet in the Yellow Saloon, and looked at her watch.

At 10.30 a.m., the Italian girl whose sister had been murdered (Frederica), was putting on a yoga lesson especially for the guests. Also very nice. Bunny, small and perfectly formed, in her mid-thirties, knew her body well. She would need time to digest her breakfast before the class began. Putin needed to get a move on.

'Are you winning, Poots?' she called out, adopting the

coaxing tones she always used when ordering her husband to do things.

But he was almost thirty years older than Bunny, and quite deaf. He didn't reply. She didn't really expect him to. She sighed.

Splish splash.

'Putin?'

The sound of giant water waves hitting the carpeted floor. Putin Rostovsky was the size of whale, and he was getting out of the bath.

Bunny was about to knock on the bathroom door, but then – something happened.

She felt a cool breeze on the back of her neck. A smell of methane. And in the corner of the room – *was that a wisp of green smoke?*

There stood two figures. Clear as day. The first was a small, stocky gentleman with a long curly beard. He was dressed like a Renaissance dandy (Bunny noted), in a velvet beret, dark stockings and pinkish buttoned tunic. Beside him there stood a slim and elegant woman, much taller than he was, dressed, it seemed, from a more modern era. She wore flowing pantaloons and an astrakhan coat in deep red. The two figures had appeared from nowhere, in their almost matching outfits. And they were peering at the inside of her suitcase. This was not the first time Bunny had seen them. She had seen them before, of course, in Rospo.

'Leo!' cried the elegant woman. For it was the ghost of Geraldine, Lady Tode (1907–1971), with her new holiday friend, Leonardo (1452–1519), whom she'd met and lured back from Rospo last summer. They were virtually inseparable.

'Leo darling,' she said, 'do look!'

21

Leonardo did look. Gravely, he shook his head.

Green smoke from the deep red astrakhan.

Bunny stared.

Leonardo stared.

Lady Tode stared.

And then, as suddenly as they were there, they were gone.

Bunny closed the suitcase. She locked it. She told herself it was nothing to worry about, and then she waited, quietly, for her husband Putin to emerge from the bathroom. Which he did, at last, his massive sixty-four-year-old body only partially wrapped in its massive towel.

'Are you all right, Money-Bunny?' He sniffed the air, but if he smelled anything he didn't comment. He chortled. 'You look like you've seen one of your ghosts again, my love!'

'Not me!' said Bunny, who lied as a rule, told the truth only ever in exceptional circumstances.

Putin unhooked the towel (modesty preserved by the overlapping belly) and dried his big, fat face.

'I wonder what they'll give us for breakfast,' he said. 'I'm starving.'

At that moment, Putin Rostovsky did not use his Russian accent. This, because he wasn't Russian, as his wife Bunny knew well, so what would have been the point? Actually, he was a British-born, RADA-trained actor from Stevenage, called Derek Hunter who, for about three months, in 1987, had played a guy called 'Mick' in *EastEnders*.

THE GARDENER'S HOUSE

10.33 A.M.

Through an archway in the old wall that separated the North Lawn from the Rose Garden, at the end of a pathway lined by ancient apple trees, there stood a small, honey-coloured cottage of such prettiness it ought to have belonged in a fairy tale. This was the Gardener's House.

For many years it had stood empty and mostly unused. Geraldine, Lady Tode (of the red astrakhan) had enjoyed free run of the place. She had made it her ghostly base since shortly after she died, more than half a century ago, and for the time being, at least, she showed no signs of moving on. This, despite the fact that for the past four years, and much to her annoyance, she'd been forced to share the house with Tode Hall's 'Organisational Coordinator', Alice Liddell.

Rather, Alice Liddell, as was.

Last June, to add salt to the wound (house-sharing with the staff), Alice Liddell had married Geraldine Tode's favourite grandson, Mad Ecgbert(Sir), aka 12th Baronet Tode of

23

Todeister. Alice Liddell became Lady Tode. *The* Lady Tode, in fact. It was something which her housemate, Geraldine, Lady Tode (1907–1971) was struggling to come to terms with.

Nowadays the Gardener's House was far from empty. Alice and Ecgbert(Sir), who were very much in love, the ghost of his snobbish grandmother and the ghost of her new best friend, anatomist and water engineer, Leonardo (1452–1519) were all squeezed in there together. And on the whole they got along.

It helped that Leonardo and Lady Tode were often away on little voyages.

Please note that in this story there are –

Two E-berts:

- Ecgbert(Sir) – recently married to Alice Liddell
- Egbert(Mr) – still married to the beautiful India

And two Lady Todes:

- *Geraldine*, Lady Tode (1907–1971) – A ghost. Grandmother to both the E-berts (also grandmother to Esmé and Nicola)
- *The* Lady Tode (née Alice Liddell) 1967–? Still very much alive. The title doesn't suit her. She will never be referred to as Lady Tode again, unless it's to annoy Geraldine. This will be clearly signposted

Also please note, there is a family tree on page x.

24

Alice and Ecgbert(Sir), the newlyweds, were eating breakfast
in the Gardener's House kitchen together: some delicious
scrambled egg and smoked salmon, also toast and marmalade, sausages and (in Ecgbert's case) chocolate cake. It was,
as Egbert(Mr) had already highlighted, a beautiful day for
October. The windows had been thrown open and a bird was
singing. Alice and Ecgbert were mulling on nothing much,
enjoying this rare moment of privacy. It wasn't often they
were alone together, and so far, at least, neither India nor
Egbert(Mr) had 'popped in' for one of their impromptus.
Better still, the ghosts were apparently on one of their safaris.
Geraldine, Lady Tode (1907–1971) and her new summer hols
friend, Leonardo (1452–1519) had taken themselves to London
for a day or two, to 'look at the buildings'.

Ecgbert was peering through a pair of binoculars. They
were unneeded, because the objects of his interest were
human size and standing only about 10 metres from the open
window. His focus wobbled between somebody's nose and/
or somebody's forehead. He wasn't certain what belonged to
whom, but there was dry skin involved. Something he'd not
noticed before.

'Am I being mad?' Mad Ecgbert asked his wife.

'A bit,' replied Alice.

'But Trudy, they're taunting us. They won't leave us alone.'

'I don't think that's it,' Alice said mildly.

'They're obsessed.'

'I don't think they're even aware that we exist, most of the
time. They're very wrapped up in themselves.'

'What? What do you mean?' Ecgbert(Sir) lowered the binoculars, the better to confront this new, idiotic proposition. 'That doesn't make *any* sense, Trudy. Of course they know we exist! They've plopped their yoga mats right in front of our window! Are you telling me they haven't noticed there's a window here? They've got the whole of the North Lawn. They've got fifteen thousand acres of nice, fresh farmland to plop themselves. So why, if it wasn't to torture us, Trudy, why would they plop their mats right here, in front of our kitchen window? It's a scandal.' He looked at the two figures again, this time without the binoculars to confuse him. 'Also, how many mats do they actually need? They're only two people.'

Piers Slayer-Wilson-Tite and Frederica Ranaldini stood head to head – arguing, as usual. They were a fine-looking pair: Frederica, with her shiny hair, her big brown eyes, perfect nose and perfect bosoms; and Piers, with his . . . Piers, especially, was exceptional. With his high cheekbones, his bright blue eyes, his flowing black hair, he looked like a tall, fit, extra-handsome vampire. Both were dressed in sportswear, and in front of them, spread out in a welcoming semicircle, were a lot of yoga mats.

' . . . Utter bastards . . . ' muttered Ecgbert(Sir).

'It is a bit annoying,' conceded Alice.

'Also, by the way, Piers pretends to be this great expert but I don't think he has the faintest idea how to do yoga. Do you?'

'He was never much good at it at Rospo, no . . . Frederica was very good, though.'

'I should think *I* probably do yoga better than Piers does, Trudy,' he said. To illustrate the point, Ecgbert(Sir), who had very long legs, extracted one from beneath the breakfast table, stretched it out in front of him, and, with surprising ease and

26

grace, lowered his nose to his knee. It was incongruous, what with his middle age, his thick, grey woolly hair and his old-fashioned corduroy suit: also it was impressive.

It certainly took Alice by surprise. 'Ecgbert! I had no idea you could do that!'

'Double jointed,' he said. 'Always was, always will be.' Encouraged by his wife's reaction, he stood up, took hold of one leather-brogue'd foot and lifted it until his legs were 180 degrees apart, and the 12th Bart was doing the standing splits.

Alice stared. 'Good God!'

He dropped the leg and sat down again. 'I bet Piers Slayer-Wilson-Tite can't do that. I watched him at Rospo. He couldn't do anything. He just flopped around, saying pointless things and confusing everyone . . . And if your instincts are anything to go by – and they usually are, Trudy – when he wasn't doing *that*, he was murdering poor old Elizabetta . . . Unless of course Nicola murdered her . . . Or Frederica . . . Or one of the Russians . . . Or Esmé, I suppose. Or the dreaded Adele . . . Or young Tippee . . . Or . . . I dare say Charlie Tysedale might've had a motive. We just need to find out what it is. We can't rule any of them out.'

But Alice was still reeling from the gymnastic display. 'Ecgbert,' she said, 'you could be in the circus! That was amazing!'

'I think you're right, though. I bet it *was* probably Piers . . . Question is, why haven't Egbert and India seen through him yet? He's a fraud and a bounder. As the Organisational Chief of this set-up, Trudy, I really do think you should find a way to get rid of him. Before someone else gets done in. How do we know who he might suddenly want to kill next?'

'I'm pretty sure *we're* safe,' Alice said, but not with as much

27

confidence as Ecgbert(Sir) would have liked. 'Anyway,' Alice continued, 'I think we're stuck with him for the time being. I don't think he's got anywhere else to go ...'

This was true. He didn't. Both his parents were dead, and now so was his wife. He had no money of his own and no discernible qualifications.

After what happened at Rospo, nobody had quite known what to do with him. Elizabetta's grieving parents, well known in the Rospo area as a family not to be fooled with, came and whipped away their daughter's body and advised – or requested – that the Todes close Rospo's famous gardens to the tourists for the rest of summer. Mr and Mrs Ranaldini asked the Todes and their guests to return to England at once, taking their other daughter, Frederica, along with them ...

Ask no questions. That's what Egbert(Mr) had said to himself. He was more than happy to comply with their wishes. After all (he reminded himself), Mr and Mrs Ranaldini were being 'extraordinarily kind', in dealing with the paperwork, the body, the local authorities, etc., while keeping the Tode family name out of any gory headlines. It was the least the Todes could do in return.

The only problem that remained was the widower, Piers. With the house and gardens closed, he was rendered homeless and jobless in a single sweep.

Which situation, in turn, left Egbert(Mr) feeling cornered. Because, as previously mentioned, Piers Slayer-Wilson-Tite wasn't just any recently unemployed, recently widowed unfortunate. He and Egbert had been at school together: in the same house, in the same year.

So – despite not having liked Piers *one bit* at Eton, Egbert(Mr), ever dutiful, ever bountiful, had felt double-duty-bound to help him out. He offered Piers a cottage on the estate while he pulled his life back together – in exchange for which, the silver-tongued Piers had suggested to Egbert(Mr) that he could act as an adviser to the estate on 'eco grants for wind farms, etc.'. Piers knew nothing about eco grants and did nothing to find out. His advice was non-existent. But he was handsome and very charming, recently bereaved and recently unemployed, and India, who missed parties and suntans, liked having him around.

Woolly haired, double-jointed Ecgbert(Sir), who did not go to Eton and would not have thrived there due to his unruly mind, lifted his binoculars once again.

He said: 'I think we should do something, Trudy. We can't just sit here while they put their mats on our lawn. We should counter-attack.'

'Counter-attack in what way? I don't think they're attacking us, Ecgbert. I honestly don't think they're thinking about us at all. Maybe they decided to set up in the Rose Garden so the tourists didn't interrupt them. Or most likely, they're hiding from Nicola.' Alice chortled. 'She'll find them, though. I give her ten minutes ...'

Alice had underestimated her new sister-in-law. As she spoke, the troubled Nicola, dressed for business in plastic visor and waterproof, visibility trouser suit, stomped between the apple trees and into view.

'Ah-ha! Talk of the devil!' cried Ecgbert(Sir). 'Good old Nicola! Here she comes! This'll put the wind up them ...'

In the aftermath of the murder-before-last (what the Tode family generally referred to as 'Nicola's funny turn'), it had been decided that she should be given a role of some sort on the estate. 'A role,' decreed her bountiful, dutiful cousin Egbert(Mr), 'will give her a sense of purpose and keep her out of trouble.' And so he and India, Alice and Ecgbert(Sir) had set to work, thinking what she might be able to do. Egbert(Mr) had suggested a job overseeing litter management in the Eastern coach park area, but Nicola had thought this was beneath her. She was quite angry about it. Instead, she designed herself a safe working uniform (see above) and appointed herself Officer in Charge of Visitor Care, Healthfulness, Wellbeing, Safety Awareness and Good Hygiene; and in that capacity she now roamed Hall and parkland each day, spritzing surfaces, forestalling fanciful hazards and, above all, irritating everyone she encountered. She was a nightmare. On the other hand, she was probably happier – or less unhappy – than she had ever been. Either way she would be bound to want to sabotage Piers and Frederica's yoga class.

'Did you even know they were doing one of their yoga classes?' Ecgbert(Sir) asked Alice, training his binoculars on Nicola's approach. 'I thought they'd stopped all that rubbish since Rospo.'

'It was Esmé's idea. He wanted them to do it especially for this weekend. He thinks it'll be good group therapy. But then Frederica decided to do it when everyone was meant to be out shooting. So . . . '

Ecgbert(Sir) nodded, as if this made sense. He was feeling quite pro his brother Esmé at the moment. Also, sorry for him about Australia. 'Well – then I think we should join the class.'

'What? But you were only just complaining . . . ' Alice paused. She disliked arguing. She also disliked exercise. 'Not me.'

'What? Why not?'

'Because it's stupid,' she said. 'I've done yoga before and it's awful.'

'Well, but I haven't.'

Alice said: 'You go ahead, then. I'm not doing it.'

At that point, quite unexpectedly, Mad Ecgbert leaned across the cluttered breakfast table, and said to his new wife: '*We* could be yoga teachers, Alice!'

Alice sat back, the better to read his face. Was he joking? Impossible to tell. She laughed anyway.

Sir Ecgbert ignored this. 'We could open a yoga holiday resort. For people. People do that, you know. They go on holidays and do yoga ...'

Alice was aware of this. But she didn't like yoga, and she was perfectly happy being an Organisational Coordinator. Added to which, in Frederica and (arguably) Piers, there were already one-and-a-half underexploited yoga teachers living on the estate. Why would they need any more?

'Good point ...' said Ecgbert(Sir). He thought about this for a moment. An idea struck. He put the binoculars down, took Alice's hands in his and whispered – or attempted to whisper: it was something he had never attempted before, and it came out at more or less the same volume as normal ... '*But what about if we did it at Rospo?*'

Alice Tode/Liddell, had spent her first fifty years living in Clapham, South London, a single mother of triplets just about making ends meet by teaching people to cook. Until she came to Tode Hall she'd led a fruity life but not, by any means, an easy one. Her and Ecgbert(Sir)'s honeymoon at Rospo nel Buco, until it was so rudely interrupted, first by the unwanted guests and then by the murder, had been the most glamorous, the most

31

elegant – the most magically, uncomplicatedly wonderful time of her life. There was nowhere on earth – or at least no corner she had ever visited – that could match the beauty of the Villa Rospo and its famous gardens. Plus, of course, there was the weather. And the food. And the weather. And the food . . .

Alice blinked. It took a lot to shake the new Lady Tode's sangfroid. After the life she'd led, nothing much amazed her. However, *this* . . .

Ecgbert(Sir) noticed the blink, he thought he caught an understated gasp. He rubbed his hands in glee.

'You see?' he said. 'They call me Mad Ecgbert. But I'm not as mad as they think! Imagine it, Trudy! We could live at Rospo! I should think Egbert and India would be quite pleased to see the back of us . . . Or at any rate, no. Not you. But definitely the back of me . . . You can teach people cooking, like the old days. If you want. You're the world's best cook. I can teach the yoga. Between us we can offer tours of the garden, and so on, once we know our way round it. People will come from miles around. It will be astonishing!'

If Alice had been a different sort of woman, she might have laughed at the idea. Because – really – it was silly. Ecgbert(Sir) had never had a job in his life, not even for one day. He couldn't speak Italian (and nor could she). He'd not attended a single yoga class in his life and yet here he was, fifty-six years old, and on the strength of a single leg kick, declaring he might launch an entire career.

Then again, a different sort of woman might never have married Ecgbert(Sir) in the first place. He was quite an acquired taste.

Alice beamed at him, sending a shot of electricity through his long body.

'Why not?' she asked.

He stood up: he jumped to his feet. 'I *adore* you!' he said, and he kissed her, dislodging one of her earrings in his exuberance. But it didn't matter. They loved each other vastly. It was a very happy moment.

She said: 'Well, you should probably go and join Frederica's yoga class, see if you like it ... You might discover you hate it ...' She noticed his corduroy trousers. 'Do you have anything stretchier?'

'Hmm?' Ecgbert(Sir) glanced at his trousers. 'Certainly not,' he said.

He turned back to the window. 'Wait for me, Frederica,' he shouted. 'Don't start without me! I'm coming out ...Wait! *Save me a mat!*'

THE ROSE GARDEN

10.45 A.M.

Having seen his new wife's smile, and decided on his career as an Italian yoga teacher, it was essential that nothing and no one prevented him from joining the class. He had just noticed four more figures approaching through the apple trees and he feared there may not be enough mats.

Tripping neatly towards the mats, with characteristic purpose, there came the dreaded Adele and her creepy son, Tippee; and behind them, panting and wheezing, the moustachioed sixty-four-year-old flesh mountain, 'Putin Rostovsky', accompanied by his much younger wife, Bunny (last seen in Queen Charlotte's Bedroom, tucking stolen objects into her suitcase).

Bunny resembled a domestic rabbit, with her white-blonde hair and her starey eyes and her little, bouncy body. Hence the nickname. She looked far stupider than she was, and she took care to keep it that way. 'Bunny Rostovsky', actual name and age unknown, was the sharpest, the wiliest, by far the cleverest, of anyone staying at Tode Hall that weekend. And the bar was quite high.

She and her husband had been among the honeymoon gate-crashers at Villa Rospo last June, when Elizabetta's body was found face-up in the moonlit waters. With no alibi between them, except each other, and (had anybody checked) no official record of their existence before April of the same year, Bunny and Putin were lucky there were so many other suspicious characters also present at the time, or they might already have been behind bars. So.

This morning, in the meantime, they were enjoying their freedom, and dressed to please, in top-to-toe Mark of Marylebone athleisurewear.

Nicola never dressed to please. She had removed her visor and was unbuttoning her luminous jacket. This suggested to Ecgbert(Sir) that she might be intending to join the class, as opposed to sabotage it. Fearing the worst vis-à-vis mat alloca-tion, he cut to the front of the queue by climbing out of the kitchen window.

'Nicola!' he shouted. 'Back off! You won't like it. Anyway, you're meant to be working. That's my mat. I'm doing it. I said it first.'

Nicola said: 'Actually nobody's doing it, Ecgbert. *Sorry.* Unfortunately it's against estate rules. No yoga in the Rose Garden.'

'What? Since when was that a rule?'

'Since yoga was invented in this country.' Nicola planted her feet a half-metre apart on the mat she was hogging, and settled in for the squabble.

Frederica Ranaldini and Piers Slayer-Wilson-Tite paid no attention. They were engaged in a fight of their own, and theirs was more vicious, because they were sleeping with each other, and there was a lot of baggage in their relationship. What with one thing and another, it was a miracle – and to both their credit – that they hadn't murdered each other already.

As the battles raged around her, Adele focused on organising her and Tippee's yoga mats. She and Tippee had brought a couple of their own. She unrolled them and arranged them neatly on top of the mats already laid out by Frederica and Piers. When she was satisfied that the job was done correctly, she produced a small atomiser from her fawn-coloured athleisure knapsack, and sprayed thoroughly. Tippee watched and waited. She nodded. *It was now safe for him to proceed.* Mother and son took their places.

Spines straight. Eyes in front.

Toes together, heels slightly apart.

They breathed.

And then there was Bunny. She glanced at the squabbling duos, but didn't blink. (She rarely blinked.) She settled onto one of the mats and arranged herself into *savasana*, also known as 'corpse pose'. She closed her eyes.

And breathed.

Putin, already sweating from the exertion of crossing the lawn, dropped to his knees on the mat beside her. Closed his eyes and panted.

'Hey, you two.' Ecgbert(Sir) turned to Frederica and Piers. 'Are you running this class or aren't you? We don't have enough mats. What are you going to do about it? Nicola, *get off the mat.*'

'No.'

'Oh my Gadd, Ecgbert!' snapped Frederica, turning

away, briefly, from her own fight. 'Jus' do it on de grass. Are you a baby?'

Ecgbert considered this. *Yoga on the grass*, he thought. *Why not?*

'Fair enough,' he said. 'Let's get started.'

'Three seconds,' gasped Putin. 'I need to lay down.'

Nicola cleared her throat. 'I'm sorry, people,' she said. 'Much as I'd like to, I cannot, in good conscience, permit this class to go ahead.'

Nobody paid any attention.

And then, out of nowhere much, a mini explosion between Piers and Frederica. Frederica yelled something in Italian. She lashed out and slapped her lover across the face.

Those with their eyes closed in corpse pose quickly opened them in time to see the mark, the outline of Frederica's fingers turning red against Piers' cheek. Nobody spoke. This, after all, was the Reunion of the Suspects, so not a good weekend to reveal a violent temper.

Piers touched his cheek. He looked at Frederica – his expression oddly blank. He turned away from her, and she turned to face the group. The eyes were still blazing, but in other respects, she seemed calm. She said:

'All right. Every-baddy is here. We are goin' to start. Nicola, if you are here, you can please fackoff. We don'want you here. Please fackoff.'

Nicola didn't move.

Everyone else stood.

'I'm sorry,' Nicola said. 'I can't allow this to continue. You don't have a permit, and if something happened – fingers crossed it *wouldn't* – but if one of you got injured, or slipped and fell, then I would not be able to forgive myself. Apologies, but I happen to value my sleep. I am banning this yoga class from continuing.'

Ecgbert(Sir) said, 'Get lost, Nicola.'

Frederica said: 'Everybaddy, feel your feet on the earth. Feel the energy from the earth coming through into your feet and ap through your baddy. Take a deep breath . . . '

Nicola said: 'EXCUSE ME!'

Frederica glanced at Piers. Something passed between them: an agreement of sorts, in spite of everything. Piers smiled at Nicola. He put his arm around her, and in a cajoling, flirtatious manner, muttered something in her ear. Whatever it was, it had the desired effect. He led her away, between the apple trees, through the arch in the wall, across the North Lawn, through the estate office car park to the family's private entrance in the East Wing.

Distances being what they were at Tode Hall, by the time he had returned to the yoga class it was well underway.

'What did you do with her, Piers?' cackled Putin. 'Bury her in the vegetable patch?'

The comment seemed to please his wife Bunny. She awoke from her goggle-eyed yoga trance and giggled loudly.

He said, 'Oh, *Bunny!*'

Everyone else pretended not to hear, because it reminded them how Ecgbert(Sir) and Nicola's mother had been found murdered in the mausoleum not so many years back, and this made them feel sad/embarrassed and/or a little spooked.

Frederica said: 'Take your left foot wid your right hand, tuck your chin, open chest, look up to your sky and *pull*. Remember to breathe . . . '

'We are surrounded by love,' mumbled Piers, roaming miserably between the mats, touching people with his sexy vampire hands, mostly on their lower backs. 'Feel the love with every inhalation. Inhale, *love*. Exhale, *gratitude* . . . Inhale, *love*—'

In the distance, shots rang out. 'Is that the sound of your husband and my father, Charles Tysedale, annihilating the local birdlife?' asked Tippee Tysedale of his mother (to annoy).

Adele said: 'Focus, Tippee. Please.'

'Inhale, *love* . . . '

Ecgbert(Sir) inhaled.

' . . . exhale, *gratitude* . . . '

Ecgbert(Sir) exhaled.

Enough of this.

He left the others lying on their mats, breathing deeply and connecting with the earth, and hurried back to the Gardener's House, to report back to Alice, that *yes* – as far as he was concerned, the new career plan was a go-er. He would become a yoga teacher as soon as he could. But, he wondered, was Alice certain she was happy to return to the old 'teaching cooking' gig as a career?

'Why not?' said Alice amiably. She thought about it a tiny bit more. 'There are quite a lot of good cooks in Italy, though. Perhaps I should think of doing something else? Maybe I could get involved with the garden?' As a life-long Londoner who, until moving to Yorkshire, had spent much of her life avoiding the outside (a bit like Tippee Tysedale), the suggestion was on a par with Ecgbert's yoga plan. But it didn't matter.

Italy was beautiful, on the whole.

Villa Rospo was standing empty.

And the famous garden was amazing.

Why not?

Only one reason why not. The house and villa were part of the Tode estate. To proceed, they would need a green light from dutiful, bountiful Egbert(Mr).

'But that won't be a problem,' Ecgbert(Sir) assured his wife. 'Considering everything he's gained from me being too useless to inherit . . . I don't see how he can refuse.'

Nobody in the family had ever bothered much with Villa Rospo. After his mother bought her own place in Capri, the Todes had never gone there again, and India and Egbert(Mr), though they were obviously aware of Rospo's existence, much preferred Greece. The villa was quite run-down, plus there was no swimming pool. Added to which, as part of a complicated pact with the Italian government, the famous Rospo gardens were meant to be open to the public most of the year. Tode family members, when they ventured from the Tode base, traditionally preferred staying in more private spots. In fact, until the day of the murder, Egbert(Mr) and India had never once looked in on Rospo, and when Alice and Ecgbert(Sir) came up with the idea of staying there for their honeymoon, Egbert(Mr) had actually needed to be reminded where in Italy it was.

Ecgbert(Sir) had plenty of reasons to believe it would be a straightforward enough request.

THE SHOOTING PARTY

Thanks to Frederica and her capricious/malicious scheduling, it had been a diminished shooting party that set out from Tode Hall that morning. First, as Frederica's yoga assistant and love slave, Piers Slayer-Wilson-Tite had been obliged to withdraw. And then Adele had dropped out, taking Tippee with her; and then, much to Egbert(Mr)'s irritation, Bunny Rostovsky had persuaded Putin to do the same.

Over breakfast in the Chinese Dining Room, Bunny Rostovsky, who was still a bit shaken post her encounter with the ghosts, had said to her husband, Putin:

'Why don't you do the yoga with me in the morning, Pumpkin; and then you can have fun shooting the birds in the afternoon? How about that? Baby, I want you to do the yoga with me. It's good for your heart. Hmm?'

Putin had glowed (it was the Bunny effect). 'I'm a lucky man,' he told everyone, while also remembering to sound Russian. 'She's not letting me alone when there's still maybe a murderer among us and everyone's carrying loaded shotguns. Isn't that right, Bunny?'

Bunny laughed. They were sitting side by side at the dining table. She patted his arm.

Egbert(Mr) wasn't amused. 'I can assure you,' he said primly, 'I've got no intention of murdering you.'

Putin, balancing a mountain of marmalade onto a thumb-size piece of toast, chortled so merrily his shoulders shook, his lungs wheezed, and the marmalade fell off the toast. He said: 'You say that *now*, Egbert, dear. You might want to murder me by the end of the day! Most people do! HA HA HA – eh, Bunny? – HA HA HA!'

Egbert(Mr) thought he might want to murder him by the end of breakfast. But he didn't say it aloud. He was more concerned with wanting to murder Frederica for changing the time of her ruddy yoga class. He would have liked to ask her *why*, when she knew she was interfering with the shooting day. *Why* would she do something so wantonly obstructive? What was *wrong* with her?

But there was something about Frederica – the volcanic temper, the yoga skills, the extended family back in Rospo – that made Egbert(Mr) tend to tiptoe when she was about. She made him nervous.

In any case, one way or another it was settled. Adele, Piers and Putin would join the shooting party after lunch. This was highly irregular and, for Egbert(Mr), very irritating. In the normal run of things, a shooting day was strictly and tradition-ally structured, beginning on the dot, and with all participants present and feeling grateful. Shooters wore special clothes and

42

turned up when they were told to turn up. Frederica knew this, and so did every one of his freeloading guests.

... However. So it went. As Egbert(Mr) tramped up Black Dog Hill en route to his next peg, he was feeling utterly infuriated by everyone and everything; and above all, by his cousin Esmé, who wouldn't leave him alone.

'Beautiful day, isn't it?' Esmé said, panting along beside him. A bit like a Labrador.

'Stunning!' Egbert(Mr) said, walking a little faster.

Esmé Tode was several inches smaller than his strapping cousin Egbert(Mr) and not as fit as he was when he owned gyms in Australia. 'Still on for the Big Ol' *"Confabulation"* a bit later?!' Esmé asked Egbert(Mr), in annoyingly jovial tones.

'Absolutely I am,' said Egbert(Mr). 'You bet! Six o'clock in the study, right? You and Charlie. I'm looking forward to it.'

'That's right! Six o'clock in the study. With the revolver, ha ha ha.'

Egbert didn't laugh. *Not funny.*

'Oops. Anyway. Charlie and I have got some very exciting ideas. You're going to love them, Egbert. We're thrilled to bits. We think you're going to be over the moon. Basically it's ... '

Egbert(Mr) picked up the pace.

'It's based on the premise that *leisure* ... ' Esmé upped his own pace to stay abreast, ' ... is where it's now at. In the age of AI and all that ... it's all about, y'know, what the hell [Esmé began to pant] we're gonna *do* with ourselves, with all this ruddy leisure time. You know? As I'm sure you're aware ... '

Egbert started jogging.

'And that's *why,*' Esmé continued, 'Tysedale and me are such a great fit ... Plus ... [pant, pant] ... you know Tysedale, don't you? Weren't you both in the same ... house at Eton?'

43

'But he was four years above,' snapped Egbert. 'So not really. We hardly spoke.'

'Slow down, Coz!' Esmé cried, pretending to laugh. 'Charlie Tysedale,' he continued, 'otherwise known as ... the man with ... the Midas touch!' Esmé had a stitch. '... Of course, you're aware ... of his athleisure-to-workwear ... brand?'

'Of course I am.'

Esmé's heart was pounding. 'Very ... very, very ... superb ... brand. So ... therefore ... a thrill ... doing business with him ... Mr Midas, ha ha ...'

'Yes, I bet.'

'... I feel passionate ... about, as will you ... Drawing on my ... experience ...'

Egbert stopped.

Thank God.

He turned to his cousin. 'Esmé, I don't want to be rude, but seriously, can it wait? I'm so looking forward to hearing all about it, but – you know – here we are: on this beautiful day in this beautiful place ... loads of birds to shoot ... We are just so fortunate to be here. I thought maybe we could concentrate on that until ...'

'Oh, *absolutely!*' Esmé had folded over now, resting hands on knees. He was panting freely. 'I just wanted to sort of *fluff* you, as it were ... In preparation.'

'*Fluff* me?' repeated Egbert(Mr).

'You're going to be thrilled, that's all I really wanted to say,' Esmé said. 'Rospo's such a valuable asset ... I said to Tysedale ... it's almost criminal the way we leave it rotting away like that.' Esmé straightened up, wiped away some sweat. 'We do believe there's potential to make ourselves a *lot* of money, Egbert. You, me, Charlie – and the *estate*, obviously! With a bit of . . . ' But he'd lost his confidence. Lost his slickness. He felt half the man he'd been in Australia, before his life was ripped apart. Esmé made a boxing move, on the hillside, in his wellington boots: a double fist jump-and-pump. 'With a bit of clever thinking. There's gold in them there hills! Know what I mean? Charlie's got a lot of fab contacts in Italy, as you're probably aware . . . So.'

Egbert(Mr) was not aware that Charlie Tysedale had a lot of fab contacts in Italy. Why would he be? He was about to ask for the second time that they save the conversation for later, but then his phone rang.

'Ah!' Egbert(Mr) cried, smiling apologetically. 'Saved by the bell as it were! Ha ha ha!'

'Ha ha. Absolutely!' laughed Esmé, not in the least offended. '*Please*, go ahead!'

But by the time Egbert(Mr) had removed his gloves and accessed the correct pocket on the inside of his outer jacket, the phone had fallen silent.

And by the time he had put the phone back in the correct pocket, it had started up again.

Egbert(Mr) rarely swore, but now he couldn't resist. 'Bloody *hell*,' he muttered.

'Oops!' said Esmé. 'Looks like someone seriously wants to get hold of you!'

'Yes, well, it's only Ecgbert,' snapped Egbert, who so rarely snapped. 'I'm not sure why it can't wait until lunch.'

But the phone kept ringing. It stopped, it started again. It stopped. It started.

Esmé laughed. 'He's not going to give up. Might as well answer.'

Esmé was right. With an irritable sigh Egbert(Mr) reached

for the inside pocket and took out the phone one more time. 'Ecgbert!' he cried, sounding positive. 'What can I do you for? As they say. I'm actually – at my peg, as it were. Can't it wait? Are you and Alice coming for lunch?'

'Yup. No. Good,' boomed Ecgbert(Sir), nonsensically. 'You picked up.'

'What's cooking, Coz?'

'Right. We've got big career changes going down over here, Egbert. Big, big decisions.'

'Right-oh . . . ' replied Egbert patiently. 'Sounds interesting!'

'Very, very interesting. Alice has decided she wants to be a professional gardener. That's the plan and you and India must *not* take advantage of her kind and easy-going nature to make her feel bad about it.'

'What's he saying?' Esmé sniggered. 'What's he saying about "careers"?'

Egbert(Mr) covered his ear. 'What's that? A gardener?'

'She's very interested in gardening,' Ecgbert(Sir) said again.

'Who is?'

'*Alice*. Is very interested in *gardening*. She's going to be a great *gardener*. And I'm – actually don't laugh – I know it probably sounds a bit sudden . . . But I'm actually going to . . . erm . . . ' But then he lost confidence. Suddenly the prospect of putting his own career plans into words felt *a bit much*, as his bountiful cousin Egbert(Mr) might have put it. Ecgbert(Sir) decided not to finish the sentence. 'Point is, Egbert, you're going to need to find a replacement for Alice. As your Organisational Sovereign. Don't tell her I said so. I know she wants to tell India herself. But we've decided we're going to shift anchor to Rospo.'

'Rospo?'

46

'Correct. What do you think? Nobody uses it much, so it should be fine. We're actually doing the estate a favour, if you think about it ... Alice and I have decided it's where we want to live. So – that's our headline news. I just thought you needed to know. All right. See you at lunch. Have fun with the birdies.'

'Ecgbert? Wait! Ecgbert, slow down! What are you talking about?'

'Hmm?'

'You can't just drop this on me!'

'What? Actually, sorry, Egbert. Sorry. Sorry sorry sorry. Got to go.' Alice had told him he should wait. Hearing the panic in his cousin's voice, Ecgbert(Sir) wished he had heeded her advice. Too late.

'Ecgbert? This is terrible news! India's going to be *distraught* ... So am *I*. Ecgbert?'

The line went dead.

As previously noted, Egbert(Mr) hardly ever swore. But this had been a bad morning, and this was bad news. India adored Alice. Without Alice – as India often said – her life at Tode Hall would be insufferable. On the other hand, Ecgbert(Sir) didn't ask for much. If he and Alice wanted Rospo, he could hardly refuse them, all things considered. '*Fuck*,' Egbert(Mr) muttered.

Esmé sensed negative developments afoot. On the back of his neck, hairs were prickling. He said: 'What? *What?* What does he want? Did he say something about Rospo?'

'No,' replied Egbert(Mr). 'I mean, *yes*. Yes, he did. Look. Let's talk about it at six o'clock, shall we? It's suddenly all getting a bit complicated ... '

A shout from the beaters. Not far off, the sound of wings flapping and birds in distress. Egbert(Mr) took aim and

47

fired – twice. Two birds fell, reunited with the earth's energy once and for all. He said to Esmé, as he reloaded the gun, 'You'd better get to your peg, Es. Seriously. Or you'll miss all the fun.'

We don't know what happened between the two of them after that but they must have come to blows, because there was no sign of Esmé at lunch. Not until after the body fell to the floor, and everyone started screaming.

That's right.

THE GARDENER'S HOUSE

11.05 A.M.

A lice returned from the lavatory. Or possibly the village shop. Ecgbert(Sir) had lost track of time. He was at the breakfast table, his phone in his hand. Outside, the remains of the yoga class were still fussing on or around their mats. Piers and Frederica stood to one side, squabbling. The class looked as if it had finally finished.

'Trudy, I've done something stupid,' Ecgbert(Sir) said to his wife. 'Please don't divorce me. I am very, very sorry.'

Alice laughed. 'I'm certainly not going to divorce you. We've only just got married,' she said. 'What have you done?'

'I called Egbert while you were on the bog. I told him about our plan to move to Rospo.' He saw the laughter fade away. The smile collapsing. His heart *sank*. 'But I told him not to say anything to India. He promised me he wouldn't tell India . . . At least I think he did.'

'Well, *of course* he's going to tell India! Oh Ecgbert . . . Oh, *Egbert* . . .'

There came a cool breeze, a faint smell of methane, a wisp of green smoke. And from a corner of the room, not quite attached to her elegant frame, the voice of Geraldine, Lady Tode (1907–1971), still wearing Lanvin: the same deep red astrakhan cape, the same, or certainly similar, flowing velvet pantaloons with embroidery edgings. Magnificent as ever.

'Never apologise, Ecgbert, darling, and never explain,' she said to her grandson. 'Alice, to keep a husband happy, you must allow him to *express himself freely*. Husbands like to express themselves.'

Ecgbert(Sir) said: 'Not now, Granny. I've made a dreadful mistake.'

'Don't be silly. Of course you haven't. Alice, mark my words, he'll leave you. Husbands *must* be allowed to feel masters of their own house.'

'Hello, Geraldine,' said Alice, wearily. 'I thought you and Leo had gone to London to look at buildings?'

'Alice,' said Geraldine, raising a long, bony finger, and leaking – as she tended to, when annoyed – fresh wisps of green stink, 'I worry you're turning into a bully. Nobody likes a shrill. Take my advice—'

'Granny,' said Ecgbert(Sir), 'this is none of your business. And Alice does not need your advice.'

'No one is perfect, Ecgbert. Not even Alice. And please don't be impertinent to your grandmother.'

'Oh for goodness' sake,' snapped Alice, running out of patience.

Lady Tode moved quickly on. 'More importantly, Leo and I are here with some sensational news. Concerning one of the Russian guests. Possibly both. Alice, as Organisational Director, or whatever you call yourself, you may find it interesting. Don't you think so, Leo? She might find it interesting?'

Alice looked around the room. Lady Tode and her holiday friend were never far apart. 'Where is Leo?'

Lady Tode indicated a space beside her – but he was gone. 'Leo? Oh, bother! Oh, Leo, do wait!'

'Crikey! What's he up to?' Ecgbert asked, peering through the window.

Leonardo was outside in the Rose Garden already, unseen among the yogis and their yoga mats. He was staring at Bunny Rostovsky.

Bunny Rostovsky lay on her mat with eyes closed and legs in the air, exhaling. Beside her, Putin lay flat on his back, also with his eyes closed. Piers and Frederica stood barely a metre away from them, locked in their never-ending squabble. The dreaded Adele, though she didn't know it, actually merged her tight buns with Leo's tunic as she bent to roll up her mat . . . and the sky could have fallen on Tippee and he wouldn't have noticed. He sat cross-legged on his mat staring at his phone. Life went on.

Leo bent over Bunny's torso and stared at her face. His luxuriant white beard rested on her stomach, and his mouth was so close to her head it looked, to Alice, as if he was whispering into her ear.

Except he wasn't whispering. '*Madame!*' he boomed. '*Signora Rostovsky!*'

The words came out very loud indeed, to those that could

hear them. They filled the Rose Garden. They reverberated over the breakfast table in the Gardener's House kitchen, making the coffee pot rattle.

Bunny's eyes shot open.

'Know this, young madam!' he cried. 'Lady Tode and I are aware of the contents of your suitcase! We have alerted your hosts!'

Bunny sat up.

He nodded. His curly beard shimmered.

Bunny glanced about her. Nothing had changed. No one else appeared to have heard him.

He said – and again the words filled the Rose Garden. The leaves on the apple trees shook. 'That's right, Madame. The Roman coins you have taken from the exhibition panel in the Long Gallery, the sixteenth-century prayer book from the chapel, the gold and ruby—'

She screamed. In a single bounce, she was up on her bare feet. Adele, Frederica, Piers, Putin – even Tippee – paused to take a look.

Leo continued: ' . . . the gold and ruby communion cup and plate, also from the chapel, the Zhou dynasty Chinese amber contemplation beads stolen by you from the Sing-Song Room . . . '

'*Þegiðu!*'* shouted Bunny, leaping away from him.

Putin, struggling to sit up, looked quite concerned. He said to Bunny, 'Are you OK, pet?'

'She's a thief,' Leo stated.

But of course Putin couldn't see or hear him. 'Honey-Bunny?'

Leonardo inhaled. 'She has gathered into her valise

---

* 'Shut up' (Icelandic)

52

artefacts of great value,' he said importantly. (Though brilliant in many ways, and always keen to experiment, Leonardo had no ear for language.) 'And at sunrise, unless prevented, she will pass them to her co-workers out yonder and leave this shack with a swagbag of irreplaceables. Her host will soon know of this, and I swear before God Almighty and my liege King Francis of France, I shall alert the pigs in a jiffy, and they shall bung this lady *in carcere* until fair justice is served.'

Geraldine, Lady Tode chortled. 'Isn't he absolutely *marvellous?*' she said. 'Lives in a world of his own!'

Alice said: 'Is it true, though? Has Bunny stolen all those things? That's quite serious.'

'Absolutely, she has,' answered Lady Tode. 'Or she's trying to. Leonardo and I have just been on a tour of all the guests' bedrooms. For obvious reasons.'

'Brilliant of you, Granny,' Ecgbert(Sir) said. 'Did you find any clues vis-à-vis the killer?'

For some reason, the question annoyed Lady Tode. She said: 'We were delayed by the contents of that young woman's *valise*. We intend to continue with our murder investigations as soon as we've dealt with the immediate crisis.'

'Good thinking,' Ecgbert said. He turned to Alice 'What do you—'

'We must intercept the suitcase at once,' said his grandmother. 'As you know, Leo and I are unable to do that.'

There came a cry from the garden. They all turned at once.

Leonardo the ghost (1452–1519) stood on Bunny's mat, hands on hips and legs apart. Bunny, attempting to swipe at him, had – of course – found no resistance, lost her balance and tumbled to the ground.

And now she was clambering to her bare feet again. She was running through the old apple trees and disappearing through the arch in the wall without looking back, leaving poor old Putin behind her, still floundering to get up from his mat.

THE NORTH LAWN

11.09 A.M.

'Hi there, Putin!' India had a soft spot for Putin. She didn't know why. Something about fat, flirtatious men made her feel even more benign than she usually did, and India felt unusually benign, most of the time. 'Is your poor wife all right? I've just seen her rushing by. She looked terrified!'

'I'm trying to catch her myself, India,' he replied. 'I think she's seen one of her ghosts again.'

'One of her ghosts – *again?* Seriously! Are you sure she's OK?'

'Oh, she's fine,' Putin said, patting India's shoulder. 'She sees them all the time ... Mind you,' he winked, 'they don't normally give her such a fright. Normally she takes them in her stride. What kind of ghosts do you have in this place?'

India did not really believe in ghosts. In any case, she was more interested in locating her children, Passion (7) and Ludo (8), who'd taken to sneaking off to play either in the mausoleum, which was *very* much out of bounds, or in the kitchen garden greenhouses, which, though less gruesome and far less dangerous, tended to annoy Weatherstaff, the head gardener, and were therefore equally forbidden.

'Goodness, Putin, we don't have ghosts at Tode Hall,' India said. 'Don't suppose you happen to have seen the children going this way?'

Putin had not seen the children. Nevertheless, he liked to be helpful. Also, like his wife, he only told the truth if there was no lie available. 'I saw a couple of young scallywags scampering along that way,' he said, pointing at random. 'They looked about the right age.'

'Oh, they are *naughty*,' India declared proudly. 'Weatherstaff will be on the phone in half a second, complaining . . . Well – I'd better go after them. Want to come? You might like the glasshouses. Very old. Very big. I mean, they're amazing, really. I can't blame the children for wanting to play in them. They're like the palace in *Frozen* . . . if you're familiar with that film? And with stuff to eat inside. *I'd* play in them given half a chance!'

'Would you now!' said Putin, lighting up. Winking furiously. 'Well now! I'd love to play with you in your glasshouses, India!'

India chortled. And off they set. She said: 'You know what, though, Putin. I must say, for a Russian, you're very good at English . . . Imagine knowing the word for scallywag!'

'Maybe,' said Putin, 'maybe *I'm not even Russian*!'

India burst out laughing.

56

THE ROSE GARDEN

11.12 A.M.

Tippee was dragging his feet, as usual. The dreaded Adele had half a mind to leave him to it. Let him find his own way back to the house. He could hardly miss it, after all.

But no. She couldn't do that.

What if he didn't find his way back to the house properly? He never did anything properly. He never had, and – if he was anything like his pathetic father – he probably never would.

Adele stood irritably beneath the stone arch that separated the Rose Garden from the North Lawn, waiting for her charmless son to join her. She watched India (dim) and Putin (dirty) disappearing together over the horizon, and wondered how their togetherness might, in any way, impact on herself, or in any way suggest that she might on some level be missing a trick. And then she was distracted. From inside the simply accessed velcro'd outer pocket of her fawn knapsack there came a ring tone which informed her, specifically, that her weak-willed, almost-bankrupt husband was attempting to make contact.

57

'Charlie. Has something happened?'

'It's me.'

She waited.

'Esmé's a fucking idiot ... Turns out getting Rospo's not going to be quite the slam-dunk he promised. There's a fly in the ointment.'

Isn't there always? thought Adele. 'Isn't there always?' she said. 'What do you need?' *As long as it's not money.*

She'd been propping him up lately, and that was never – *NEVER* – meant to be the deal. She'd bailed him out with £1 million in the spring. Had she yet seen a penny of it back? She had not. Mark of Marylebone athleisure-to-workwear was dying. And almost every time her husband looked at her, this harsh truth floated in the air between them, the request for more of her money hovering on the tip of his tongue.

It was out of the question.

On the other hand: she couldn't allow him to sink altogether. To be brutal about it (which she never was, explicitly) her own business depended on keeping a particular image afloat. To Round the Unicorn Circle, or whatever it was she and Baby Mouse claimed to be doing, she could hardly be seen to leave the Ape to drown.

So. There was a lot going on when she asked him the question: *What do you need?* And a lot of poison flowing between them.

Fifteen years, they'd been married. The dreaded Adele had set herself up as an expert on the subject. She'd founded an international career instructing people on what it took to make a marriage work. What *she* needed was a marriage that at least looked as if it worked.

'What do I need?' snarled Charlie. 'I don't *need* anything ...

I was just ringing to give you an update. Turns out everyone in the whole of fucking Yorkshire wants to get their hands on Rospo. As of this morning, Sir Ecgbert Waste-of-Space himself has decided he wants to move there with his new wife . . . '

'*What?* Why? That's absurd! What's he going to do there?'

'Christ knows. Fuck all, if his track record is anything to go by.'

'But it's not fair! Why should *he* get it? He's useless. You and Esmé might actually make something of it.' She sighed, exasperated by so much incompetence. 'Well, you'll just have to explain to Egbert why he has to give it to you and Esmé, and not to anyone else. Who else wants it, anyway?'

The sound of gunshots.

Charlie said: 'I'm not sure. I'm fairly certain Wilson-Tite is angling . . . Look, I have to go. I just thought, maybe – might you have a little word with India? Explain the situation to her? You're so brilliant. Maybe you can help her to see how much better it would be for the family if they gave it to us. Could you do that?' . . . More shots. More shouts . . . 'I've gotta go, Adele. We'll catch up at lunch, right? See what you can do . . . I'm counting on you.' He made kissing noises into the phone, which were not reciprocated, and then he hung up.

Adele disliked her husband vastly and had very little interest – actually, minus interest – in his overall happiness. Nevertheless, Mark of Marylebone athleisurewear was going bust. That much was obvious. Her husband needed a project and the Rospo Garden Spa Retreat (working title) suited her purposes for several reasons:

- It would require only minimal added investment from her.

- With the eco emphasis (to be insisted upon) it fitted the Adele Tysedale narrative. During interviews and talks with her fans, she would be able to chatter about her husband's eco-retreat with pride.
- It would keep the idiot busy.

In the meantime, here was Tippee, keeping her waiting, still dragging his useless feet. And there, over the horizon, was India, with the flesh mountain Putin beside her ...

Adele was not the type to procrastinate. She needed to catch them up. She needed to dispatch the flesh mountain back to the house, and have a quiet word with India. Now. Before lunch. Before Sir Waste-of-Space and his drab little bride stole a march on everyone, and ran off with the prize.

'Tippee,' she said, 'I want you to head back to the Hall on your own. Can you manage that?'

Over her shoulder, across the wide lawn, the seventh largest house in Britain loomed close and clear. It would be hard – impossible – for him to get lost. On the other hand ...

'I don't know which door I'm supposed to use,' he whined. 'I won't know how to get in.'

She pointed to the front door, which itself was the size of a small villa. 'Try that one,' she said. 'If it doesn't open, just *sit*. Sit right there on the steps in front of the door, and I'll come and find you.'

He mumbled something surly and wandered off, intent on doing anything at all, except for that.

THE GLASSHOUSES

11.18 A.M.

P utin's desire to hang out with India in the Tode Hall glasshouses was at odds with his desire to lie alone on his bed
and drink water. He'd already taken more exercise this morning than he generally took in a month, and it turned out the
kitchen garden was some way from the North Lawn.

'Are we nearly there?' he asked, after ten minutes of winking
and flirting and struggling to keep up.

India said: 'Come on, Putin! The walk'll do you good!'

But Putin wasn't like India. He was almost thirty years
older, and possibly three times her weight. He said: 'India,
there's nothing I want more than to play in your crystal palace,
heheheh . . . '

He took it too far. India smiled, but she felt a bit queasy.

'However, I think if I carry on I may have a heart attack!'

'All right,' she said abruptly. He walked too slowly anyway,
and it was all very well being *flirty*: there was no need for him
to be *gross*. 'I'll see you back at the house then, shall I?'

He was slightly shocked. He'd not expected to be released so easily. It felt more like a dismissal.

Upper-class snobs, he thought. *Scratch the surface and they're all the same.*

In any case, he waddled off back to the house, having only got halfway to the kitchen garden. He spotted the dreaded Adele as she bustled past. They had nothing to say to one another, and nothing obvious to gain. They nodded but didn't bother to speak. She broke into a run as soon as she knew he wasn't looking. She didn't want to miss her chance.

India was roaming between the glasshouses, half-heartedly calling out her children's names, when Adele caught up with her. (She was unlikely to get an answer since they were currently building a camp on one of the empty coffin shelves in the mausoleum at the very opposite side of the park.)

Adele said: 'Ooh, hello, *India!* I thought that sounded like you!' As if she hadn't come all this way, especially to find her. 'Are you looking for the kids?'

'Oh, hello,' said India. 'Don't suppose you've seen them? Putin said he saw them coming this way, but I think I may have missed them ... How was Frederica's yoga?'

'Super! So much fun! Tippee adored it. Frederica is a *star*, don't you think? A real treasure!' Adele wrinkled her nose (symmetrically). 'I wish I could just *pack her up in my suitcase* and take her home with me, so Tippee and I could enjoy her yoga lessons every day!'

'I wish you would,' India said. But then she noticed the look of bewilderment on Adele's symmetrical face – and quickly backtracked. 'But no, yes. You're so right. She's incredible. I love her to bits. Did she and Piers have one of their fights? I bet they did.'

'Maybe a teeny weeny one!' giggled Adele. 'Young love, eh?'

'Not that young. *Actually.* Piers is the same age as Egbert. I just wish they'd . . . ' She stopped. Smiled. 'Anyway. Have you come to see the famous glasshouses, Adele? They have tomatoes and everything. People love them.'

'Tomatoes? In October? My goodness, I would love to see that, India. Thank you so much! What a wonderful hostess you are!'

India said nothing. Maybe this weekend wasn't going to be such fun after all. The two women fell into step. After a while, Adele said: 'So lovely to see Sir Ecgbert has found happiness. It must be such a relief for you and Egbert, to know there's someone who can share the responsibility.'

India said: 'Do you mean by marrying Alice?'

'She seems like such a lovely lady.'

India said: '*Alice?*'

Adele hesitated. ' . . . Yes . . . '

India said, 'Of course she is.'

Adele tried again. 'How is he managing, with you and Egbert in the Hall? Does that work well? I bet it does! He is so fortunate, to have you both there, *in loco*, looking out for him. You and Egbert do such an amazing job, keeping him busy, keeping him out of harm's way . . . I am truly . . . lost in admiration. So is Charlie!'

India said: 'He keeps himself out of harm's way. He's not a baby.' But she wasn't terribly interested. 'You'll never guess what Putin just said to me . . . '

Adele understood that to control a dialogue, you had to allow space for a little contraflow every now and then. (Especially when dealing with fluffy-headed morons like India Tode.) So, instead of pushing the Rospo agenda *just yet*, she paused it, offered up a cosy titter and said: 'Oh India! I'm not sure I want to hear it, do I? Go on, tell me – what did he say?'

'He said he wanted to pay Egbert and me three million pounds to rent Tode Hall for one year. I'm not sure if he was serious. But I mean ... I said to him ... *why not?*'

'My goodness!' said Adele, yet again. She was trying to work out in what way this information might be useful. 'Well, I should think that would be the going rent ... Does it include bills?'

'What? I've no idea ...' India sighed. 'I don't suppose Egbert would entertain it but imagine what fun it would be! We could spend a year in Greece. Or Italy. We could spend the year at *Rospo*. Build a pool. Learn Italian ...'

'Rospo? I don't think that would work,' Adele said sharply.

'No, probably not ...' Another sigh. 'Never mind. He was probably talking out of his you-know-what – out of his arse-hole – I don't suppose he meant it for one second. Look! See?' India said. In front of them, rows of thriving tomatoes. 'Not bad, eh? For boring old rainy Yorkshire.'

Adele said: 'On the subject of Rospo ...'

AFRICA FOLLY

LUNCHTIME

You could look down onto the whole of Tode Hall from the south-facing windows of Africa Folly. See the house splayed out in all its glory. From the opposite windows you could look down onto the matching dome of the family mausoleum. Africa Folly was a single-storey castellated affair, built in that spot – with the magnificent views – by the 7th Sir Ecgbert, specifically for shooting lunches.

Inside was just one room (aside from a lavatory, added in the 1970s). The table, which ran the length of the room, was covered in a white linen cloth, and had already been laid for lunch. At the end of the room, a roaring fire burned.

It was not a large party. Only fifteen guests were expected:

- India and Egbert(Mr) Tode
- Alice and Ecgbert(Sir) Tode
- Esmé Tode and his safety-conscious sister, Nicola
- Bunny and Putin Rostovsky

- Frederica Ranaldini and her vampire-lookalike love-slave, Piers Slayer-Wilson-Tite
- The dreaded Adele Tysedale and her seedy, almost-bankrupt husband, Charlie
- Tippee Tysedale and his mobile device, and finally –
- (Rarely mentioned but never completely forgotten) India and Egbert's young children, Passion and Ludo Tode

At this point everyone but Esmé was present. Passion and Ludo, covered in cobwebs and woodlice, were stealing bread off the long table before anyone had sat down. Nicola, who didn't generally bother to turn up to shooting lunches, was yelling at them to stop, from behind her dirty visor, and they were ignoring her. Same old, same old.

But where was Esmé?

Egbert(Mr) said to India, 'I think we'd better start without him.'

'For some reason Charlie and Adele say they want to wait,' India told him. 'By the way, Putin's come up with the most amazing idea—'

'Frankly I don't care what they want,' snapped Egbert.

India was quite shocked.

He apologised at once. 'Oh Gosh, Munch, I'm *sorry*. I really am . . . It's been a difficult morning . . . First Frederica mucking us all about, for her own . . . dark . . . reasons. And then Esmé won't shut up about wanting to take over Rospo for some sort of eco-tourism venture with Charlie . . . which would have been fine. A really good idea, probably. But now Ecgbert and Alice want it, too. So someone's going to have to be dreadfully disappointed . . . Unless they take it on together, which isn't ideal.

Plus ... ' He pulled at his dark hair (greying, India noticed, and quite quickly, these days. He needed to relax more). 'Plus ... '

'Alice and Ecgbert want it?' India repeated. (Sharp as a knife.) 'Whatever for?'

'What?' *Damn.* He'd not meant to tell her that. Not until he'd had a proper chat with Alice and Ecgbert. 'Sorry, did I say that? That's not what I meant.'

'Oh good. Because I was thinking maybe *we* should take over Rospo,' she said. 'Turn it into a lovely place for the summer. Putin—'

'*Us?* Oh God, *please*, India ... ' He looked – and this was extraordinary: Egbert(Mr) hadn't even shed a tear when his mother died – but in that moment he looked as if he might be about to cry.

'I say, Egbert ... Have you got a sec?' Still clasping his fore-lock, Egbert turned to see Piers looming towards him.

'What do you want, Piers?'

Piers raised an eyebrow. 'Just a sec of your time,' he said defensively. 'If you've got one to spare ... '

'I suppose so ... ' Egbert pulled himself together. 'I mean, *of course*. Sorry. What's up?'

'Frederica's going nuts.'

Egbert looked politely concerned.

Piers laughed. 'I'm not joking. She actually beat me up this morning. In front of half the guests ... ' Piers tilted his remark-able face, tapped his pale cheek just below the cheekbone. 'You can still see the mark ... '

'Crikey,' said Egbert. He giggled, embarrassed. 'What the hell did you do to annoy her?'

Piers said it wasn't what he'd *done*, so much as what he hadn't done. 'She's determined to go back to Italy.'

'Right you are,' said Egbert. (He certainly wouldn't miss her.)

'She wants to go back to Villa Rospo,' he said. 'To be honest, so do I ... We were pretty happy there. I mean ...' He had the grace to look a little awkward. 'I'm not saying it was a conventional kind of happiness ... But – you said yourself before it all happened, what a great job we were doing ... Ask Alice and Ecgbert. They'll tell you. We had the place running like clockwork. Can't we go back, now it's autumn? Get the thing back up and running?'

Egbert sighed. His shoulders dropped. 'Piers, we've already discussed this.'

'But that was *then*,' said Piers. 'I haven't mentioned it for a month. For fuck's sake, Tode. She harangues me. Constantly. Every fucking day – Just ... *please*.'

'Piers.' Egbert(Mr) dropped his voice. He spoke extra slowly. 'I mean, really ... there's the matter of *tact*, vis-à-vis the tragedy. And respecting the parents' wishes and all that. One can't simply ride roughshod ...'

Piers waved this aside. Egbert was getting the wrong end of the stick. 'She wants to go back to Rospo. And so do I. And I don't see why you won't let us. And neither does she. *Please* ... At least say you'll consider it ...'

Egbert sighed. '... Piers ... There are so many reasons why it can't happen. As I say, I'm pretty sure her parents won't allow it. Plus ...' Egbert stopped. 'By the way, have you seen Esmé?'

A moment passed. Piers, his beautiful hands in his back pockets, glared at his old school friend. His old school acquaintance. They hadn't been friends. With his silver tongue and his vampire beauty, Piers had been in another league when they were teenagers. In fact, despite being in the same year and the same house, he and Egbert had barely spoken. Back then, Egbert had known his place. Now ... Now, here was Piers. *Begging.*

He spun on his winkle-picking boot, and left without another word.

Egbert(Mr) sighed in relief. That was that. Now it was time to eat. Lunch had already been transported from the Hall by Mr Carfizzi, and his wife, Mrs Carfizzi (returned from her extra-marital adventures several months back, a stronger, happier woman, and a better cook). Roasted pheasant and sundry extras awaited the guests' attention. They had been laid out in silver salvers along the length of the table for almost half an hour now, and were already quite cold.

Egbert(Mr) clapped his hands. 'Come on, everyone! Nosh-time! Let's eat!'

The dreaded Adele did not eat roasted pheasant, let alone sundry extras. She had spent forty-five minutes in the Hall kitchen before dinner the previous evening, explaining to Mrs Carfizzi (74) her own and Tippee's weekend dietary needs. Mrs Carfizzi had nodded throughout, and pretended, as was her wont when feeling obstructive, that she didn't speak or understand English. In any case, Adele didn't travel anywhere without a catering tray arranged with her gluten-, meat- and dairy-free menu favourites. She gave the tray to Mrs Carfizzi, who dumped it in the larder and left it there. So. While the others tucked into the pheasant, Adele made a fuss about the missing catering tray. Egbert(Mr), full of apologies, called back to the Hall and asked for it to be brought up.

There followed a bit of a stand-off between Adele and Tippee, because Tippee was hungry and wanted to eat what was already on offer. Adele forbade it.

'He has a very sensitive stomach,' she explained to Bunny, who happened to be nearby, and who couldn't have been less interested.

Bunny, dressed in a short mink jacket and tight leather trousers, nodded understandingly. 'You can't be too careful,' she said. 'Back in Minsk where I grew up –'

'*Minsk?*' said Adele, wrinkling her nose. 'Goodness. How fascinating!'

'– my grandmother was also very particular. Too many colours on a table alerted the bob demons, she used to say. "Rakshasa." That's what she said.' Bunny shrugged. 'And maybe she was right.'

'That's so fascinating,' said Adele.

'Potato soup was also a big no-no. Same rationale.' Bunny looked back at Adele, deadpan. It was astonishing to her how much gibberish you could speak in polite society without being called out. She did it, often, in situations like this, only to stop herself from falling asleep, with the boredom.

Adele thought Bunny was dressed like a prostitute. 'How fascinating to come from Minsk,' Adele said. Her book sold very well in Norway. She liked Norway. (Was Minsk in Norway?) 'I do think we, in the West, are very casual about what we put inside our bodies.' Adele mimed putting something into her mouth.

Bunny nodded. 'Rakshasa,' she said.

'Rakshasa,' repeated Adele.

70

Lunch ground on.

Still no sign of Esmé.

India had messed up on the seating. Rather, she'd not bothered with it at all, so now she, Bunny and Adele were stuck together in a triangle of politeness, at the bottom of the table.

India's eyes wandered the room.

Piers and Frederica looked furious. (Nothing new there.)

Ecgbert and Alice looked sad.

Eggzie looked stressed.

Charlie Tysedale looked shifty.

Putin looked – actually Putin looked quite upbeat. He was trying to flirt with Frederica, rocking on his big fat bottom, laughing at his own feeble jokes – not in the least put out by Frederica's brutal refusal to respond.

India wished she'd sat herself next to her children. They were in a world of their own, ignoring everyone but each other, talking loudly and confidently about what it might feel like to be stabbed, and intermittently pushing each other off their chairs. Unlike anyone else in the room they at least looked like they were having fun.

India smiled. Sighed. Caught her husband's eye, at the far end of the table. He pulled a face, indicated the door – she didn't know what it meant, but then he stood up and left the room. She wondered where he was going.

Pudding arrived. Lemon meringue pie for everyone except Tippee and Adele, who had something Adele called 'quinoa-flake tap'.

India said it looked delicious.

Tippee, on the other side of his mother, said, 'It tastes like sick.'

And lunch ground on.

'There's a super place in Dover Street,' Bunny said to Adele, 'which scans the body with electro genomic themesis detectors. Identifies *all* the gremlins and zaps them in one go. Super state-of-the-art; I can't recommend it enough.'

'Sounds amazing!' Adele said.

Bunny nodded. 'Catalysing Titration,' she said. 'It's a fourteen-week course. So it's a bit of a commitment. But I swear, you come out feeling amazing. I'll give you the details.'

And it ground on.

Where the hell was Egbert? She couldn't be expected to do this alone!

India was reminding herself that he'd never wanted the weekend to happen in the first place: she was just thinking what a very nice man he was, and how much she loved him. She was trying to persuade herself that the weekend might yet improve. Also, that Putin's offer of £3 million might come to something. Also, that somewhere among this roomful of – mostly – not very nice people ... there may even lurk a killer.

And then—

From just outside the door there came a noise: an ear-splitting BOOM! A most violent explosion. Louder than a shotgun. Louder than anything anyone had ever heard.

The door opened. The room fell silent.

And in staggered Egbert(Mr), covered in blood. Blood pouring from his head. Blood everywhere.

He stood stock-still, behind his chair at the head of the table.

No one spoke.

And then, behind him, ashen-faced, in stepped Esmé, also spattered in blood. He was carrying something in his hand.

Egbert swayed.

Everyone stared.

Egbert said: 'I've been a ruddy fool. I'm so sorry.'

India screamed. The children screamed.

Egbert(Mr) collapsed to the floor.

From somewhere, in the micro-second of stunned silence that followed, before the humans present had time to comprehend what they had witnessed, there came a chilling cry, not heard by many. It was Leonardo the anatomist (1452–1519). He swept through the room at the speed of – not as fast as light, but faster than sound: very, very quickly indeed. 'The killer has struck again!' he cried. 'Let me see! Let me see!' He bent over the body. 'Move! Out of my way! *Fatemi vedere il collo! Cosa gli hanno fatto,* these monsters?' It seemed to Lady Tode that he might have been either weeping or giggling. But she didn't understand what he said.

There was only one person present who could see him and hear him, and who understood. Without another word, Bunny Rostovsky picked up her handbag and sidled out of the room.

Leonardo didn't notice. He was glowering at Egbert(Mr)'s prone body, just as he had glowered at Elizabetta's when she was pulled from the moonlit waters of the Rospo four months before. Nobody paid much attention to him on that occasion, either. He was quivering with curiosity; already convinced that the two incidents were linked.

And perhaps he was right.

Let's rewind, then. Let's travel to beautiful Rospo, and rejoin the party at its happiest point, or at any rate, to a time when everyone involved was still alive.

ITALY

VILLA ROSPO
ROSPO NEL BUCO
FOUR MONTHS EARLIER

A NICE DAY IN JUNE

VILLA ROSPO'S FINEST BEDROOM

10.15 A.M.

'Well, I must say, Trudy – one thing I will say. We're jolly lucky with the weather and all that,' Sir Ecgbert Tode, 12th Bart, newly married to the love of his life, gazed from the open balcony window down onto Villa Rospo's famous gardens.

'Italy in June,' said Alice, sipping coffee, sighing blissfully, still lying in the bed. 'The best weather in the world, the most beautiful place in the world . . . Not so bad, is it, Ecgbert?'

'Seriously, though. Do you think I'm being mad? Or do you think they might actually be spying on us?'

'I think you're being a bit mad.'

'But there *must* be somewhere else they could set up their ruddy mats? There's only three of them, Trudy. They're laughing at us. I swear . . . Look at them! They're looking purposely ridiculous. They're messing with our minds.'

Alice climbed out of their giant bed and padded across the cool red-tiled floor to have a look for herself.

Ecgbert might have a point.

Villa Rospo was nothing special: quite big, quite pretty, quite run-down; built from scratch at the end of the nineteenth century by the couple that transformed the surrounding patch of land into the giant pleasure garden spread out below them this morning.

But the pleasure garden – it was something else. Directly beneath Ecgbert and Alice's bedroom balcony, set around the ruins of an ancient city, lay 40 acres of a landscaped wonderland. Lawns and streams and fresh-water pools separated the flower-decked ruins of a Roman tower, a Roman pigsty, a crumbling street of Roman terraced houses, and the remains of three large medieval churches. There were ancient fruit groves, and a giant bamboo forest, and ancient bridges and nineteenth-century 'contemplation huts' along the curving riverbanks. It was more than beautiful. It was spectacular. The famous Gardens at Rospo deserve a full description – some other time. First: there was the matter currently exercising Sir Ecgbert.

Directly below his bedroom balcony, perhaps 5 metres from the house, lay three rubber yoga mats; and on them, their bottoms in the air, two familiar figures, and a third figure, who (sadly) would very soon be dead.

Piers Slayer-Wilson-Tite, folded into an *adho mukha svana-sana*, bottom pointed balcony-ward, was sandwiched between two beautiful women: Frederica Ranaldini, and her sister, Piers' wife, the soon-to-be-dead Elizabetta.

The Ranaldini family had been involved with the gardens for generations – since long before Egbert(Mr) and India had any connection with the place. In fact, since before any Tode had any connection with the place. They knew it inside out, better than anyone. And the Todes were traditionally, eternally grateful to them. The Ranaldinis managed everything, from the cleaning and cooking in the villa to the organisation of VIP garden tours for visiting dignitaries. Elizabetta was a qualified accountant with a master's degree in landscape ecology and conservation. She was currently Rospo's General Manager, and also, more humbly, its housekeeper. Her sister, Frederica, meanwhile (a little more beautiful but not quite so clever, also notoriously bad tempered), had numerous diplomas in yoga. Frederica still lived with her parents a few miles up the road, but due to a shortage of willing yoga students in the area, she tended to be around a lot. She had her own little apartment at the top of the house. When the villa was occupied, by Todes (almost never) or by paying tenants (not often), she offered her services as a private cook.

Nobody was quite sure when or how Elizabetta had hooked up with Piers Slayer-Wilson-Tite, but somehow he had inveigled himself into the Ranaldini set-up. He'd made himself delightful and/or useful (the former, most likely), got himself a not-too-taxing role in the running of things – and along the way, married the boss.

Normally, they lived peacefully in the villa, undisturbed by Todes or tourists. Government subsidies flooded in, money flowed and accounts were filed, and – to be fair – the gardens were immaculately maintained. But, except for the occasional VIPs – visiting politicians, Hollywood stars or whatnot – tourists were kept at bay. It meant Piers and Elizabetta usually had the house and garden to themselves. This week, while Ecgbert and his bride were enjoying their honeymoon, they had quietly moved back into their official apartment on the ground floor, behind the kitchen.

And so, while his wife specialised in everything and his

sister-in-law specialised in bad-tempered yoga and cooking, Piers specialised in doing nothing. Through handsomeness and sleight of hand, Piers lived his life from one day to the next, looking like a vampire, smoking weed, drinking lager, occasionally burying himself in conspiracy theories involving UFOs; and getting laid. He led an unusually pleasant life. Despite the fact that he hadn't a penny to his name. Piers was always on the scrounge, and he was always broke.

'Why would they want to stick their bottoms in the air – right in front of our window?' Ecgbert asked. 'Don't they know it's our honeymoon?'

Of course they knew. Alice and Ecgbert had been in residence a week already: a wonderful week, because they loved each other and because the famous garden at Rospo might well have been among the most romantic, most beautiful spots in the world. Nevertheless, Elizabetta, Piers and Frederica were used to having the place to themselves. They would have much preferred Sir Ecgbert and Lady Tode to have enjoyed their honeymoon somewhere else – obviously. And whether by design or otherwise, they had made the newlyweds feel like intruders.

'There's something weird about them always being together,' Ecgbert said.

Alice agreed. 'There's a weird dynamic.'

'Sexual.'

'A little bit . . . '

'Granny calls it a *ménage à trois*. I think she may be on to something. Shall we go and have breakfast?'

The terrace, thankfully, was on the other side of the house, and Frederica had laid out a fine breakfast for them. There were slices of melon and some *cornetti* still warm from the baker, and freshly squeezed orange juice awaiting them. Also present, dressed in turban and Emilio Pucci leopard-skin swimming costume, tapping her imaginary teacup, gazing over the cypress trees – was Geraldine, Lady Tode. Rubies dangled from her earlobes, catching the sun and emphasising her long, slim neck.

She waited until Alice and Ecgbert had sat down before deigning to acknowledge their arrival.

She said 'Good *morning*,' as if, somehow, they had already done something very wrong. And in a way, they already had. She was still angry about the marriage. Despite her fondness for Alice. Yes, she was fond of Alice, and yes, she loved her grandson. Nevertheless.

Ahem.

Nevertheless ...

The fact of the matter was – Alice's grandmother had, for many years, worked at Tode Hall as Geraldine's lady's maid. This, in fact, was how Alice, living in Clapham, came to hear of the job vacancy in the first place. (Her grandmother saw the advertisement for Organisational Director advertised in *The Lady*, and, worried by Alice's empty days and empty bank account, had applied for the job on Alice's behalf, without actually telling her.)

Geraldine, Lady Tode would learn to live with the situation in time. But at this point, it was only a week after the wedding, and she was still sulking.

'Morning, Granny,' said Ecgbert equably. 'You're up early.'

Geraldine, Lady Tode said: 'Ten fifteen is not early, Ecgbert.'

Ecgbert said: 'I beg to differ,' and poured himself some coffee.

Alice said: 'Well, it's –

[Geraldine, Lady Tode inhaled.]

81

– *quite* early. If you're on holiday.'

'"On *holiday*",' repeated Lady Tode. '"On *holiday*", indeed . . . Only bus drivers and secretaries go *on holiday*, Alice dear. One doesn't go *on holiday* . . . One goes *away*.' Lady Tode sighed, and it caused a brief windstorm over the breakfast table. A *cornetto* rolled onto the floor.

Alice chuckled. She didn't care.

Lady Tode returned her attention to the Cypress trees. She said: 'I met someone in the garden last night. Interestingly, the Duke of Milan dispatched him here, many years ago, to do something about the swamps . . . There were dreadful swamps. Mosquitoes and TB and whatnot. Half the city was dying of TB. Well—'

'What are you talking about, Granny?'

'If you could do me the politeness to be silent for a single moment, Ecgbert, I would tell you,' replied Lady Tode. 'You might even find it quite interesting. The point is he's been here on and off for over four hundred years, and he knows *all* the gossip. Added to which, he's an extremely distinguished gentleman. Even you might have heard of him, Ecgbert, dear . . . '

Like a dancer, inviting her co-star to share the applause, Lady Tode raised a long slim arm. 'Leo, darling, are you ready?' she called out . . . 'Alice and Ecgbert, I would very much like you to meet . . . '

He appeared from the other side the wall, tiptoeing and giggling; the same dark stockings, pink tunic, ludicrous pink hat . . . Clearly, the entrance was something they had prepared. Lady Tode inhaled:

'May I introduce . . .

'The *anatomist*

'The *engineer*

'The *inventor of helicopters*

'Not to mention ... '

'Te-dar!' cried Leonardo, who couldn't wait any longer. He lifted his beret and bowed. 'Leo Da Vinci,' he declared. 'I am at your service!'

Neither Alice nor Ecgbert, nor, in fact, anyone alive or dead, had seen Geraldine, Lady Tode laugh with such merry abandon. She and Leonardo giggled like two gleeful schoolchildren.

Finally, Alice said: 'Gosh. Well, that's ... Crikey, is it really ...? It's a pleasure to meet you ... '

'I told you!' snorted Lady Tode. 'I told you they'd be amazed! These children continually underestimate one!'

Alice was dazzled. It didn't happen often. She was dazzled, and impressed. She struggled to remain cool, and sadly, failed completely. 'It's an honour to meet you,' she said. 'I went on a school trip to France once, many years ago. We had to queue for hours and hours with our long sandwiches – you know those long sandwiches?'

He nodded. Yes, he did.

'We had to queue with these massive sandwiches outside the Louvre,' she said again. '... Until finally ... *finally* we got to see the – the –' Her mind went blank. She couldn't remember its name. It was the most famous painting in the world. And she had seen it on the school trip. And it was called ... '... The *painting* ...' Alice stopped. '... It was amazing. Golly. I'm so sorry. I'm gabbling ... You can imagine ... Why are you ...? How come you're ...? Why?'

Lady Tode looked quite delighted. She said, 'I bet you're happy I came to Italy now!'

'Wouldn't go that far, Granny,' Ecgbert(Sir) replied. 'Most

83

people don't take their granny on honeymoon. Even so ... very nice to meet you, Leonardo. Very nice. If a bit weird, as Alice says. What brings you to Rospo?'

Leonardo said he'd grown fond of the place over the centuries. He often popped in. It was wonderful, he said, to see how it had been transformed through the years. 'Of course,' he added, 'I only witnessed the last few yesteryears in the physical dimensions. Like you, the first 1.5k ... calendar years ... are ... a *mind trip scenario*, Sir Ecgbert. We must have to imagine it together.'

Lady Tode gurgled with laughter again. 'Of course. Even Leo can't time travel,' she said.

A little history:

The town of Rospo had been around and thriving since before the Romans built the Appian Way. However, when they built the Appian Way (around 340 BC) they by-passed the thriving town of Rospo by twenty-odd miles, as a consequence of which, the town lost much of its through-traffic, and fell into disrepair ... Evidence of Rospo's ancient beginnings could be seen, even now, from Alice and Ecgbert's breakfast terrace.

Rospo's fortunes ebbed and flowed through the centuries, eventually evolving into a stinking, diseased, swamp-ridden medieval city – and the ruins of that, too, could be seen from the breakfast terrace. There were the three ruined churches in Rospo's famous garden, the ruined Roman street of terraced houses, and many ancient graves. Even today, the Rospo gardeners turned up human bones.

A hundred years ago, the Todes hitched their marital wagon to the Italian heiress who owned the land, and between them, they transformed the ruins of the two abandoned cities into an English aristocrat's pleasure garden. And so –

Here they all sat.

'As Lady Tode was just attempting to drill into you hobos, the first time I visited this place, it was 1489,' Leonardo said. 'I was dispatched here in great urgency by his Grace the Duke of Milan to see what I might do to fix the swamps . . . Everyone was dying . . . ' Leo paused. He chuckled to himself, picturing the stinking mess that had greeted him.

Lady Tode said, 'I've already told them about all that, Leo. Tell them about the Ranaldinis! He has some exceptional information regarding the Ranaldini family.'

'And I will be direct with you, groovers,' Leo said, wholly ignoring the interruption, 'it was a gross-fest.'

'What was a gross-fest?' asked Alice. She was confused.

'In 1489 the city of Rospo was a gross-fest, Alice.'

'Do you mean the Ranaldinis, as in Frederica and Elizabetta, currently outside the bedroom window, doing the yoga?' Ecgbert(Sir) asked. 'What have they got to do with this?'

Leo raised a hand. A very small hand, Alice noted. She tried to imagine the hand holding a paintbrush, painting the famous picture whose name she still couldn't remember. '*Patience*,' said Leonardo, 'is a virtue. And virtue is a grace . . . '

'What?' said Ecgbert. 'What are you talking about? I'm completely lost. Can we redirect pointward? I say, Trudy, is there any coffee in that pot?'

But (as His Grace the Duke of Milan, and his Liege the King of France had both learned to their cost) Leonardo did not like to be hurried, let alone redirected pointward. 'His Grace the Duke implored me to pull together an activity team. Urgent activity was required to fix the city of Rospo's drainage crisis. At the time I was engaged in building a remarkable self-propelling metal canon for His Grace the Duke. It would have been the first ever known to mankind ... However. As luck would have it, he begged me to set this aside and to come to Rospo to rescue the stinking situation here. This I did ... Well.' He looked momentarily disappointed. 'Well – no, I didn't ... I of course had the ingenious masterplan within a short time, but unfortunately this was rendered unworkable by its human components ... We employed a Ranaldini to manage and oversee the activity ... and of course it came to pass that he couldn't be trusted. Antonio Ranaldini – I see him here, kicking around the place sometimes. So I assume that his actions of 1489 continue to haunt him, as they do me ... The sly dog took the gold and he disappeared! The Duke sent men out in search of the scoundrel. *Ovviamente*. But from what I understand no one ever saw him, or the gold, ever again ... ' For a moment, Leonardo looked quite furious. His mortal life had been littered with unfinished projects. He might have learned to come to terms with them by now. It was just that, for once, his inability to achieve anything here at Rospo had not solely been down to his failed attention span. 'You understand,' he said, 'if the villain Ranaldini hadn't made off with his Grace's gold, who knows what a glorious city might be standing here now?'

Alice clapped her hands on the table: 'The *Mona Lisa*!' she cried. 'Oh my goodness, how could I forget that? I swear I couldn't remember its name ... Leo – may I call you Leo?'

He nodded, with his heavy head, still brooding on his foiled drainage plans. It wasn't only Ranaldini who was to blame, and he knew this. ' ... A tragedy of titanic proportions. A titanic tragedy,' he said. 'Of course, I might have stuck around. Perhaps I could have persuaded the Duke to send more cash. Instead I convinced myself at once that the ball game was a bust, what with the mosquitoes sending me demented with their ceaseless buzzing, and thus – I bounced. Or scarpered, as you say. Back to that wicked young man. I never *finish* things, you see.'

Alice laughed. 'But you achieved so much! Most people don't even *start* things. Let alone finish them. And you finished so many things . . .The *Mona Lisa* . . .'

He shook himself. Looked up at the sun and the cypress trees and the big blue sky. 'The important thing is this: always, my friends, *always* you must follow the blood . . . Antonio Ranaldini preferred to take the money and leave his town to sink into disease and swamp. Those girls would do the same. *Do not trust those girls* . . .'

'Are you sure?' Ecgbert said. 'It was five hundred years ago, after all. That's a lot of years . . . Do we even know if it's the same Ranalilinidis?'

'Ranaldini,' Leo corrected him: 'Sir Ecgbert, believe me, there will only ever be *one* Ranaldini family in Rospo nel Buco. They are bad people. Wicked people, may God have mercy on their vibrations. Do not trust them.'

And then, because he was a genius who quickly tired of things, Leonardo became a sparkle: a flash of fire, and he disappeared.

'Oh! Leo! Wait!' Lady Tode, being a less-practised immortal, took longer to vaporise. She left behind a foul-smelling cloud of green.

And silence.

Over the coffee and orange juice, Alice and Ecgbert looked at one another.

'Crikey,' said Ecgbert. 'Not sure what to make of all that.'

'Me neither.'

'Sometimes, you have to ask yourself if you're dreaming.'

Alice nodded. 'How could I forget the name of the *Mona Lisa*, Ecgbert? We went on a school trip, all the way to Paris! ... And we had these long sandwiches ... ' She'd already told him that. Not that it mattered. Such was married life. She laughed, thinking about the sandwiches. 'Baguettes. We thought they were so funny!'

'What shall we do today, Trudy?' Ecgbert said. 'Shall we go to the sea?'

HOTEL DE RUSSIE

ROME

7.15 P.M.

ndia Tode was explosively happy when Alice and Ecgbert(Sir) announced their engagement, back in the spring. She prided herself on having a nose for these things and, as she mentioned several times to Egbert(Mr), she hadn't been remotely surprised by the news. Not even *remotely*. Despite the fact that Alice and Ecgbert(Sir) sprung it on them out of nowhere, before they'd even come clean about being in a relationship at all.

'I knew it!' India had said. 'I *always* knew there was something a bit special between you two! Didn't I say it, Eggzie? Ages ago?'

'You certainly did, Munchie,' her husband agreed.

And to be fair to India, she did normally have a nose for these things. She loved it when her friends got together. She loved it when they were happy. She loved Alice. She loved Ecgbert(Sir).

She loved weddings. She loved it when love-conquered-all. And so on. India was a very warm and kind individual.

Nevertheless, she was only human. Once the wedding was over, she felt a bit put out.

Ecgbert and Alice had insisted on keeping the party small: just Alice's grown-up triplet boys, difficult Nicola in her PPE, trying her best to be nice, and a hotchpotch of their old friends (for a couple in their fifties, a lot of their friends were already dead – a reflection of their dishevelled lives, no doubt, and, indeed, of how alike they were in spirit). In any case, once India had thrown the last of the confetti over their departing car, she had turned to her husband and said: 'Eggzie, seriously, we don't look at each other the way Alice and Ecgbert do . . . Do you think we're getting bored of each other?'

Egbert(Mr) was appalled. 'Certainly not!' he said.

The upshot was – an emergency mini-break, far away from boring old rainy Yorkshire. India had observed to Egbert(Mr) that Alice and Ecgbert(Sir) going to Rospo reminded her of how lovely Italy was. She'd suggested a weekend in Rome. Immediately. At once. To cheer themselves up about having been married for so long. (Nine years.)

Egbert(Mr) cancelled his meetings, told his biking pals he wouldn't be biking this weekend . . . And booked the two of them into the most elegant hotel in Rome. Seven days after Alice and Ecgbert(Sir) tied the knot and flew off on their honeymoon, India and Ecgbert(Mr) checked into the Russie.

And here they were. India and Egbert(Mr) were showered and changed, and had just ordered drinks to be brought to them in the Hotel de Russie's famous garden bar. All was well. It was better than well.

India leaned back on her chair and sighed with contentment.

The air was filled with the scent of jasmine and everywhere she turned beautiful people were ordering beautiful drinks.

'This is the life!' she said to Egbert(Mr).

He was checking his phone. He was tapping out a message to the Estate manager about – something to do with permits for added retail space in the pottery gallery. Something urgent. It had been quite a commotion for him, getting away at such short notice. So he didn't reply to India at once.

After nine years of marriage, India was quite used to this. 'Imagine if Alice and Ecgbert suddenly walked in!' she continued. 'Wouldn't it be funny! What would they think? They'd be amazed ... They might think we were stalking them.' She laughed, not expecting feedback. 'Maybe we *are* stalking them ... I don't *think* we are ... Are we? ... Yikes ... '

The drinks arrived. Two Negronis. Beautiful colour and very strong. India said '*Grazie mille*' in her finest Italian, and she beamed at the handsome waiter, with all her shiny blonde hair, and he beamed back; and Egbert, scowling at his phone, tapped out:

viz a viz drop in footfall etc. Best regards, ET

He pressed send.

'What's that, Munch?'

Her attention had been caught by a couple on a nearby table. Up to no good, she assumed.

'Look at those two. Over there,' she said. 'I bet you a million pounds that's not his wife.'

Egbert(Mr) was checking his weather app.

The man looked a bit seedy; grey hair, crumpled linen suit, puffy face: prematurely aged – like someone (India thought) who spent a lot of time and money with hookers. English, she reckoned. Public school, obviously ... Might have been quite good-looking once ... and most definitely not with his wife ...

'Says it's going to be gorgeous tomorrow ...' Egbert(Mr) said. '... twenty-seven degrees ...'

The woman looked far younger than him. Italian, obviously. And – so far as India could see – beautiful: shiny hair, big brown eyes, perfect nose, perfect figure. She looked less dolled up than most of the women in the bar ... but very self-confident. Sexy, India thought, and probably *not* a prostitute, despite the way the man was looking at her. Also, India noted, the woman wasn't flirting. Quite the opposite, in fact. She looked almost disdainful.

'Intriguing,' India said to herself.

The man pulled out a thick envelope and slid it across the table towards her.

India gasped.

The woman took it swiftly, slipped it onto her lap and began to check the contents.

'Do look, Eggzie!' India whispered. 'He's passing her an envelope! I think it's got – She's – Oh my goodness ... it's got money in it. She *must* be a prostitute. But she doesn't look like a prostitute, does she?'

At the word prostitute, Egbert(Mr) looked up. 'Who?' he said. 'Where?' He followed India's gaze ... Looked. And then looked again. 'Oh my goodness! Oh, *hell*.'

'What?'

'Shhh!'

'What? Eggzie?'

Egbert hunched his shoulders. He dropped his voice and muttered through the side of his mouth, 'India, seriously – the

92

guy with the – the *guy*. We were at school together. For God's sake, don't let him see us. He'll ruin our night.'

'Egbert!'

'He's horrid—'

'*Eggzie!!*'

'Tysedale. Four years above. Charlie Tysedale. He was in my house.'

India said: 'Do you think that's his wife?'

Egbert curled up a little smaller. 'Shhh!' he said miserably.

'Eggz!' India laughed. 'This is not like you . . . '

From his ball-like position he peered at the woman. 'No,' he whispered, finally. 'That is definitely not his wife. He married that girl – you'll have heard of her – she writes those books about relationships. And *he* – Tysedale – made a mint, selling gents' sportswear. He's got all those shops at the airport.'

Egbert(Mr) considered this. 'Or he did. Now I think about it, I haven't seen them for a while.' He sounded hopeful. 'Maybe they went belly-up?'

India said: 'Well, he can't be completely bust or he wouldn't be drinking at the Russie . . . And passing envelopes of cash to strange women.'

'Good point.'

India continued to stare.

'Please, darling. Try to be subtle. This is our romantic weekend. We don't want it ruined. Please, please don't catch his eye—'

'OH. MY. GOD.' India put down her drink. '*Egg! Egbert! LOOK!* Look who's just joined them! . . . *Wow! He looks terrible.*'

They'd last seen him four years ago when life was peachy. He had come home for a whistle-stop visit, golden brown from the Aussie sun, and brimming with health and fitness. The

93

updated version of Esmé Tode, just now settling himself down at Charlie Tysedale's table, looked thinner, sadder, slyer. He was hardly recognisable.

'Good God!' exclaimed Egbert(Mr). 'It's Esmé. I don't believe it! If he was already in Europe, why the hell didn't he come to his brother's wedding last week?'

'Let's find out!' India replied, and before Egbert(Mr) could stop her, she was up on her feet, steaming across the garden to greet him. In fact, she barely knew Esmé. He'd come home for his mother's funeral, but other than that he'd only visited Tode Hall on one occasion since India had been in residence. This didn't matter. For India, who loved suntans and parties, it was thrilling to be bumping into people in glamorous spots like the Russie. It made her feel less like a boring old rainy Yorkshire *hausfrau*, and more like an active member of the international jet set. So she whooped with delight as she approached the table. 'Esmé Tode!' she called out. 'How absolutely amazing to see you! What are you doing in *bella Roma*? We thought you were still slogging it out Down Under. Congratulations on finally escaping! And how lovely to see you!'

India was too busy being an active member of the international jet set to notice Esmé's reaction. It wasn't great. He looked bewildered at first: *who was this noisy Englishwoman? Did he know her?* When he realised who she was, his expression turned from bewilderment to horror.

'Crikey, Esmé! What a mad surprise!' she continued. 'What are you up to, you old rogue?' She didn't wait for an answer. It was fortunate because he would need a moment to think of one. 'Egbert and I have come over just for the weekend. We're "renewing our wedding vows" , as they say in Hollywood. Ha ha ha!' India glanced behind her. Egbert, pulling a polite face, was putting his phone away and slowly making his way over to join them. 'Here he comes!' she said. 'I swear. Forty-eight hours in the most beautiful hotel in the most beautiful city in the world, and I'm struggling to get him to look away from his phone! *Come on, Eggzie! Come and say hi to your cousin!*'

She glanced at Charlie Tysedale and the mysterious woman. Neither looked welcoming. Charlie, surveying her from a superior position, leaning back on his chair, looked especially surly. India didn't care. She liked suntans and human beings and, much as she loved him, Egbert(Mr) on his own could – sometimes – be a teeny bit boring. 'Shall we join you?' she said, casting around for a chair. To Charlie Tysedale, she said: 'Hi, I'm India Tode. We haven't met. I'm married to Esmé's cousin, Egbert.'

At that, Tysedale's body language transformed. He sat up. He may even have blushed. His eyes swivelled from India to Esmé, and then to Egbert(Mr), still approaching the table. He recovered himself.

'Egbert Tode, as I live and breathe!' he drawled. 'Must be twenty years at least.' He grinned. It wasn't at all attractive. 'Haven't you *grown*!'

'Ha ha, very funny,' said Egbert. 'Good to see you, Tysedale. Long time no see ... And what a surprise to see you here with Esmé! Esmé – what on earth are you doing in the Northern Hemisphere?!'

Handshakes and backslaps followed. Nobody introduced the Italian woman, who sat very still, watching the proceedings. Eventually India said to her, '*Buona sera*, I'm India!' and held out her hand. But the woman turned away.

In the meantime, Esmé had yet to come up with a satisfactory

95

explanation for his presence here in Rome.

Egbert(Mr) asked once again: 'But what brings you to Rome?'

Esmé said, 'Oh, you know, always had a soft spot for the Eternal City! Not doing anything much . . . Business. Charlie and I are cooking on an idea. I'll tell you about it later. But didn't you know Charlie from Eton? Charlie knows Italy well, don't you, Charlie? Plus . . . the other amazing thing about Charlie: he speaks fluent Italian! So – jolly useful. In Italy. Sit down, Egbert! Sit down, sit down . . . India tells me you're here to renew your wedding vows!'

Egbert(Mr) looked disconcerted.

India felt compelled to clarify that she'd been joking.

Egbert(Mr) said, 'Thank goodness! Crikey! Leave that sort of mumbo-jumbo to the people of Tinsel Town, ha ha ha!' Two waiters appeared from nowhere carrying two extra chairs, and he and India sat down. ' . . . Quite tricky, doing business with the Italianos, so I'm told . . . ' Egbert(Mr) said. He tapped his nose. 'Got to be quite careful, if you know what I mean. Without wishing to be . . . you know . . . ' He glanced awkwardly at the unfriendly Italian woman, and quickly changed tack. 'But what *fun!* What sort of a business venture, may I ask?'

Fortunately for Esmé, he was prevented from giving a more fulsome explanation by the arrival of –

The dreaded Adele.

'ADELE!' cried Charlie Tysedale, who hadn't greeted his wife so warmly in years. 'And little Tippee-toes Tysedale! Hello, my darlings! We weren't expecting you for at least another hour! *How was the Colosseum? Was it amazing?* Adele, darling, you'll never guess who we just bumped into. This is Egbert Tode. Of Tode Hall. Esmé's cousin.'

The beautiful Italian woman, without a word and with

minimal movement of the air around her, picked up her handbag, now with the envelope inside it, slid off her seat and slipped away. Almost no one noticed.

Adele told Charlie that Tippee had been fascinated by what he'd seen and learned at the Colosseum, and Charlie, who didn't usually engage his son in conversation, asked him lots of follow-on questions, quite loudly: all of which Tippee answered in monosyllables, if he answered them at all.

Adele ordered some chilled lemon water with a little slice of lime and *no ice* for herself, and some coke, 'as a special treat', for Tippee. 'All that sugar! He'll be climbing the walls!' she snickered.

India asked Tippee if this was his first time in Italy.

Tippee said, 'No.'

Adele said: 'He's been to Portofino several times, haven't you, Tippee? And then we went to Florence, didn't we, last half-term. Tippee loved his visit to the Uffizi.'

'Did you, Tippee?' India said. 'Crikey. Clever old you! I couldn't pay my kids to visit an art gallery. They hate museums more than life itself.'

'Tippee, tell Mrs Tode which was your favourite painting in the Uffizi. Can you remember, darling?'

Tippee looked at his mother as if she was mad.

'Come on, Tippee,' Charlie chipped in. 'We spent a bloody fortune on that ghastly guide. For Christ's sake, tell me you can remember at least one bloody painting.'

Tippee said: 'Are we going home tomorrow?'

Adele said: 'Tippee, you know *perfectly well* we are *not* going home tomorrow! Tomorrow, we're going on a special outing to look at Daddy and Esmé's exciting new business venture—'

Esmé and Charlie started talking at once.

Charlie said: 'I think I'll have another Negroni. Anyone else?'

Esmé said, for the second or third time, 'Charlie, weren't you and Egbert in the same house at Eton? Did you overlap at all?'

'What business venture?' asked Tippee. He had a nasty look in his eye. Charlie, who'd never much liked or trusted his son, assumed, wrongly, that Tippee knew what he was doing. Tippee didn't know – or not exactly. He had no idea, for example, that Charlie and Esmé had specifically met, here in Rome, in order to continue with their already quite developed, as yet secret, plans to take over the management of Rospo nel Buco, and to transform it into a six-star private members' eco-health-spa for billionaires. Tippee did not know what 'business venture' his mother was talking about, because he tried, always, to mute every word she or his father ever spoke. But he sensed he was on to something troublesome, and that they wanted him to stop asking questions. He smiled slyly and added: 'Do you mean the *secret* venture that no one's allowed to know about?'

Egbert(Mr) said: 'Yikes! Well, now I really am curious!'

India said: 'OMG ditto! Do spill, Esmé! I hope it's got nothing to do with the Mafia! Ha ha ha! Super scary!'

Tippee, now quite over-excited, said: 'I bet it does, knowing my father,' which gave his father an excuse to intervene.

'Don't be so bloody impertinent, Tippee,' he snapped.

He must also have sent some sort of message to his wife under the table, in the form of a kick, because at this point she came to the rescue. She backtracked on the 'business venture'.

'Silly me, I'm getting confused,' she said, tapping her head in a way that didn't muss the hair. 'It's nothing to do with the business venture. That's on Friday! Tomorrow we're going to the *gardens*, aren't we, Charlie? The famous, haunted gardens! With the human bones in the flower beds . . . Where Leonardo da Vinci once went to mend the drains!' She tittered, symmetrically. 'Remember, Tippee, I told you? You were thrilled about it.'

Tippee hadn't the faintest idea what she was talking about – but for Egbert(Mr), the penny dropped – or it almost dropped. Where had he heard of gardens with human bones in the flower beds? What was the— 'Esmé! You're not going to Rospo! As in *our* Rospo? How weird! Why?'

Esmé blinked. Why indeed?

Egbert(Mr) said: 'You do realise your bro is there *right now*? On his honeymoon. Ecgbert and Alice are on honeymoon at Rospo!' He looked from Charlie to Esmé and back again. He looked from Adele to Charlie to Tippee to Esmé and back again. He looked at India, who looked as bemused as he did. What the hell was going on? 'Esmé! Will you explain! Did you realise Ecgbert was at Rospo? Is that why you're going?'

Esmé blinked. Was it?

'*Yes*,' Charlie said. 'Of course he realised! Esmé wanted to surprise him! You were sorry you couldn't make the wedding, isn't that right, Esmé? . . . *Esmé*? Wakey-wakey!'

'That's right,' Esmé replied, at last. 'It's a surprise. I wanted to surprise him.'

'But that's so sweet!' India said. 'That's adorable! I'm not sure if you're really supposed to barge in on people's honeymoons – but even so . . . I suppose if he's your brother and you live in Australia . . . I bet he'd be happy to see you.' She didn't sound convinced.

Four more Negronis arrived. Adele stuck to her lemon water and told Tippee to sit straight. Charlie proposed a toast to the newlyweds, even though they weren't there. He told India and Egbert(Mr) that Esmé had generously agreed to let the Tysedales tag along for the trip because young Tippee had been so excited when he heard about the human bones in the flower beds. And because Adele was very interested in gardens.

Adele said, 'So true!'

India, Egbert(Mr), Charlie and Esmé slugged back their very strong, very expensive drinks –

[⅓ gin
⅓ Campari
⅓ sweet vermouth]

– and quickly loosened up, to the point, even, in spite of everything, where they became quite jolly. Charlie Tysedale ordered another round.

The question of dinner – what, where and with whom – inevitably bubbled to the surface. In the end it was too much effort for anyone to extricate themselves from the group. Egbert(Mr) tried it, half-heartedly. Esmé, too. The dreaded Adele adopted her usual passive-aggressive approach when socialising with her husband's people. She sipped on her lemon water and said she'd be 'happy doing whatever', which meant the opposite. She was never happy, whatever. Charlie didn't care much either way. He'd decided, three Negronis in, that India was rather attractive. So.

They ordered the bill.

Phew, what a scorcher.

Charlie and Esmé made a little show of reaching for their wallets, but their wallets never quite appeared. In the end, Adele and Egbert(Mr) split the bill.

Egbert(Mr) said: 'Crikey. Bit steep!'

Adele smiled symmetrically, with lips together.

India said: 'How much? Let's see!' She looked over Egbert's shoulder, said: 'WOW! It *was* yummy, though,' and promptly forgot all about it. If, later in the evening, anyone had asked (which they didn't) what was the Negroni bill at the Russie that night, she wouldn't have been able to tell them: not within the nearest €100.

The four drinkers, accompanied by Adele and Tippee, rolled merrily through the sweet-smelling garden, out through the hotel reception, and onto the street. Charlie said he knew of a very nice trattoria just off Via Ripetta, but he couldn't exactly remember which end. Esmé said he knew of a super little place on Via Laurina or was it Via della Fontanella? Egbert(Mr) checked his weather app.

They stood outside the Russie, a little drunk and a little loud, arguing about where to go next . . .

It was when they were spotted by the Rostovskys.

VIA DEL BABUINO

ROME

9.15 P.M.

I
t so happened that Bunny and Putin Rostovsky were window-shopping on that very same street at that very same time. Had they been window-shopping on another evening, at another time, they might have bumped into a different set of rich and inebriated tourists with wallet pockets a-bulging, loudly wondering where to go for dinner – and this would have been a very different tale. But they bumped into the Todes. And so this story unfolds.

They were walking arm in arm, feeling mellow and positive about the world, wondering how to spend their mysteriously acquired riches. Putin/Derek liked to play the big spender when Bunny was about. Bunny was happy with that. She kept her own mysterious stash tucked away, and rarely spent a penny of it. Not in front of Putin, anyway. He wouldn't have tolerated it. He would have seen it as an assault on his manhood. And Bunny – who knew what Bunny really thought? In so far as she left any clues at all, it seemed that she was in agreement: spending money was a man's job.

Bunny Rostovsky was many things, most of which would always remain hidden. Age, nationality, name, personal history – they could only be guessed at – even by Putin. Especially by Putin. He didn't mind. Or he told himself he didn't. He said to himself: 'I know all I need to know about my wife: she's gorgeous.' Also, clever, discrete, mysterious. And he adored her. That much no one could deny.

So they were window-shopping outside Chanel, Armani, Kenzo. Walking arm in arm, gazing through brilliant glass at some of the more expensive clothes in Europe. They had paused outside a store called Gente. Putin was saying:

'This would look *gorgeous* on you ... Oh my God! I'm getting hard *just thinking* about you in that frock, Money-Bunny ... you gorgeous thing ... What do you think, Bun? Shall we come back tomorrow and buy it? Would you like that, Bun?'

Bun surveyed the dress: skin-tight, emerald-green satin, plunging neckline. There was nothing subtle about it. She thought he was probably right. She would look gorgeous in it ... Then again, Bunny looked gorgeous in almost everything. She shrugged.

'We could,' she said. 'After we've visited the catacombs maybe?'

'You what?' He chuckled: a chuckle of joyful, indulgent wonder and worship. 'You culture-vulture you!'

A happy moment. They'd not been married for long – if, indeed, they were married at all. At the sound, just behind them, of upper-class English voices, engrossed in a noisy discussion about restaurants, both snapped to attention. They turned towards the sound together. Bunny and Putin stayed very still and watched silently as their drunken prey settled on restaurant and route, and ramshackled off down the street.

'Well I never,' murmured Derek/Putin to his mysterious wife. 'You know who that was, don't you, Bun?'

Bunny had recognised Adele from an interview on *Good Morning Britain*. The others, she couldn't yet place. But – she was intrigued. She could smell money.

Putin put his arm around her shoulder. He would have had to stoop to reach her waist, so this was more comfortable. 'Well, my dear,' he began, 'if that gentleman, with the slicked-back hair, if he isn't the multi-millionaire founder of Mark of Marylebone, UK's leading gentlemen's athleisure-to-workwear clothing label, I will eat my hat. And if that lady with him isn't his wife, Adele Tysedale, the internationally best-selling author specialising in couples' therapy, then, trust me, Bob is not my uncle. Know what I mean?'

Bunny said she did. The party was disappearing from view. She wanted to know who were the others. Putin was happy to furnish her with the information – of which he was quite certain. The younger couple were Mr Egbert and Mrs India Tode of Tode Hall stately home – the famous murder mansion. Where people kept dying in mysterious circumstances.

'Ah-ha,' said Bunny. 'Yes, of course.' Without discussing it, both had turned away from the green satin dress and were making their way, slowly and charmingly, in the direction of their prey. 'And the little chap?' she asked.

'Is Mr Esmé Tode, the second son of the baronet who passed away some five years ago, and of course of the ma who died in mysterious circumstances in the family mausoleum shortly afterwards ... *He* is recently divorced, Bun. But don't go getting any ideas. He's a Tode with a Turnip!' Putin laughed very hard.

'Ah-ha,' Bunny said. ' ... What do you mean?'

'I mean he hasn't got a bean. Recently divorced from the gorgeous, but nowhere near as gorgeous as you, Aussie bikini model turned full-time mummy, Chelsea-Reine Molasses. Their marriage unfortunately hit the rocks soon after Esmé's string of Sydney-based luxury gyms went bust in the so-called pandemic ... '

'Poor guy,' she said.

'That's as maybe,' Putin replied. 'And by the way, the reason I know all this,' he added, picking up the pace a bit, 'is because ... Well, it's my business to know all this, isn't it, Bun?'

'It is,' she agreed. 'Even so, that wasn't bad! The only one I recognised was the author woman. Mind you, she's worth a mint on her own, Derek. She's a toughie from what I've seen of her. Hard as nails. And not completely stupid, either.'

'Not as clever as you though, eh, Bun!' Putin replied. 'They don't know it, do they? But *no one's* as clever as you ... Come on, Mrs Rostovsky. Let's have ourselves a bit of fun!'

Bunny laughed.

And off they set.

The happiest couple in Rome.

It was still warm at 9.15 p.m., this being June. Putin was sweating quite a bit by the time he and Bunny caught up with the

English party. They were turning into Piazza del Popolo, and had paused on the Santa Maria portico to confirm, once and for all, what they wanted for dinner and which direction to take.

'Hello, hello, hello ... I *thought* it was you!' declared Putin loudly, in a Russian sort of way, and aiming the comment at any one of them, except Tippee, who was irrelevant. 'Fancy bumping into you in the middle of Rome! Are you looking for somewhere to have the dinner this evening? Want a recommendation?'

They all turned, but Egbert(Mr) was the closest. Putin managed to get a hold of his right hand and was pumping it with assurance and warmth.

Egbert(Mr) said: 'Hullo. Err ... Sorry. Have we met?'

Putin said not. He laughed at the idea. He explained to Egbert(Mr) that he was a great friend of Egbert's cousin *Nicola*.

This should have been a red flag. Nicola had no friends. Certainly no 'great' friends. And in fact, even if the bonhomous Putin Rostovsky had been the last human on earth, he would never have been accepted into Nicola's non-existent friendship group. She would have loathed him on sight.

However. As usual, nobody was paying attention. Plus, they were fairly drunk and preoccupied with the whats and wheres and lack of reservations for supper. So Egbert(Mr) said, 'Jolly good. What fun!' And then somehow, before he knew it, Putin and Bunny had not only joined the party, but were leading it back up Via del Babuino to a different restaurant entirely; this one, looking down over Rome from above Piazza di Spagna.

It was a fifteen-minute walk. Putin assured his new friends that they wouldn't need reservations because the owner was a great personal friend. And sure enough, they were welcomed in. Putin embraced most of the staff, and even a few of the customers; and though the restaurant was full, a perfect space was found for them outside on the terrace, with an uninterrupted view of floodlit Rome below. As the group settled at their table, everyone present – even the dreaded Adele – felt grateful to Putin for taking control of the situation, and thoroughly delighted that he and his wife had joined the group.

Eventually somebody – India – thought to ask Putin about his relationship with Nicola. Where, for example, had they met?

Putin said: '*Ah.*' He glanced across at Bunny and said to her: 'Bun? Do you want me to say?'

Bunny shrugged. 'It's up to you. For me, this is not important.' She gazed back at him, her expression deadpan. Something passed between them. A secret joke. Tippee Tysedale clocked it.

He said: 'What's so funny?' But nobody paid attention.

'Bunny and myself we met Nicola in Arizona,' Putin said solemnly. 'My darling wife, who saved my life, was a therapeutic nurse at this time. I am correct, my darling?'

Bunny shrugged.

'Nicola and I both we were ... I will say we were clients at the same resort-hospital in Arizona for persons whose souls are troubled. It is a very, very special place. A very nurturing place. This place ...' Putin glanced lovingly at Bunny. 'It has brought me back my life. That is true.'

'Oh!' said India. 'You were at the rehab together! That's amazing! ... It looks like it really worked for you ... which is great ...' She stopped there, to prevent herself from saying anything disloyal about Nicola.

'That's marvellous,' Egbert(Mr) said quickly, in case his wife changed her mind. 'Nicola gained so much from the experience. She's doing really well.'

Putin nodded, as if this came as no surprise. 'Nicola and myself we did a lot of group therapy together. So – I owe Nicola my thank-you for what she has done in my own personal recovery. And I think Nicola agrees the same about me ... We went through a lot of very difficult emotions together. And Bun was there for us both through this. Weren't you, Bun? You were "guiding us through" ...'

Tippee, suddenly interested in the adult conversation, asked Putin: 'Guiding you through what? What was wrong with you?'

Adele said: '*Tippee!*'

But Putin brushed it aside. 'No, no,' he said. 'The boy ask a question. It's fair, isn't it? Suffer the little children, as your great man said. As I learned. Or the Bible maybe. Et cetera ...' For a moment Putin lost his footing. But nobody seemed to notice. They were only half listening in any case: those that allowed gluten in their diet were wondering what pizza to choose.

'I'm not a little child,' Tippee said. 'Why were you both in the resort-hospital? What is a resort-hospital anyway?'

Adele said: 'Never you mind, young man. Now then – have you chosen your pizza? Or shall we ask if they can do you a special burger?' She turned to the table. 'Tippee doesn't like pizzas, believe it or not!'

Nobody cared.

The conversation moved on to more pressing concerns: who was going to eat what and, once that was resolved – everyone's plans for the morrow.

As things stood: Esmé, Charlie, Adele and Tippee were due to rent a car and drive out to Rospo for the day. Putin and Bunny officially had no plans, and Egbert(Mr) and India were keeping theirs to themselves. But then Putin happened to know off the top of his head that the commuter train from Rome to

Rospo would be a much simpler and more enjoyable option than renting a car. Putin also remarked that he and Bunny had been wanting to visit the beautiful gardens at Rospo nel Buco 'for years'.

An awkward silence settled. It was all very well, allowing an unknown Russian to help them sort out a good table for dinner. It didn't mean they were friends. Enough was enough . . . Tippee suggested the Rostovskys join them on the trip to Rospo.

There came another awkward pause.

Little shit, thought Tippee's father, and the thought was written all over his face. Tippee grinned at him.

'Oh my goodness. What a very generous suggestion, young man!' exclaimed Putin. 'I'm touched!' He looked at Bunny. 'Bun?'

Bunny shrugged.

Putin said: 'Might be fun?'

She acknowledged that they had nothing else planned for the day, and that she had always been curious to see the gardens at Rospo.

' . . . We wouldn't want to intrude,' said Putin.

Esmé tried to redirect the conversation. He asked India what she and Egbert(Mr) had planned for the following day. It was a mistake. Because it turned out that if everyone else was going to barge in on Ecgbert(Sir) and Alice's honeymoon, India didn't see why she and Egbert(Mr) shouldn't barge in, too. Also, she didn't like the sense she might be left out. Also, a day trip on an Italian commuter train sounded like fun. Also, she'd never been to Rospo. Also, also . . . She said to Esmé, 'Well, if everyone else is going to Rospo then I think we should come too! Don't you agree, Eggzie?'

109

He did not.

On the other hand, since it was a part of the Tode Estate, he was actually responsible for the place. He would have to drop in at some point, and truth be told, he'd been avoiding it until now – knowing, as he did, that his old school contemporary was out there running the show. Did he want to spend the day at Rospo nel Buco, pretending to get along with Slayer-Wilson-Tite? Not in the least. But now that it had been presented as an option – and by his wife, no less – he felt duty-bound to take it.

'I must admit I do feel a bit – well, actually, *jolly* remiss,' Egbert(Mr) said. 'I probably should have checked into Villa Rospo by now . . . poor old Wilson-Tite has been slogging away, managing the show, ever since your ma . . . you know . . . '

'Died,' said Esmé.

'That's right . . . ' Egbert(Mr) looked apologetic.

Esmé said: 'Why don't you just leave it to me? You and India enjoy your weekend. I can check up on the situation and report back. If you'd like that?'

The suggestion made Egbert(Mr)'s ears burn. Made him sit up. Cemented his resolve. 'No, no. Thank you, Esmé. Very kind of you. But no. Really, I feel I ought . . . '

'It's absolutely no trouble . . . ' Esmé's ears were burning, too.

Tippee said he thought it would be fun if Egbert and India came too. Helpfully, he pointed out that since they would now be taking the train to Rospo instead of renting a car, it didn't really matter how many people tagged along.

'The more the merrier!' Tippee said.

Charlie said: '*Quite.*' His face added another *little shit*. Tippee gurgled with delight.

Charlie turned to his beloved wife. Mimed an injection. Said: 'Has he had his shot?'

Adele scowled. 'Of course he has,' she snarled; and then, to the table: 'Tippee has very acute ADHD.'

Nobody cared.

Esmé gave it one final try. He suggested that intruding on his brother's honeymoon, unannounced, with a party of eight guests (as opposed to four) might perhaps be seen as a bit of an imposition . . . But India swept that objection aside. Esmé and Charlie had already planned the intrusion. By bringing along a larger group, at least it turned the intrusion into a party.

'They'll be delighted,' she said. (And she believed it. India loved people. She couldn't imagine not feeling delighted by the arrival of more, even on her own honeymoon.)

And so it was – thanks mostly to Tippee – that Esmé and Charlie's long-planned business trip, Egbert(Mr) and India's romantic getaway weekend, and Alice and Ecgbert(Sir)'s honeymoon were all destined to be derailed.

'What a hooley!' said India.

Putin Rostovsky called for the bill.

Not everyone at dinner was 'fortunate enough' (as Adele explained to Tippee) to be staying at the Russie that night. It being the smartest hotel in Rome, not everyone could afford it – whether they admitted to it or not.

Esmé, pockets recently emptied in an ugly divorce, claimed to have rented a 'stunning apartment' overlooking the Forum, which he said he much preferred. The Rostovskys swore something similar – but, conveniently, in the opposite direction: theirs overlooked the Trevi Fountain.

So after dinner, Esmé and the Rostovskys shuffled back to their secretive, less expensive hideouts, and India, Egbert(Mr) and the Tysedales returned together to their smart hotel. It was agreed, after quite a lot of irritable discussion (Esmé, still hoping he could somehow lose the hangers-on altogether, and certain among the hangers-on being quite determined to stop that from happening), that everyone should reconvene at the Russie for breakfast the following morning at nine.

THE GARDEN AT VILLA ROSPO

9.15 A.M.

Another morning in paradise for Ecgbert(Sir) and his new bride. Their eighth since married life began, and their seventh at Rospo. They were enjoying the famous garden, lolling by the stream in the morning sunshine, amusing themselves watching the grapefruits float by.

Alice had never seen grapefruit anywhere before, except in a supermarket. These ones looked bigger, fatter, more swollen, less yellow. There was something hypnotic, even slightly disgusting, about them.

'They look like skulls,' she said.

'They look like decapitated babies' heads,' said Ecgbert.

Lady Tode and Leonardo had not made their presence felt since lunchtime the previous day. It was *nice*, Ecgbert(Sir) and Alice agreed, that Lady Tode had at last found a new friend. Nice for Lady Tode – who was clearly smitten – and very nice *indeed* for the newlyweds, to be left in peace.

'What do you imagine Leonardo sees in Granny?' Ecgbert

asked Alice, as they splashed in the crystal waters. 'It's not like they have terribly much in common ... She likes paintings, I suppose. But she's not very bright.'

'I suppose they're both dead,' said Alice. 'Which is something. Dead and stuck here on earth, in the earthly dimension ... or something ... That's probably quite a big thing ...'

'Correct,' he said. They thought about that. '... I hope,' said Ecgbert, 'that if we both die, we can spend eternity being dead together in this garden. Don't you think, Trudy? It wouldn't be such a bad way to be dead.'

'It would be paradise,' Alice replied.

Her phone pinged. A text message from Egbert(Mr).

'... Oh *no*,' she said.

'What?'

Ping. Another text message – this one from India. And then lots more pings from India, one after the other.

'Oh goodness ... Oh my goodness.'

Ping.

PS Tippee Tysedale is a VERY weird kid ☹

Ping.

BTW SORRY for the intrusion on your fab
honeymoon ☺

Ping.

Miss you both SO MUCH!!! ☹☹☹
Cant WAIT to see you!!! ☺☺☺☺☺

Ping.

> BTW Charlie Tysedale – GREAT fun! ☺
> WIFE ... hmmm ... ☹ IMHO jury's still out!!
> *Bit* of a 'cauchemar' ☹ if you know what I
> mean !! ☺☺☺☺

Ping.

> And not sure WHAT you'll make of the Ruskies! ☺

Ping.

> They're NUTS! ☺☺☺☺ See yu L8er!!!

'You're not going to believe this, Ecgbert ... They're ... Really, they are *unbelievable*. India and Egbert are actually in Rome!' Alice laughed. 'They literally cannot survive without us for *a week*! Absolutely – *bloody hell!* They're coming to lunch – today – with six guests. *Six!*'

But when Ecgbert(Sir) learned that his brother Esmé was among the invading army, and that he had intended to surprise him, he was actually quite touched. He'd not seen Esmé for almost five years – in which time, Ecgbert(Sir) had accrued various things he was keen to boast about: a driving licence, for example. Not to mention a wife.

The party of eight uninvited guests were demanding not only to be fed, but to be fetched from the train station in Rospo nel Buco, a twenty-minute drive away.

Alice and Ecgbert's blissful honeymoon was over.

THE SUPERMERCATO

ROSPO NEL BUCO

12.23 P.M.

There was not enough food in the house for eight surprise guests. Ecgbert(Sir) had been given a shopping list. He was at the bread counter trying, loudly but not successfully, to communicate to the sales assistant his desire for focaccia – all the focaccia in the store – when he was approached by a smiling man, slim and dapper, in his early sixties.

'Signor Tode?' said the silver fox. 'You are having some trouble. I can help you perhaps?'

'Ah. Yes,' replied Ecgbert(Sir), forgetting to wonder how the stranger knew him by name, and happy with the improved outlook vis-à-vis bagging all the focaccia. 'I'm trying to explain to the nice lady that we've got a lot of Brits coming to lunch, and Brits love that kind of bread. It's the only reason most of them come to Italy. I suspect she thinks I'm being greedy.

Could you explain? It's not greed. It's realism . . . I'd be very grateful.' Ecgbert(Sir) turned back to the sales assistant. '*Otto Inglesi!*' he said. '*Otto* people! Focaccia, yum yum.'

With the help of the silver fox, and amid much good-natured laughter, Ecgbert(Sir) was able to buy all the focaccia he needed. But then the sales assistant, to Ecgbert's surprise, handed the bread parcel to the silver fox, who moved as if to hand it on to Ecgbert –

But when Ecgbert(Sir) reached out to take the parcel from him, the silver fox held on tight. There was a slight tussle.

Ecgbert(Sir) said: 'I say . . . '

The silver fox said: 'You are staying at Rospo, no?'

Ecgbert gave the bread another tug. 'Yes, I am . . . *I say* . . . '

No luck. The man clearly wasn't ready to relinquish it yet. 'What's it to you where I'm staying, anyway? Who are you?'

'My name is Ranaldini,' he said. 'Signor Ranaldini.'

The name meant nothing to Ecgbert. 'Jolly good. Well – grazzy mealie . . . Signor . . . Ranalalin. *Grazie* so much for coming to my rescue about the bread. English can't get enough of it, you know.'

Signor Ranaldini lowered his chin. His voice grew softer. 'I am father of Elizabetta and Frederica.'

'What? . . . OH! . . . Oh, well! How marvellous! You should have said! Very nice to meet you, Signor Ranannanni. Randy. Mr Randeney . . . Lovely girls. Splendid girls. Smashing stuff. Congratulations on your daughters. And thank you for getting the bread.'

Signor Ranaldini nodded. Still, he held on to the bread. 'I understand you are making big plans for Villa Rospo.'

'That's right. We've got this ruddy lunch. But with a bit of luck they'll be gone by teatime.'

'Good,' Ranaldini said. 'The villa is good just as it is, Mr Tode. We look after it very well. You understand me?'

'Absolutely!' said Ecgbert(Sir). 'Molto benny!'

'Do not try to change things,' said Signor Ranaldini, and Ecgbert(Sir) sensed hostility.

'Right-oh,' he agreed. 'I won't! But I must push on, Signor Renny. I have a lot of people to fetch at the station and, between you and me, I think it's going to need two journeys ... Unless you happen to know of a taxi service?'

'... Do not ...' Ranaldini tried again 'Mr Tode – *ti consiglio* ... Don't put yourself in situations where you cannot understand any persons who are involved.'

'Hmm?'

'And tell your partner the same. We do not want his money ...' Something seemed to make Ranaldini laugh. He shook his head. 'To take care of Rospo, the Ranaldinis do not need his envelopes.'

Ecgbert was confused, but not nearly as confused as he would have been had he been concentrating. He was preoccupied with the bread and the train, and getting the bread to the car, and the car to the train, and showing Esmé how well he could drive these days and Signor Rospi – though perfectly OK – was talking in riddles, and making him late.

'I must say, you're being awfully cryptic,' Sir Ecgbert said irritably. 'But other than that ... thank you so much for the help ... Grazzy *very much*. And I will certainly send your good wishes to your fine daughters. Frederica, especially, is very bendy. Isn't she? Amazing, this "yoga" people do these days. However, we can't stand here chattering all day, can we Signorina Randy? Gotta crack on!'

Signor Ranaldini smiled slightly, and with a small inclination of his elegant head, finally released the bread parcel, and stepped out of Ecgbert's way.

'Mr Tode,' he said.

'Mr Randy.'

Ecgbert, as he wheeled his trolley to the till, thought it was pretty feeble of Signorina Randy not to realise that he was actually a Sir. *Mr* Tode, indeed. *Mr indeed!* 12th Bart., *actually*, Mr Randy ... Subject of which, he must remind Alice she could call herself 'Lady Tode' now, if she felt like it. It might tickle her a bit. He pulled out his phone.

'Ah, Trudy ... Good, you're there ... news alert, in case you'd forgotten or didn't realise ... ' His English voice boomed across the *supermercato*. 'You do realise, don't you, that ever since you were so kind and generous and gorgeous and wonderful enough to marry me, you – I say! – HEY! EXCUSE ME – SCUSI *MOI*, Madame! MADAME, THIS IS IN FACT A QUEUE. Please be kind enough to form an *orderly* queue ... '

'Hello? Ecgbert?'

There followed a bump and crash and a couple more '*scusi*'s and then the line went dead. Ecgbert's news alert would have to wait.

As it happened, Alice had some quite juicy news of her own.

VILLA ROSPO

ROSPO NEL BUCO

12.48 P.M.

While Ecgbert(Sir) had been fighting over bread at the *supermercato*, Alice was wandering the garden, savouring her good fortune, her unusually fine husband and her magnificent honeymoon. She wasn't someone who spent a lot of time measuring these things, but it was possible she had never been happier. She was barefoot, it being a hot day, so she travelled in silence. She'd been collecting plums from a tree behind the villa, and after a while, both hands being full, she had turned back towards the house. As she drew closer she thought she heard a combination of giggles and grunts coming from behind the bushes, where there was a woodshed adjoining the back pantry.

Aye aye, she thought (being human). *What's going on here?* She tiptoed a little closer, as far as the woodshed door.

120

The grunting and giggling grew louder. The giggling faded, and the grunting grew more heartfelt.

Yikes... She was too close to it now. This was embarrassing. She wanted to retreat, but she worried. If she moved they might hear her. If she didn't move – they might find her, standing there. They might hear her breathing.

She was still half frozen with embarrassment, trying to muster the courage to do *something* to extricate herself from the situation, when she heard a car pulling up at the side of the house.

The grunters obviously heard it, too.

The grunting stopped. There came, in its place, whispered swearing in Italian and English. Less grunting, more scrabbling on the other side of the door.

Alice seized her chance. Quickly she stumbled a few steps back, to the other side of the bush – in perfect time to see Elizabetta Ranaldini climbing out of her car carrying an open tray of eggs. To her right, looking casual, and now fully dressed, Elizabetta's sister, Frederica, and Elizabetta's husband, Piers, stepped out of the woodshed. Alice stood between them, blushing like a teenager, pretending something fascinating was happening near her foot.

Elizabetta didn't seem to notice anything remiss. Or if she did, she didn't show it.

'Hey, baby,' said Piers to his wife. (He spoke in Italian, translated here for convenience.) 'You're back soon. How was Carlo? I thought you were staying for coffee?'

'Carlo wasn't there,' Elizabetta replied (also in Italian). 'I just took the eggs,' she indicated the tray, 'and I came home.'

She was lying. To Alice this seemed obvious. Whatever it was Elizabetta had been up to, the eggs had not been the main event.

In any case, it seemed that both parties were too busy covering their own tracks to care what the other had been up to.

The four of them, including Alice, walked into the villa together talking keenly about the weather.

Returning to the villa after a morning experimenting with what Leo called 'the ninth dimension lightness contender theorem' (his friend and willing assistant, Geraldine, Lady Tode, had no more idea what it meant than the rest of us), the two ghosts were surprised to discover the long table on the terrace laid up for ten people.

'Who on earth,' demanded Lady Tode, 'is coming to lunch?' The question excited her quite a lot more than the one about the ninth dimension. Leonardo noticed this, but because he was tactful, as well as a genius, he chose to keep the observation to himself. Also, he was curious. He'd never been married himself, of course, for obvious reasons. But he'd been led to believe it was the modern tradition for honeymooning couples to want to spend their time away from the crowd.

The ghosts could hear noises coming from the kitchen: the two Italian girls, arguing with each other, as usual. But they could see no sign of the newlyweds.

'Where is everyone?' asked Lady Tode.

A horrible thought occurred to her.

'They wouldn't have *left*, would they?' she asked. Ghosts weren't meant to feel pain, or so Lady Tode had been taught. Until this moment she'd never had cause to query it. But the suggestion, just then, that she might have been abandoned;

that her dearest friend, Alice, and her ludicrous grandson, Ecgbert, might have conspired together, in secret, to get away from her – brought to her heart-space a pain so sharp that for a moment her ghost-shape semi-pulverised.

It created a beautiful firework display, there on the lunch terrace: a ninth dimension lightness consequence in all its glory! Leonardo had his answer. But he had no sense of smell, and so his theorem vis-à-vis the tenth dimension stayed unchallenged. Thankfully, the stink of methane that Geraldine always left behind her when emotionally disturbed passed unnoticed by both of them.

In any case, of course they hadn't left her behind! Ecgbert(Sir) was just then parking outside Rospo nel Buco station to wait for the train from Rome to roll in. Alice was cowering – for want of a better word – in the ruins of an eleventh-century church at the bottom of the garden, trying to avoid Piers and both Ranaldinis, post the woodshed debacle. She was staring at the frescos (still clearly visible on the open walls) trying to be amazed by their beauty, but finding it hard to concentrate.

She heard the sound of fireworks from the direction of the house: and then, filling the clear, warm air ... the needy, outraged voice of Geraldine, Lady Tode calling her name. The leaves shook. Before the sound had finished, there she stood: Geraldine, Lady Tode and beside her, looking apologetic, Leonardo.

'There you are!' exclaimed Lady Tode.

'Ahh,' said Leonardo, seeing the fresco before her. 'You have discovered *La Conversione di Saulo*! What do you make of it? It's a wee bit busticated, exposed here in the sunshine. But it's breezy, no?'

' ... I don't know,' said Alice, vaguely. Sometimes it was hard to understand what he was talking about. 'What was that noise just now? Sounded like an explosion.'

Lady Tode definitely didn't want to go into that. She brushed the noise aside. 'Would you mind telling me why the lunch table is laid for ten people, Alice? I thought you and Ecgbert were on a honeymoon?'

Alice, who was longing to share her gossip, and hadn't yet had a chance to tell Ecgbert, didn't answer the lunch question at once. She said: 'Guess what? I just caught Piers and his sister-in-law having it off in the woodshed!'

Lady Tode said, 'I'm not in the least surprised.' Which is what she always said when she was surprised.

'Piers and Frederica were *having sex* in the woodshed!' Alice said again, unsatisfied with the reaction. 'But he's married to Elizabetta!'

A tail of smoke wafted from beneath Geraldine's Mexican sunhat. She disliked being told things she felt she ought already to know. So she didn't respond at once.

'Ah yes,' said Leonardo, who would have preferred to concentrate on the fresco. 'I have observed this too. Piers and Elizabetta. Piers and Frederica. Sometimes, if I'm not mistaken, Piers and Frederica and Elizabetta. They are not a happy triumvirate. So much ardour. So little sense. An inferno of intrigue. Sex and so on. They argue and bash constantly, have you not noted this?'

'Piers should count himself lucky,' Alice said. 'He's a good-looking chap. But he's a bit of a drip. He never really seems to *do* anything much.'

'Drip?!' repeated Leonardo, delightedly. '*Drip?*' His portly body shook with laughter. 'I don't know what it means . . . He is a ne'er-do-well. An opportunist and a slacker . . . and now he is approaching forty years old.' Leonardo looked wistful. 'He is beautiful, no? I wish I had known him when he was fifteen . . . imagine . . . '

Geraldine said: 'Leo! Are you blushing?'

Leonardo pulled himself together. 'I'm only suggesting I would have loved to paint him.'

The moment was saved (neither Alice nor Geraldine had imagined for *one moment* he was suggesting anything else) by the sound of a car horn honking, loudly, merrily, repeatedly. It could only mark the triumphant return of Ecgbert(Sir), the focaccia, and however many of the day trippers he'd managed to cram into his car.

Ecgbert spotted Alice and the ghosts before he reached the end of the drive, and skidded to a stop. The smell of burning rubber mingled with the smell of jasmine. Ecgbert opened the driver's door, unfurled himself from the car and left it there. He loped towards Alice, smiling and waving.

'Astonishing feat!' he was shouting. 'I managed to squeeze them all in . . . They're not in the best mood . . . '

'*Dear God*,' muttered Lady Tode. 'What's going *on*?'

Behind him, they could see people piling out of the car . . . One . . . two . . . three . . . four . . .

Alice squinted in the sun, not sure if she was seeing right. . . . five . . . six . . .

She chortled. They did look quite disconsolate, even from here.

'Incredible!' exclaimed Leonardo. 'How did you do it?'

... seven ... eight ...

'How many more?' he laughed.

'Who are these people?' Lady Tode asked again. 'I know India and Egbert, of course ... Good Lord, that can't be my grandson Esmé? ... *It is!* And who are all the others?'

'I've no idea,' said Alice. 'But they've invited themselves to lunch.'

NEARLY LUNCHTIME

First things first. Adele and her dreaded Tupperware boxes needed to be introduced to the kitchen staff. The pizza from the previous evening was playing hell with her digestive system; and nor was she willing to jeopardise Tippee's intestinal health for a second meal in a row. She'd ordered the staff at the Russie, who were accustomed to spoilt people's lame requests, to prepare a gluten-free picnic for the two of them. She would have liked to bring her husband on board with the healthy diet and lifestyle she shared with their son, but Charlie was having none of it. (Unicorns and Apes.)

She asked him this morning, as she was spooning fruit compote onto Tippee's granola, if he would like to nibble on something gluten free. Charlie was doing something with his phone at the time, slurping espresso and stuffing a second cream-filled *cornetto* into his face. She had to ask him the question three times, in exactly the same tone of voice. Then Tippee said to his father: 'Charlie, Mummy's asking you something.' To which Charlie replied, through the pastry and cream (it wasn't clear which family member he was addressing):

'Fuck off.' And then, after a munching pause, 'And, Tippee, don't call me fucking Charlie.' Adele had not said a word after that. No one had. Tippee had grinned into his granola and compote. The family had eaten the rest of their breakfast in silence.

She wouldn't let him divorce her. Right there, that was the elephant in the room. She needed him, for PR purposes; knowing this, and being a clever, careful, thorough woman, she had long ago organised her affairs in such a way that if he left her, he left her without a penny, and Charlie simply could not conceive of a life being penniless. He would rather be dead. So he was stuck with her. Tied to her prissiness for eternity. The dreaded Adele had made him her slave. Or that was how Charlie saw it, when feeling hungover.

Anyway, that was the happy scene at breakfast. Now it was nearly lunch. Adele had a melange of iron-, folate- and potassium-rich legume, tofu, seaweed and flax arranged deliciously in one tub; and several other tubs with similar treats. She needed to discuss them with the cook, who Ecgbert(Sir) had told her was named Frederica; also to explain to Frederica exactly how to serve them. She'd brought enough food for two meals – lunch and supper – for both Tippee and herself, just in case Charlie got drunk, as was his wont, and refused to leave in time for them to get anything healthy back in Rome. She'd also brought medication for the boy, who became, in her opinion, quite unmanageable without it; sleepwear for all the family; the first-aid kit, and any lotions required for her nightly skincare routine.

Adele liked to be prepared.

It was a small kitchen. She found Frederica Ranaldini in there, trying to cook the lunch. Adele, who'd not travelled at all until she was rich, and then only in the finest hotels, thought the kitchen looked scruffy and dirty and tried not to touch any of the surfaces. She said to Frederica, who was trying to reach around her to get to the hob, also trying to put the finishing touches to a lunch for ten people involving veal and sage and prosciutto and lemon and quite a lot of other ingredients: 'Frederica – hello, Frederica?! Sorry! I can see you're super busy, and I absolutely refuse to be a bother! But where will I find your antibacterial? I'm going to give the counters a super-quick spritz! Ignore me! Just – if you could point me in the right direction ... '

Frederica ignored her.

Adele tipped her head to one side: it was unsymmetrical, but she was a little taken aback. She waited a moment longer for a reply, until it was obvious that Frederica had no intention of giving her one, at which point, with a tight little smile and a perky little hum, she began to search for the antibacterial herself.

'*Sorry! Ever so sorry ... !*'

Cupboard doors, bumping into Frederica's shins. Despite the size of the house (six bedrooms, attics, cellars, two sitting rooms, three bathrooms, two staff flats), it came, in the Italian convention, with a remarkably small kitchen: what London estate agents call a 'galley kitchen'. Also, with the oven on and no air conditioning anywhere, it was very hot indeed. If Adele had visited a behavioural scientist with a Ph.D. on 'How to be Irritating', she could not have come up with a more efficient method.

Anyone who knew either Ranaldini sister would have stepped more carefully. Then again, when Adele set her mind to achieving a thing, an army of Ranaldini sisters wouldn't have got in her way. And Adele wanted to kill the germs in that kitchen.

'*Sorry* . . .' Adele paused. She was squatting in the middle of the floor space, holding open the cupboard under the sink. 'Do you actually *have* any antibacterial?' she was saying. 'I'm not sure – do you use it in Italy?'

It was too much. Frederica's foot moved of its own accord, lashing out behind her, as she stood there stirring delicious sauces at the hob. The foot landed just above Adele's bottom, on the small of her back. It sent Adele flying.

Frederica paused. She turned to look at Adele, now spattered on the floor. There followed a murderous pause. At that moment either one of them, had they been holding a knife, might well have dug it into the other. But the moment passed.

Instead, they laughed.

'Oh my gad, are you all right?' laughed Frederica (in English), bending her bendy body to help her up. 'This is *terrible*! I don't know what to say . . . I am such an idiot. My foot fell out – what kind of idiot I am . . .'

Frederica said she was sorry, and Adele – did not miss a beat. She stood up, straightened her sundress and matching fabric hair tie, smiled her symmetrical smile and declared brightly: 'Not a problem! Accidents will happen!'

After that Frederica had no option but to help Adele with her antibacterial quest. Not only did she locate the spray dispenser, she took the damp cloth from Adele's hand, and spritzed the surfaces herself.

'Are you sure I can't help?' asked Adele as Frederica wiped.

Frederica assured her otherwise, and urged Adele instead to join the others on the terrace, and relax. Lunch was almost ready.

'And you're OK with the ...?' Adele grimaced apologetically and pointed at the Tupperware.

'Yes, yes, yes!' Frederica cried. 'Don't worry at all. I bring it all in.'

Beneath its fragrant, wisteria-clad canopy, Villa Rospo's terrace ran the full length of the building and at this time of year, in the heat and the sunshine, all of life took place on it. At one end there was the long table, laid out with a lunch for ten; at the other end were sofas, armchairs, swing seats, small tables and large cushions and, at this moment, sundry delicious-looking pre-lunch snacks. Most of the household had already gathered here by the time Adele wandered out to join them.

Tippee was eating salami. She put a stop to that. She helped herself to some fizzy water and sat quietly on an empty swing seat while the others talked around her. She looked, thought Alice, quite miserable. Poor thing.

Alice went to sit beside her. They'd never met before, but Esmé had just updated her with a potted biography.

Alice said: 'Esmé tells me you've written the most amazing book about marriage and relationships ... I must read it.'

'I don't know about *amazing*,' Adele said, with a prickly smile. 'Has Esmé even read it?'

'Esmé?' Alice laughed. 'I'm not sure that he has. Maybe he should've done, given his circumstances ... But in any case he made it sound amazing.'

Adele said: 'Anyway, let's not talk about my book! It's such a gorgeous day! And so gorgeous of you to have us all.'

Alice ate an ovalini, offered one to Adele, who turned it down. She tried again. 'How was the train journey?'

But it turned out Adele did want to talk about her amazing book, after all. 'I'm surprised you haven't read it, Alice,' she laughed in a prickly manner. 'I didn't think there were many women left who hadn't! It's sold twenty-eight million copies worldwide.'

'*Goodness!*' exclaimed Alice, obligingly. 'Twenty-eight *million?* Then I certainly should have read it! Definitely! Esmé told me it has a wonderful name . . . ?'

'*The Ape and the Unicorn, Squaring the Me–Him Circle* . . .' said the dreaded Adele. 'I wrote it at a time in my life when I felt very alone and afraid. I looked around and I thought, I can't be the only one thinking these dark thoughts, as a woman and a mother. I realised – not everyone can afford to see a therapist, so who can I talk to? Where can I get the help I need? And you know what I did?'

'Well – I think you wrote the book, did you?'

'I wrote the book because I knew I could help myself and I could help other women too, who found themselves in the same situation . . .'

Alice might have asked something about the situation that had prompted the great work. But it was hot and also— Ah! *Here was Piers*, ambling by. Alice didn't like Piers. She hadn't trusted his smarmy ways, not from the very start: and even less so, after this morning's shenanigans. Nevertheless, he was an easy conversationalist.

'Piers,' she called out. 'Come and join us! Wouldn't you like a drink?'

But Piers said he had work to do. This was unlikely, since

work didn't appear to be any part of his remit. Nevertheless – *perhaps*, thought Alice, it was uncomfortable for him, meeting his old school companions in these circumstances . . . with him being an employee, and his wife's sister cooking the lunch. On the other hand – as Tode Hall's Organisation Director, she, too, was an employee. Who cared?

Apparently Piers did, because he kept on walking.

Ecgbert(Sir) came to join them. He'd watched Piers shamble by, pretending he had work to do, and felt offended on Alice's behalf. He said to Adele, much too loudly: 'Alice heard him in the woodshed, having it off with his wife's sister this morning. Probably why he's in a mood.'

Alice said: 'Shhhhh!'

'Don't worry,' Ecgbert(Sir) said. 'They can't hear.'

Adele blushed. For a woman who'd made her fortune discussing apes, unicorns and human relationships, she was, in fact, outlandishly prudish. For a while the shock she felt, hearing Sir Ecgbert's woodshed bulletin, robbed her of the ability to speak. So she sat on the swing seat, between husband and wife, sweat trickling between symmetrical bosoms, and wished the world would swallow her up.

Finally she said, 'So . . . *Frederica* – the lovely lady I met in the kitchen, doing such a super job with the lunch . . . is that Piers' wife, or Piers' sister-in-law? I'm so confused!'

'That's the sister,' Ecgbert(Sir) explained. 'She's very good at yoga. The *wife* . . . ' He looked around him. 'I don't know where she's got to . . . maybe she's having it off with someone else. I hope so, for her sake.'

Adele could take no more. It was exactly this sort of decadent approach she so desperately wanted to keep away from Tippee.

She said: 'Think I better pop to the ladies' before lunch is served. Tippee? Tippee! Come with me. It's nearly lunchtime. Come with me and wash your hands.'

'Righty-ho,' said Ecgbert(Sir), moving into her empty seat. He sent a bemused look to her retreating back, and turned to Alice: 'Who rattled her cage?'

LUNCHTIME

Adele was still hiding in the lavatory, scrubbing beneath Tippee's fingernails and administering his behaviour-modifying medications, when Frederica (very good at yoga) banged the lunch gong.

Finally!

Guests shunted along to the table end of the terrace. Ecgbert(Sir) and Alice plonked themselves in the middle and told people to sit wherever they wanted.

Putin, who loved new people, put himself next to Alice.

Bunny put herself next to Ecgbert(Sir).

Charlie Tysedale – who would have paid good money not to sit next to his wife, if only he still had any – quickly sat himself next to Bunny, patted the seat beside him and yelled to India: 'Come and sit next to me, darling! I haven't spoken to you *all morning.*'

Egbert(Mr), sitting down and noticing the empty spaces around him, said: 'Is Piers joining us, Alice? Do you know? I was looking forward to meeting him, after all these years! And his wife! What's she like?'

'Oh, she's lovely,' Alice said automatically.

135

Ecgbert(Sir) said: 'They've got a *ménage à trois* going, apparently.'

Charlie perked up: 'What? Who?'

Alice said: 'Ecgbert, for heaven's sake ...'

Egbert(Mr) said: 'Crikey,' but his attention was mostly on lunch.

Alice said: 'Anyway, I think they've all decided to have lunch elsewhere. I'm sure you'll catch up with Piers later.'

Egbert said he jolly well better had catch up with him later, since that was why he'd come all the way to Rospo. He tucked his napkin into his shirt, looked at the giant dish of veal laid out before him and rubbed his hands together.

'Yum *yum!*' he said. 'Gosh. What a treat! How we *love* Italy! What have we here?' It was already half past two. Everyone was hungry. There was a brief delay, as India and Alice discussed the possibility of waiting for Adele and Tippee to rejoin them, but by then Putin, having piled his own plate high, was spooning more than she wanted onto Bunny's plate, and Charlie Tysedale was already shovelling food into his mouth, and eyeing the dish for seconds.

Charlie said, wiping oil from his chin, 'There's no point waiting for Adele. She'll be ages. She knows it's lunchtime. If she *chooses* to bugger off just as the gong goes it's her lookout ...'

... *Squaring the Me–Him Circle*, indeed. The ape's hatred of the unicorn (or was it vice versa?) was impossible to miss. Everyone felt it.

Ecgbert(Sir), thinking aloud, thinking he was being tactful, asked Charlie: 'How long have you guys been married?'

Putin chortled. 'Longer than they want, I get the feeling. Longer than Bunny and me, eh, Bunny?'

Bunny shot him a look.

Quickly, with a stronger Russian accent, he diverted attention back to the group. 'What about you, Ecgbert? *Sir* Ecgbert – I understand you're in a "Week One" situation. The "honeymoon period", as they call it! But you, Mr Egbert, when have you and the beautiful Mrs India been married, huh? You seem to love each other very much . . . It's beautiful to see, am I right, Bunny?'

Bunny said yes, he was right. It was beautiful to see. But it was too late.

Egbert(Mr), though glowing from the compliments, had been reminded of what a short time he and the Rostovskys had been acquainted, and of how little he knew about them. 'When did you two tie the knot?' he asked.

Bunny looked at the table, waived the question away with a diffident smile. Luckily for her, Egbert wasn't that interested. 'Ooh, that reminds me,' he said, before she had time not to reply. 'Munchie, did you hear back from Nicola at all?'

'What's that?' said Putin.

'India sent a message to Nicola last night, telling her how we'd bumped into you!' Egbert(Mr) said.

India grinned mischievously. 'We're *longing* to hear what she has to say, aren't we, Eggzie? For example . . . we know why *she* was in rehab –'

'Oops,' mumbled Egbert. 'Bit much, Munchie.'

'– But what about you, Putin?! What were *you* doing in Arizona?'

Putin smiled bravely but there was a look of panic in his eyes, and no words to fill the space where his answer was meant to be. He came up with a laugh, but it lacked the usual gusto.

Alice, whose mother had died of a drug overdose, noted this and she felt sorry for him. She thought India was being tactless.

'Maybe Putin doesn't want to share that information with a table-full of strangers. I have to say I don't really blame him.'

'Come on, Rostovsky!' cried Charlie Tysedale, ignoring Alice, who was not important, also spraying the table with little specks of veal. 'What were you in for? You must have *done* something . . .'

But India was mortified. She said, 'Crikey – Alice, you're quite right. Shut up, Charlie. Putin, I'm so sorry. So rude of me. Absolutely none of my business. Anyway – I haven't heard back from Nicola yet. *Obviously.* She never replies to messages so I don't know why I bothered . . .'

Putin, mightily relieved, forgave India at once. The mood lightened.

Briefly.

The dreaded Adele returned. She looked dazed. She and Tippee had opened a door that she thought (or she claimed she thought) led to a bathroom, but instead led to Alice and Ecgbert's bedroom. She found a strange woman sitting on the bed, staring back at her.

'Why are you hiding in here?' Tippee had asked her. The strange woman didn't reply.

Adele wasn't someone who looked closely at people's faces, and in fact, if Tippee had not been with her, everything might have turned out rather better for everyone concerned. Unfortunately Tippee recognised Elizabetta at once.

He pointed at her. He said: 'You're the girl from—' He didn't get a chance to finish. Elizabetta pulled herself together. She tossed her head back and swept past them onto the landing, and disappeared up a nearby stairway without looking back.

As Adele and Tippee took their places at the lunch table,

it was clear to everyone that something had happened. Adele looked tense and thoughtful, and Tippee was grinning wildly. Each time Tippee opened his mouth to speak of the encounter, Adele hissed at him to be quiet. He obeyed her – twice. He was on the point of giving it another try –

But then there was no point. Elizabetta herself appeared. She breezed onto the terrace, and sat down in an empty space beside Egbert(Mr).

'Sorry I am late,' she said, in perfect English. 'I'm Elizabetta. I am married to Piers. He can't make it for lunch, but it turns out I can, after all.'

Charlie and Esmé stopped chewing. Knives and forks stopped still. They glanced at each other, and then back at Elizabetta, who was carefully not looking at either of them, helping herself to some wine.

Tippee couldn't have been more delighted. Again, he pointed at her. Again, he grinned. 'She's the girl from the hotel, yesterday, isn't she, Charlie? I recognise her.'

'Don't be silly,' said Charlie. 'And don't call me Charlie.'

'Good God,' exclaimed India. 'So you are! That's amazing! You left before we were introduced. I tried to say hello but I don't think you heard me ... Anyway I'm India. And this is Egbert, my husband. How *funny*! What are you doing here, Elizabetta? Or what were you doing *there* – or ...?' India shook her lovely head in magnificent confusion, remembering the envelope of cash, remembering how Elizabetta had slipped it into her bag; remembering, above all, the way Charlie had been looking at her. 'But OMG how *intriguing*!' she said.

'Intriguing?' repeated Egbert(Mr) 'What is? What girl? What are you talking about?'

'*Egbert*!' said India. 'Remember the *girl* who was sitting with *Charlie* last night at the *Russie*? Remember? And then *Esmé* came along? And it was all very jolly … *This is her! This is Piers' wife, Elizabetta!*'

'Oh right, yes …' said Egbert, still not really up to speed. (In matters like these, never fully up to speed.) 'Well! Jolly nice to see you again, Elizabetta. Glad you could join us.'

Elizabetta said nothing. She frowned, as if confused, not denying or confirming her identity. 'We have not met before,' she said to Egbert(Mr).

'What? No? Good. Well, very good to meet you at last.'

It was an awkward situation for everyone – except for Tippee, who was having the time of his life. Charlie Tysedale looked ready to kill someone – his son, maybe – or his wife – or Esmé, or Egbert, or Elizabetta. All or any of the above. Esmé looked as if he was trying not to cry.

Putin Rostovsky broke the silence. He introduced himself and his wife to Elizabetta, and asked if she would like any veal.

Elizabetta glanced at him gratefully. But she must have seen something that interested her. She frowned, and looked at him again.

'"*Putin*"?' Elizabetta said.

'You have heard my name correct the first time,' he said. And then he added, with a laugh and a fat, Russian-style finger-waggle. 'But you mustn't mistake me for the other Putin. Bunny and myself call him the *bad* Putin. In any case, of course, Putin is not my surname. No, no, no! I got there first!' He offered some more laughter, but as the silence around him continued, and Elizabetta continued to stare, it was developing a slightly desperate ring.

'Oh right, very funny!' said India. 'So the *wicked* Putin equals Mr Putin, whereas you are in fact Mr Rostovsky!'

'Exactly correct!' cried Putin, gratefully. 'Mr Vladimir Putin would be another man completely, I assure you!'

Egbert(Mr) said: 'Probably just as well.'

Elizabetta had not yet cracked a smile, nor had she taken her eyes off Putin. It was making him nervous. He cleared his throat. Wiped his brow. 'Anyway,' he said. 'Hot, isn't it?'

Bunny leaned across the table, smiling. She said to Elizabetta: 'We've all been longing to meet your husband. Ecgbert's been telling us all about him.'

'Have I?' said Egbert(Mr).

Bunny said: 'I meant Sir Ecgbert.'

Ecgbert(Sir) said: 'No I haven't! I absolutely have *not*. I've been very discreet.'

'Funnily enough, Elizabetta, did you know that Piers and I were at school together?' Egbert(Mr) said. 'Same house. Same year. Everything . . . '

'Oh, really?' said Elizabetta, who knew it already, and wasn't interested.

'He was a lot cooler than me,' Egbert(Mr) continued, 'I'll be honest.'

'Boo!' cried India. 'I don't believe it!'

'He actually *was*,' Egbert(Mr) reiterated. 'So we weren't really friends . . . but I mean, you know, five years in the same house – on the same corridor and all that – you get to know someone pretty well, even if you don't have a whole lot else in common . . . '

There was something about Elizabetta, her beauty, her sexiness, her cool, hard stare – that made most men feel a bit jumpy. Egbert(Mr) couldn't seem to stop himself from talking. 'You wouldn't believe how amazed I was when I heard he was out here, running the show.' Elizabetta's lips pursed, just a

141

fraction, at 'running the show'. Egbert gabbled blithely on. 'I actually feel terribly remiss, not having popped out to see him before now. So when this opportunity came up yesterday ... '
He turned to his cousin Ecgbert(Sir) and then to Alice. 'And I apologise for barging in on your honeymoon, Coz, I really do ... but seeing as we were so close, it seemed *madness* not to come and meet the guy in person ... '

And then, lo and behold, along came the guy himself, loping across the hot grass; dressed in black, on this bright blue day, looking pale and beautiful and as if, at any moment, he might just turn to dust in the harsh sunlight. He was smiling.

'Well, well, well,' he said, very self-assured. 'If it isn't Mr Tysedale and Mr Tode!' He folded himself into the last remaining empty seat and looked around him at the guests, the most laconic of smiles on his shiny red lips.

The women – except for Elizabetta – they all felt it. India, Bunny, Alice – even Adele. There was something lithe and devilish about Piers that was hard not to feel thrilled by, at least during the early encounters. The women adjusted their postures. They wriggled and leaned.

Not that the men noticed, of course. Not even Piers noticed it really. His arrival on a scene had generated the same sort of effect for all his adult life. He glanced at his wife, who glared at him. He took a final drag of his cigarette, and waited to see who would speak next.

Adele tutted. But not with the usual gusto. She tutted and smirked – and tipped her head in a way that made a lock of hair go loose.

In the end it was Esmé who stood up first to shake Piers by the hand. 'Quite the school reunion, eh?' he said. 'Except of course you're all so much younger than I am, I suppose ...

We never overlapped. Good to meet you in the flesh at last, Piers . . . And good to meet you too, Elizabetta.'

Piers stayed seated. He shook Esmé by the hand, and then he turned to Charlie Tysedale and smirked. He patted his own lean belly, and looked at Charlie's paunch. 'Good to see you've been eating well, old man,' he said.

'Ha ha ha,' said Charlie. 'Eating very well indeed, thank you, Wilson-Tite,' he replied to Piers, whose father had gone bust in the late 1990s. 'You've been managing to feed yourself, just about, have you? It's not easy, I know . . . '

So the tone was set – just as if the last twenty-odd years had never happened.

TEATIME

Two hours later, the focus of activity was still very much flopped around the lunch table. It was too hot to venture into the garden yet, and there was a sense of unease among at least half of the guests, which made them hesitate to leave their posts for fear of what they might miss, or what might be said while they were gone. The aimless eating and drinking continued.

Tippee, having been slathered in sunblock, had been permitted to wander the garden on his own, and Alice and Ecgbert(Sir) had sidled off for an afternoon nap. Ecgbert(Sir) had said to the guests, somewhat optimistically:

'Have a great trip back to Rome. Just in case we don't see you again.'

Everyone else had stayed put.

At some point Egbert(Mr) said to Piers: 'So, Piers, we really must have a chinwag before I toddle off. You can tell me all about how things are going.' He was a little drunk, due to school reunion tension. Egbert(Mr) had been the underdog back at school, and now here they were, and he was Charlie's host, indirectly, and Piers' boss. Egbert(Mr) still felt very much the underdog. He always would. He waved his wine glass, and said with a silly swagger he didn't often use and certainly wasn't feeling, 'I don't see any tourists anywhere ... Is that normal?'

Piers didn't bother to reply.

Egbert(Mr) tried again. 'I suppose you're about to tell me the place needs a terrifying injection of cash!'

Piers left a beat, because Egbert(Mr) was the underdog. He replied coldly, 'We're doing OK.'

'Oh, I'm sure you are,' said India. 'The place looks amazing ...' She was bored. Somehow the whole of lunch had passed, dominated by old schoolboy war games, while the far more intriguing mystery surrounding Elizabetta's presence yesterday in Rome/not in Rome seemed to have been brushed aside. 'Seriously, though,' India said, 'Elizabetta, you don't mind me asking. It just seems so weird. I can't work it out. Did you actually know Charlie and Esmé before today? Or ...' She frowned. 'It was *you*, yesterday, wasn't it? In Rome? I'm so confused!'

A split second passed while Elizabetta made some private calculations. Her face cleared. She laughed. 'In *Rome*? Yesterday? ... I was uncertain what you were all saying before. But no! That was not me! ... Of course I wasn't in Rome yesterday!'

'You weren't?' India was thoroughly flummoxed. She glanced at Adele. Adele said nothing. India looked at Esmé and Charlie, but they were both 100 per cent preoccupied by the stems of their wine glasses. 'Well then ... How very weird ... Where's Tippee when you need him?' she laughed. 'Tippee was convinced it was you, wasn't he? I'm *sure* it was you ...'

But suddenly she wasn't so sure, not any more. She turned

145

to Egbert(Mr) for reassurance. But he was no use. He'd been staring at his weather app. She turned to Adele ... 'It was her, wasn't it?'

Adele smiled her creepy, symmetrical smile. 'Sorry, India. I'm not sure I know quite what you're talking about.'

'But you ... Am I being mad?'

Esmé and Charlie seized on it. Yes, she was being mad. Most definitely.

'Oops-a-daisy! Loony alert!' said Charlie, into an imaginary walkie-talkie.

'Calling all doctors. Any DOCTORS in the area?' said Esmé, into an imaginary megaphone. 'Sedative needed on Ward Eight. This is NOT a drill. Urgent. Urgent. Escaped Mad Person on the Terrace at Rospo. Back-up required immediately. Send for back-up.'

Bunny and Putin said nothing. They watched and learned.

'No, but come on, guys. Be fair,' said Egbert(Mr), still not entirely up to speed, but sensing his wife was under attack. 'There was definitely *someone* ... And she definitely looked a bit like ... ' He looked at Piers. Piers smiled in a languid manner, and said nothing at all. 'Anyway, bottom line,' Egbert(Mr) finished feebly, 'I take it that it *wasn't* you, Elizabetta?'

'HA HA HA!' bawled Esmé and Charlie. 'RED ALERT! UNSTABLE WOMAN ON THE LOOSE!' ... 'DO NOT APPROACH!' ... 'STRAITJACKET REQUIRED!'

India looked as if she might be about to cry.

Putin noted this. He didn't like it. He said: 'Hey – guys – come on. Stop it ... '

He would have said more but just then, out of the corner of one eye, he spotted movement. He looked up towards the back of the house. A figure. Approaching.

146

A small figure heading towards the terrace. Stompety-stomp. Someone short and slim. Very short and very slim. With short hair, a thick woolly sweater, in the scorching heat, and a dirty safety visor covering her face.

Putin's heart missed a beat. *Could it be?* Even with the visor, he recognised her from the pictures in the paper. Under the table, he gave Bunny a small kick. Now they were in trouble.

Slowly, Bunny turned.

'Nicola Tode!' she cried. 'I don't believe it!' Bunny leapt up, and ran across the garden towards her. She opened her arms and wrapped Nicola in a tight hug.

Nicola didn't like being touched. She stood ramrod style, unable to move; her face, beneath the visor, a mask of intense emotional discomfort. Bunny did not let go.

A moment passed. Aside from Putin, nobody paid a great deal of attention. In their own ways, they were all engaged in a battle to save their skins. The arrival – albeit extraordinary and un-announced – of non-person Nicola (as Charlie Tysedale referred to her later) was not quite sufficient reason to pause. Not at once.

Bunny only released Nicola when Putin was standing by her side, in position to continue with the long embrace.

Putin held her tight. Tight enough to suffocate her, if he wasn't careful. But he was careful. He held her tight, but not too tight. 'Nicola!' he said. 'Nicola, Nicola, Nicola! Ahhh! My beautiful friend Nicola! How have you been, my friend? I am – look at me, in tears . . . ' He wiped his eyes with one hand, while maintaining his grip with the other. 'My God! What a miracle it is to see you again . . . And here in this beautiful place. So beautiful . . . '

Eventually Nicola said: 'If you wouldn't mind. It's very hot . . . '

147

He let her go.

By that time, the rest of the group had caught up and India, always happy to see people, even Nicola, also quite relieved to have the attention diverted from the brutal ribbing about being a mad person, stood next in line to envelop her in love.

India said: 'Darling Nicola! What are you *doing* here? Why aren't you in Yorkshire?'

But by now Nicola had had more than enough of the hugging. 'Please,' she said, pushing India away. 'It's incredibly hot. I came as soon as I got the message.'

'What message?' India was confused. 'I didn't send a message, did I? ... Oh. You mean last night?'

Nicola said: 'Affirmative.'

'The message about bumping into—'

'Affirmative. I booked myself onto the first flight from Manchester this morning. Mr Car-Fizzy kindly drove me to the airport. I was fortunate. As you can see, I got here as soon as I could ...' She peered around India, towards the lunch table. 'Is there any food left? I'm starving.'

There was plenty of lunch left.

She had arrived with a rucksack. She settled herself at the table, and dumped it at her feet. India went to find Frederica, or failing that, a clean plate and a wine glass from the kitchen. Egbert(Mr) introduced her to the group.

'This is my old school chum, Piers, who's doing a brilliant job as *maître d'* of Rospo house and gardens,' he began.

Nicola pulled an oily slice of tomato from the salad dish, and dropped it, seal-style, into her mouth. Grease dripped on her chin. She wiped it away with a dirty sleeve, and looked at Piers.

Nope. She didn't like the look of him. She nodded.

'And this is *another* old school chum, funnily enough. Can't get away from them this week, ha ha. This is Charlie Tysedale. We all bumped into each other in Rome last night!'

Charlie said: 'Lovely to meet you, Nicola. Welcome to Rospo!'

Nope. She didn't like the look of him, either.

'And this is Charlie's wife, Adele.'

Nope.

She dropped in another slice of tomato.

'And I think you know your brother, Esmé!'

She double-took. Swallowed the tomato. 'Esmé! What the hell are *you* doing here?'

'Ha ha!' said Egbert(Mr). 'That's what we're all trying to find out!'

India laughed, but nobody else did.

'I keep *telling* you,' Esmé said peevishly, 'I came to surprise my brother on his honeymoon. I don't know why that's so difficult for everyone to understand.'

'Too right!' said Egbert(Mr) quickly, who didn't want to fight. 'Alice and Ecgbert have gone off for an afternoon siesta, if you're wondering, Nicola ... And I think you know me and India ...'

'Such a lovely surprise to see you here!' India said.

Nope.

Egbert(Mr) continued. 'And – I'm *sorry*, I should have introduced you earlier. This is Elizabetta. Very remiss of me. Nicola, this is Elizabetta. AKA Mrs Slayer-Wilson-Tite. She has the misfortune to be married to young Piers here ...'

Nope.

'She and Piers run the show together, is that right, Elizabetta? Sort of *Maître* and *Maîtresse d'*, if that makes sense ... We were just discussing how much she resembled a lady we met in Rome last night ... But clearly it was a case of mistaken identity ... Am I right?'

'You are correct,' said Elizabetta. 'I would have loved to be in Rome last night. But unfortunately I had business here at Rospo ... I have no idea who you met at the Hotel de Russie. But it wasn't me. I have never even been there.' She glared at India, daring her to say otherwise.

'Your English is amazing!' India said instead – keen not to be dragged into all that again. 'Where did you learn to speak English so amazingly?'

'I am married to an Englishman,' she replied. Her gaze moved from the Englishman she married to Putin Rostovsky, who had been uncharacteristically quiet since returning from his fulsome Nicola embrace. 'And I always used to watch your British TV show, *EastEnders*. I used to be addicted to it.'

Putin, brilliantly, broke into a noisy, twang-filled rendition of the theme tune, during which he didn't take his eyes off Elizabetta. And though this singing sounded hearty and fun, his beady eyes sent a different message. The theme tune dragged on. Elizabetta and he eyeballed one another, on and on ... Until Bunny leaned across and gently tapped her husband's forearm. 'Enough, baby,' she muttered. 'You're giving everyone a headache.'

'Ah! Thank you, Bunny!' said Egbert(Mr). 'I thought it would never end!'

Nicola disagreed. 'It's a great tune,' she said.

'Am I leaving anyone out?' Egbert(Mr) looked around the table. 'I think that's everyone, Nicola. You'll meet young Tippee later. And of course you already know Bunny and Putin Rostovsky. They're old friends.'

Here was the crunch. Bunny smiled at Nicola. The most beautiful, warmest, sexiest of smiles.

Nicola blushed.

'*Hello, Nicola darling*,' murmured Bunny. 'Good to see you looking so well.'

Nicola looked at her hands. She swallowed her tomato.

Bunny said: 'Honestly, I would hardly recognise you . . . You look *transformed* . . . '

A tomato pip, or possibly it was saliva, went down the wrong pipe. Nicola spluttered slightly. It took a moment. Bunny Rostovsky, reading the situation with the usual laser-beam acumen, slid from her seat and moved closer to Nicola. Softly, she stroked Nicola's shoulders until Nicola stopped coughing.

Nicola didn't want Bunny to stop. Or she did want her to stop. Or she didn't. In any case – this is the thing. Nicola missed her moment. Nicola, who'd been on the road since 5 a.m., who'd packed her rucksack and rushed to the airport specifically to raise the alarm: to call out these imposters, inexplicably claiming to be her 'friends', and to send them packing . . . Nicola – lost her nerve at the crunch.

Bunny, she liked. Bunny was delightful. Perhaps, after all, Nicola was mistaken, and they really had known one another in Arizona in any case? . . . It certainly seemed as though they might have done.

There was something familiar about her. In a way. Something lovely.

Bunny Rostovsky.

Bunny, Bunny, Bunny . . .

But what about Putin? Nicola was almost certain she'd never laid eyes on the guy before now. Should she say something? What if – because actually – when she thought about it –

151

On the other hand, there was a lot about Arizona she'd purposely blocked out. Or genuinely forgotten. And after all, it had all happened over two years ago. So much had happened. People – nurses and patients – had been coming and going all the time.

Bunny watched Nicola's face and read most if not all of these thoughts. She kept her hand on Nicola's back and deepened the caress. 'Are you OK now?' she said, leaning in and leaning over.

'Yep. Yes. Yep.' Nicola tried to sound OK. But the tumult of senses and emotions awoken by Bunny's voice and touch had sent her into another coughing fit.

People were getting bored.

India said: 'It's absolutely lovely to see you, Nicola. Amazing you managed to get out here so fast! What made you decide . . . ? I suppose – actually, I don't blame you. I suppose I would have felt a bit left out, knowing everyone was here.'

Nicola slurped on her wine. She was conscious that the entire table was looking at her. She could feel her face burning. She was furious. How dared India imply she had come out to Rospo because she felt *left out*? How insulting! 'Negative. I did not feel left out. The fact is . . . '

At the end of the table, behind Egbert(Mr), standing quite casually by the door that led to the sitting room, Bunny Rostovsky noticed two figures. A tall majestic-looking woman dressed in a Russian mink hat and diamanté shift dress (Mary Quant), and a stout little man with a long beard, in a pinkish tunic and floppy velvet hat. They were staring at her. The majestic woman seemed to be emitting a faint haze of green vapour from neck and armpits; somehow this (minor detail) dimmed her overall majesty not one bit. She looked back at Bunny and smiled slightly. She lifted one bony finger to her lips:

'*Shhhh*,' she said.

'It had nothing to do with "feeling left out", as you call it,' Nicola was saying. 'The fact is—'

Bunny said: 'This place is haunted.' She pointed to the ghosts. 'Can anyone else see them?'

But nobody could. And when Bunny looked back, they were gone.

After that, which caused a minor stir and a lot of joshing, and more talking into imaginary walkie-talkies from the men, the guests wondered if it was time to have a wander round the famous garden, seeing as they'd come so far. The sun was still hot. On the other hand, they couldn't sit on the terrace all afternoon, and they needed to think about getting back to Rome.

The prospect of squeezing back into Ecgbert(Sir)'s rental car wasn't thrilling. Plus, now there was the added body-plus-rucksack in the unwashed form of Nicola.

Nicola had asked Esmé if she could 'doss down' in his fantastic Rome apartment tonight, to save money. She said it would be great for the two of them to spend some 'quality time' together. He'd said, 'Yeah, sure', but obviously he hadn't meant it.

Esmé needed money. He badly needed this Rospo venture to work. What he needed, right now, was 'quality time' with Charlie and Elizabetta, here at Rospo. And yet, it seemed to him that from every direction, there leached more hangers-on, bent on obstructing his progress. The last thing on earth he needed at this moment in his life was to spend a pointless night with his sister, in his imaginary 'fantastic apartment' in Rome.

What with one thing and another there was an idea growing in everyone's minds, for a variety of self-interested reasons, that

153

perhaps it might be more convivial to spend the night at Rospo after all, and return to Rome in the morning . . . The question was, how to get this past Alice and Ecgbert(Sir), who were meant to be enjoying their honeymoon. Also, how to persuade somebody, somewhere, to organise making up the extra beds.

It was agreed that the group should spend a few hours doing their own thing, and that they would reconvene 'a bit later, to discuss trains and things'.

Bunny and Putin left the table together.

India turned to Egbert(Mr). 'Shall we explore?' she suggested. Egbert looked slightly resistant, until India reminded him that this was meant, after all, to be their romantic weekend getaway. (Egbert might have reminded her that it was India who had insisted on joining up with the big party. But he didn't do that. It wouldn't have been kind.) He said, 'Right you are, Munchie! Let's go and find some ghosts!' He turned to Piers as he was leaving. 'And we really must have a chinwag at some point . . . ' he said.

Piers agreed. Yes, he said, they must.

Without quite looking her in the eye, Esmé asked Elizabetta what the situation was vis-à-vis Frederica possibly providing them all with dinner.

Elizabetta said, 'Of course.'

Elizabetta and Esmé got up from the table together. Esmé, with Elizabetta standing beside him, said to Charlie: 'Fancy an amble, Tysedale?'

But Adele, alert now, and noting Elizabetta's presence, decided that this was not to be. She stated that Charlie had promised Tippee they would explore Rospo's medieval church ruins together.

'Isn't that right, Tippee?'

Tippee, returned from the garden and now immersed in an electronic game, didn't look up from the screen. But from the ambient sound/his mother's voice, he had learned long ago when was the moment to nod. He nodded.

'He's super-excited, aren't you, Tippee?'

Tippee nodded.

Adele said: 'He never gets to spend quality time with his daddy. Do you, Tippee?'

Tippee nodded.

Esmé and Elizabetta were standing, waiting. It was too bad. Charlie said to Esmé: 'I'll catch up with you later.'

APPROACHING DRINKS TIME

The gardens at Rospo were not flat or small. They stretched for 40 acres or more. And as Bunny led the way ever further from the house, Putin tried to hide from her how he was struggling to keep up. They needed a shady spot, far from prying eyes, and Bunny worried that unless they moved quickly, Nicola would try to join them and after what had happened, she and Putin needed a moment alone together to regroup, agree on the way forward, etc.

Behind the ruins of the Roman pig shed (400 BC), in the shade of an old plum tree, they found a clear-spring pool, and they settled down beside it. They removed their shoes, dipped their feet into the cool water, and allowed themselves to think.

Bunny's emotions, such as they were, never showed. But on this occasion, beneath the porn-star perfection, there lay a heart that was beating very fast indeed.

'What now?' Putin said, after a while. 'That was bloody close.'

Bunny laughed. They both laughed. 'Which bit?' she asked.

He shook his head. Good question. The whole of it. 'You

were amazing, Money-Bun. *Amazing*, watching you at work there. I'll be honest, you got *me* in as much of a lather as young Nicola. And *I* knew you were only putting it on!' The comment didn't impress Bunny, for a variety of reasons, and Putin, who longed to impress his wife, regretted making it very much. 'Not that she's 'specially young,' he added. '... Anyway ...' He gazed unhappily at his hot and swollen feet, cooling beneath the crystal waters. 'I think,' he said, 'the greater danger might be Elizabetta. She could be a big problem.'

Slowly, Bunny nodded. 'She recognised you,' she said. 'That's obvious ... So why didn't she say something? What's she up to?'

Putin said: 'More to the point, Bunny, what are *we* up to?'

They laughed. He'd made her laugh! Putin's heart soared. Whatever it was they were up to, it was wicked, and fun, and they were up to it together.

Putin said: 'Oh Bunny, I feel lucky to have met you, I do, I do!'

Bunny nodded.

Putin said: 'I don't think Nicola's going to say anything, do you? I think we've – I think you've mesmerised her, Bun. I don't think we need to do anything more with Nicola. Agreed?'

Bunny nodded again. 'No. Let's just be sweet to her. Poor old thing.'

'Let her enjoy her holiday.'

'Exactly.'

They fell silent. Bunny looked into the water, so clear and so still, and – who knows what thoughts passed through her brilliant mind? Putin looked at Bunny and remembered their earlier days when, at moments such as these, his fat old body would spring to life. He would have been all over her. Not any more. He wondered what Bunny did for sex these days, and the thought terrified him.

'I'd be lost without you,' he said. 'You know that, don't you, Money-Bun? I'd do anything for you. Anything at all.'

Money-Bun ignored the comment, if she heard it at all. Putin's vocal adoration was Bunny's white noise. She said instead: 'The one we need to worry about is Elizabetta. She'll be asking us for money before the end of the day. Mark my words.'

Charlie and Adele were still at the table. They ignored Frederica as she cleared the remains of lunch from around them. They wished she would leave them alone, so they could squabble in peace. It seemed to Charlie, who always assumed the worst of people, that she was clearing the table in that slow and surly fashion specifically to antagonise him. He didn't want anyone overhearing the way Adele spoke to him when no one was around. Rather, the way she spoke to him about money.

Nowadays it was Adele who made the money and Adele who controlled his purse strings, not only domestically but – since the big Mark of Marylebone bailout – in his business, too. Charlie dreamed of cutting loose. And if only he could get Rospo up and running, he'd be back on his feet again. He'd lose some weight. Stop smoking. Make his own money. Get rid of his wife once and for all.

Adele, meanwhile, longed more than anything to claw back the money she had loaned him in the bailout. She longed to be married to a winner again. Had she thought about it, which she certainly didn't, she would have longed not to be married to him at all, but Adele's fortune depended on maintaining a good domestic front. The *Ape and the Unicorn* indeed. No circle was ever less squared. They loathed each other.

In the meantime:

'I must admit I was a little confused. Was that lady – Elizabetta – *was* she the one in Rome or wasn't she? She disappeared off so quickly, whoever she was ... Tippee seems to be convinced ... Don't you, Tippee?'

(From his place on the cushions, at the far end of the terrace, Tippee nodded.)

Charlie didn't choose to reply. So she asked him again.

He said: 'Oh for Christ's sake, Adele.'

'I'm afraid "for Christ's sake, Adele" isn't an answer. Who was that girl? Why were you drinking with her? Why didn't you want to introduce me to her last night? What's going on, Charlie?'

He said: 'Why are you suddenly so interested? What do you care?'

'I care, Charlie,' she said patiently, 'because—'

He slapped his hand on the table. Tippee looked up from his screen, briefly.

'Adele,' Charlie snarled. 'Do *not* talk to me like I'm a fucking child.'

Adele paused. Inhaled. 'I care, Charlie,' she continued, 'because you are my husband, and the father of my child and ...'

But by then Charlie had already left the table.

Tippee sniggered.

Adele said: 'Charlie? Come back here. At once.'

159

He didn't. But he did pause. 'I'm going to find Esmé,' he said. It was a different tone: less defiant. Without Adele, he couldn't even pay the Russie hotel bill. Without Adele, there would be no money for Rospo. They both knew it. 'Elizabetta is nothing you need to worry about,' he added. 'She couldn't be less important. I swear.'

'Good,' said Adele.

And he half turned towards her, awaiting her dismissal. Adele nodded. The cicadas broke into song once again. Charlie plodded out into the sunshine, his prematurely aged, over-indulged, alcohol-soaked body shimmering with self-pity and rage.

Charlie wondered what he'd ever seen in Italy. It was too hot. And how the hell was he supposed to find Esmé and Elizabetta in this massive garden? It was ridiculous . . .

'Esmé?' he called.

From behind one of the church ruins, he heard a man and a woman. At the sound of his voice, they fell silent.

Were they plotting behind his back? Were they going to try to cut him out of the deal? 'ESMÉ!' he roared.

There came India's voice, laughing at the sound of his fury. 'Only me and Egbert, Charlie,' she said. 'Having a romantic moment . . . I think Esmé went off with Elizabetta, didn't he?'

Charlie wandered away. He brought out his phone.

No answer from Esmé. *Bastard*. Where was he?

The heat, the alcohol, his dreaded wife, his appalling financial situation – they were all conspiring against him. Charlie felt very angry and very put upon. What was he supposed to do now? He looked up from his useless phone and saw Elizabetta, standing alone. She was waiting for him.

Charlie said: 'What have you done with Esmé?' It was an odd way of putting it. He must have seen something in her face.

She shook her head. Nothing.

She said: 'Esmé's an idiot.'

'He isn't, actually,' Charlie replied. 'And even if he were – he's a useful idiot. What have you done with him? Where is he?'

She took a step closer; glanced about her, beckoned him to follow her further into the garden. She said: 'My father is very angry. He spoke to Ecgbert in the shop. He thought it was Esmé.'

'Ecgbert? Or Egbert?'

Elizabetta shrugged. 'Who cares?' she said. 'My father is very angry.'

'But why? How? What did he say?'

Elizabetta shook her head impatiently. 'He thinks we are lying to him.'

Charlie said: 'Well, but I mean . . . What am I supposed to do about it? He's your father, Elizabetta. We're not lying, are we? *Are* we? Are *you*?'

She didn't confirm who was lying to whom, or even whether they were. Charlie assumed, rightly, that in fact everyone was lying to everyone.

Instead of answering the question, Elizabetta looked him in the eyes and said: 'I need more money.'

Charlie laughed. 'What's the problem?'

The problem was she wanted more money. Lots more.

'The problem is,' said Charlie, 'this is the second time you've done this to us. How do I know you won't do it again?'

She gazed up at him with her cold, brown eyes and her shiny

161

hair and her perfect body. She kissed him on the mouth – and
in the confusion, what with the sun and the alcohol, and
Elizabetta being amazingly sexy, and his rich wife being so
dreaded, he didn't stop her.

'Where will it ever end?' he muttered.

Elizabetta smiled.

'Ah! Tysedale! There you are! Good. Been looking for you
everywhere. Did you find Elizabetta?'

Charlie was still recovering from the kiss. The whole ridiculous encounter. He was furious with himself, and somehow,
quite unreasonably, even more furious with Esmé. Angry
and hot, and feeling stupid, he told Esmé how, once again,
Elizabetta was asking for money.

Esmé already knew. He said: 'Yes. She's greedy. We're going
to need to think about that. She may be more trouble than
she's worth. However – look, now that we're *in loco*, as it were,
finally, I really want us to focus on the vision. Forget about
Elizabetta for a second. We should never have trusted her. Too
bad. This doesn't have to be grubby. We don't have to make it
grubby. Come with me . . . '

He led Charlie away, down the hill towards the stream where
the grapefruits bobbed on by. 'I used to spend so many hours
playing in this stream, Charlie . . . ' he said, bouncing off his
heels, bouncing off in front. 'Before Mummy got the house
at Capri we used to come here a lot . . . I remember this little
bit of the garden like the back of my hand. And this – *here*,'
he said, coming to a halt by a small forest of giant bamboos,

'this is where I envisage a sort of Roman-style ... The water is *icy*. Feel it ... See? It's coming up direct from the spring, deep in the earth. I don't think there's cleaner water in the whole of Italy. I see plunge-pools, natural. All natural ... And then the crescent of eco-rev "love-pods" right here, among the bamboos ... and then ...' He led Charlie further into the trees. '... *Here*,' he said, 'This is the – you remember the drawings ... Well, *here* ...'

Esmé loved this place. Charlie hadn't realised. Not that it mattered much. Yes, Charlie had seen the plans. He'd seen the projections. This garden, with its clean-water pools, its ancient ruins, its giant bamboos, its seamless transport links to Rome's two international airports – this could be the health and wealth retreat to beat them all: the most exclusive, most romantic, most luxurious private club in the world.

Yes, it could.

There were just a handful of obstacles that needed to be cleared first.

DRINKS TIME

'Have they gone yet?' asked Alice, from her lovely bed.

Alice and Ecgbert(Sir) had dispensed with their afternoon rest period and would have liked, under other circumstances, to venture out in the fresh air again. But Ecgbert, peering through the shutter slats, noted sadly that, no, they had not gone yet. Far from it. The place was 'still swarming' with unwanted guests.

'Couldn't we just herd them into the car?' Sir Ecgbert suggested. 'We could order them to get in.'

Alice thought about it. 'Maybe, if we had the engine running . . . '

'Trouble is, now there's Nicola. I'll be honest with you, Trudy. It was quite a battle squeezing eight of them in. They complained a lot. With the addition of Nicola, small though she is, it may actually be impossible.'

'Couldn't we get Elizabetta or Piers to take their car, too? Or Frederica? Or isn't there a taxi service?'

'Possible,' Ecgbert(Sir) agreed. ' . . . Problem is – getting anyone to *do* anything . . . ' He fell silent. He could see them, scattered in little huddles and pairs around the garden. There were Charlie and Esmé, among the bamboos, talking to one another intently. And there was Elizabetta – what was she up to? Heading south, by the look of things. Making a bee-line for the Russians at the far end of the garden . . . Yes. And there, to the east, Egbert and India were swimming in one of the fresh-water ponds . . .

'Yikes,' said Sir Ecgbert. 'I think India's naked.'

'Nooo!' Alice laughed. 'She can't be! Egbert would have a fit!'

'Well, there are clothes in a pile . . . I think Egbert's naked too.'

'Don't be ridiculous!' Alice climbed out of bed to take a look. Together, they peered through the slats.

It turned out that Mr and Mrs Tode still had their underwear on.

'Boring,' said Ecgbert(Sir).

His attention moved on. 'Seriously, Trudy. How are we going to get rid of them? They're spread all over the garden. They've obviously got zero intention of leaving tonight . . . Is that *Nicola*, with the Russians? Do you think they know she's spying on them? . . . She shouldn't do that . . . ' At that moment, Nicola was crouched behind the Roman pigsty, staring at them as they flopped and splashed in the water. 'I thought they cured her of all that in Arizona . . . Oops. And here comes Elizabetta! This could be interesting . . . '

Not to Alice. She was more concerned with getting the unwanted guests back to Rome before dinner. She said: 'If we could somehow get the message to Frederica or Piers – we could have the cars waiting and then just not really give them a chance to think about it. Bundle them all in. Maybe have all their bags in the cars ready and waiting ...' It was obvious from the tone of her voice that she didn't believe any of this was feasible. But she ploughed on. 'Has anyone even checked when's the last train back to Rome?'

A tap on the bedroom door. Alice and Ecgbert looked at each other in alarm. There was no one out there they wanted to speak to or see. They were trapped.

Another tap, this one accompanied with a sing-song: 'Anyone there?'

It was the dreaded Adele, giving them bad news about trains: the last one had pulled out of Rospo nel Buco station about three minutes ago. She didn't want to be a bother – she knew Charlie and Esmé had a lot of business to discuss ... And in fact, she'd suspected this might happen even before they left Rome this morning. Fortunately she'd had the foresight to bring her and Tippee's overnight things as a precaution. So there wasn't a problem. She was only concerned because she'd been an idiot and left the almond milk behind ... Might Frederica, for example, be popping to the shops, now that there would be thirteen for dinner? And if so, would she mind ever-so-much popping some almond milk into her trolley ...?

Ecgbert(Sir) said: 'Thirteen? By the way – you do realise this is our honeymoon?'

Adele assured him that she couldn't apologise enough. She said, 'Who would have known the trains back to Rome stopped so early? Meanwhile I'm paying for two rooms at the Russie, Ecgbert. And Tippee and I have tickets for the Vatican Museum at nine a.m. tomorrow. But you know how it is with Charlie ...'

'I don't. Not really,' he said. 'I've never met Charlie before.

I'm not even sure why he's here. Do you know why he's here, Trudy?'

Alice agreed that she didn't know him, or why he was here, either. (Also, she didn't add, from what little she'd seen, she wasn't terribly enthusiastic about getting to know him any better.)

Adele said: 'He and your brother are hatching a super little plan for the gardens.' She smiled. 'I know he wants to talk to you about it.'

'But this is our honeymoon,' said Ecgbert.

'The other thing,' said Alice (grasping at straws), 'I worry the shops around here won't sell almond milk ... Maybe you should all get a taxi back to Rome. It's not that far.'

Adele said: 'Believe me ... the situation is not ideal for me either. But we are where we are.'

Ecgbert said: 'What about the taxi idea? Can't you all just get a taxi?'

'There aren't any,' lied Adele.

If Adele had wanted a taxi, she would have found one, but she had a few reasons she preferred to stay at Rospo: among them, the prospect of spending an evening alone with her husband and son back in Rome. It was better here. There were other people around. Charlie would have to be a little less disagreeable. 'I'm just wondering if you might be able to tell us where we're sleeping? Not so much for me, but Tippee has brought a teeny bit of school work with him. He doesn't concentrate well in strange environments, so the sooner I can get him settled the better ... '

167

Out in the garden, guests were beginning to realise that they were thirsty. They'd forgotten the time – or so they claimed – what with lunch having been so late. India and Egbert(Mr), fully dressed once again, and looking on their phones at the train timetable, realised the situation vis-à-vis getting back to Rome tonight and were horrified: truly embarrassed to discover the trains had all finished for the day.

'You'd have thought,' said Egbert(Mr), 'that someone might have looked into it.'

'Well, I suppose we all thought someone else would.'

'Yes, that's all very well,' Egbert replied, sounding tetchy. They squabbled.

'Watch out, Eggzie,' India said. 'You're sounding awfully pompous. You know you could have perfectly well checked the trains yourself.'

She was right. Of course she was. 'Oh God, Munchie,' he said, his face crumpling. 'Forgive me. I'm being insufferable. I just – I suppose I'm just terribly disappointed to be stuck with these awful people a moment longer than we need to be . . . This is supposed to be our romantic weekend away. But now here we are, with these dreadful people. Obviously I don't mean Alice and Ecgbert . . . Or Esmé . . . Munchie, unless we can somehow organise a taxi, we're going to have to spend the *night* here . . . And we've got that gorgeous room at the hotel, waiting for us. Honestly, I'm not even sure why we came here in the first place. I can't seem to get a chance to speak to Piers. He keeps sidling off . . . Plus – even if I could persuade him to stick around long enough, I'm not sure what I'm supposed to be saying to him. As long as Rospo ticks along I don't see why I need to worry . . .'

'Touché!' cried India.

He sighed. 'It's an almighty cock-up.'

'They're not all dreadful,' India said. 'I quite like the Russians.'

'Plus, I feel very, very guilty about poor Ecgbert and Alice. We've barged in on their honeymoon. They can't want us here . . . It's too embarrassing.'

India agreed that they should try to organise a taxi. They were, after all, only 40 or so kilometres outside Rome. It couldn't be impossible.

They ordered not one but two taxis, or they thought they had – from a number that claimed to be a taxi service in Rospo nel Buco. However, it was hard to be sure quite what they'd done, since neither of them spoke any Italian, and the Italian who answered the phone at the taxi office didn't speak English.

From what they could make out, the request for the cars not to arrive for at least an hour seemed to have been clearly understood. This was excellent news. It gave them plenty of time, they thought, to gather everyone up and get them organised and maybe, if Alice and Ecgbert could be lured out of their bedroom, for everyone to enjoy a farewell drink.

There's nothing like forbidden sex on a sunny June morning, just before lunch. Except more of the same on a sunny June late afternoon, in the run-up to dinner.

Upstairs in her little staff flat, the incredibly bendy Frederica Ranaldini and her handsome brother-in-law, Piers Slayer-Wilson-Tite, were at it again. Rather, they had been until about ten minutes ago. They'd been enjoying a lull, listening to the cicadas, and catching their breath.

But now they were arguing again. Between Piers and Frederica there were really only two states of being. This one or the other. Actually, three states. Also the one where they pretended, in front of Elizabetta, not to be secret lovers at all. Frederica was getting very tired of that third state. Hence the argument.

She'd had enough of the *ménage*. Why wouldn't Piers leave Elizabetta and run away with her? Why?

Piers didn't have an answer. Or not one that would have satisfied Frederica.

Piers enjoyed a remarkably good life here in Rospo. Sometimes, when Frederica started up on this topic, yet again, he found it quite hard not to giggle. How deluded must she be, to imagine he would ever want to change it?

Frederica's phone was ringing. It was her father, calling for the third time in an hour. She switched it off.

Frederica said to Piers [Please note: the following conversation took place in Italian]: 'You think you know everything, Piers. But you don't have the slightest idea what's happening around you. So much is happening and you don't see it. Because you're an idiot. An English idiot.'

Piers, complacent fellow, gave his lover a sexy smile, and asked her, without the slightest intention of listening to the answer, *what she meant*. What, exactly, was happening around him, that he didn't know about?

For a while, she didn't reply. She laughed, and looked at the ceiling. She wasn't sure he deserved to be told.

'Well, *for example*,' she began, 'I suppose you know why those men are here today? The two English men – Charlie and Esmé.'

'Charlie Tysedale and Esmé Tode? My old school chums?' Piers said. He reached for a pack of cigarettes, lit himself one. 'I would imagine,' he said, 'from the way they're prowling around the place with dollar signs in their eyes ... that they've got some sort of scheme in the works regarding Rospo ... Why? Do you know something I don't?'

Frederica said: 'Maybe I do. Maybe I don't.'

Piers laughed, underestimating her again.

'Cute,' he said.

Frederica gazed at the ceiling. He offered her the cigarette. She took a drag and passed it back, and calculated things. For example, what to tell her lover and what to leave out. All men were slightly stupid (she calculated). It was only a matter of knowing how best to put them to work.

After a while she said: 'And where do you think this will leave you and me and Elizabetta, Piers? And my family? Do you think their "scheme" will have any impact on us? The way we live our lives?'

Piers shrugged. 'I would imagine not much,' he said. 'Plus, you know – I mean ... we're talking about two English men – they haven't the faintest idea ... They can scheme and plan as much as they like. But nothing's ever going to actually happen. We all know it ... ' He took a long, complacent pull on his cigarette. 'This is Italy.'

Frederica watched him from the corner of her eye.

She laughed: 'You think you understand Italy and the Italians?'

'Nope,' he said. He was bored. It was time to get back downstairs. Elizabetta would be wondering where he was, and he couldn't have that. He passed Frederica the cigarette, reached for his T-shirt. 'Do you think you understand the English?'

It might have been better they didn't speak. When they weren't having sex they really did not like each other one bit.

Frederica stubbed out the cigarette. She had made a decision. In a sudden, surprising move she reached for something beneath the bed and slapped it onto the sheet between them.

An envelope, filled with banknotes.

Piers paused. He looked at the envelope. And then at Frederica. She watched him. And no, she did not understand him – any better than he understood her. Piers Slayer-Wilson-Tite was impossible to read. Everything about his insubstantial existence depended on it. *Had he seen the envelope before this moment?* Frederica couldn't tell. *Did he know who had given his wife this money, and why? Did he know more or less than Frederica did?*

'Where did you get that?' he asked. And then: 'How much is it?'

'I counted. It's twenty thousand euro. Your friend Charlie Tysedale gave it Elizabetta in Rome, last night . . . '

'Really?' said Piers.

Frederica watched him closely and it occurred to her that maybe he wasn't quite so hard to read, after all. She thought: *He knows.*

He bent over the bed, took the envelope, flicked through the wad of notes. It was a lot of money. 'Where did you find it?' he asked.

She didn't answer. She left him there, the money in his hand. She took a shower, dressed, switched on her phone again, looked silently through her messages.

Still, he lay there, holding the money. Irritably, she snatched it back.

'What are you going to do with it, Frederica?' Piers asked her. 'Are you going to put it back? It's not yours. It belongs to Elizabetta.'

172

'I am certainly not going to put it back.'

'Well ... I think you should. You can't just take it. What am I going say to Elizabetta?'

'Say whatever you like,' she replied. 'Or don't say anything at all. She's your stupid wife.'

'C'mon, baby ...'

But the conversation was over. Frederica was already at the door.

'Don't – c'mon – don't just flounce out!' he said.

DINNER TIME

The taxis did not arrive. After one hour plus thirty minutes, India began to chase them. She tried three or four times, and then Egbert(Mr) took over. Egbert(Mr) could hardly believe it. He was stunned by the sheer *hopelessness* – the mind boggling *irrationality*. (*Why* would they not turn up when they said they were going to? *Why?*) But no matter how many times he or India or anyone else dialled the number, no one at the 'taxi service' ever answered the phone again. The guests were going nowhere.

Alice decided there was no point in making the evening more disagreeable than it needed to be, no matter how irritating the situation. She rummaged in the kitchen while Frederica and Piers were still upstairs, squabbling and shagging, and managed to put together some arrabbiata which even Frederica, who despised the English, had to acknowledge, when she finally emerged, didn't smell too bad.

As the sauce did its slow simmering, the unwanted guests gradually reconvened on the terrace. Ecgbert(Sir) said: 'I suppose you all want a drink?'

And funnily enough, yes they did.

It was a big enough crowd that nobody noticed who exactly was present, where or when. People came and people went: to the bog, to recharge their phones, to look at the sunset, to medicate their son, to make a call, ask for water, squabble about where they were going to sleep.

While Ecgbert(Sir) was spilling things into different glasses, ineptly fixing people's drinks, Alice asked if he'd seen his grandmother or Leo.

Sir Ecgbert replied: 'Hardly a glimpse all day, Trudy. I think Granny has fallen in love. Do you think she knows – do you think we should tell her she's barking up the wrong tree?'

Alice said: 'No, no, no. Let's definitely stay out of it.'

'Of course it probably doesn't matter much in their situation anyway . . . If you think about it . . . Can ghosts have sex?'

Green vapour. A smell of methane. The voice of Geraldine, Lady Tode: 'Don't be *revolting*, Ecgbert.'

Alice giggled. Ecgbert said, 'Oops. Sorry, Granny. Didn't realise you were—'

And then, from behind them, there came an almighty crash. Bunny had dropped the ice bucket.

'Are you all right, Money-Bunny?' asked her husband.

'Absolutely,' she said. 'Absolutely fine.'

She disappeared after that, to do something about the icy cold water on her dress.

The pasta was ready. The table was laid. It was unlikely that anyone was very hungry, since lunch had only been finished a few hours earlier. But there was nothing else for them all to do, except squabble and get drunk. It was supper time.

There was too much pasta to fit into a single receptacle. Alice and Ecgbert each carried a fine-smelling, steaming dish out onto the terrace. They laid one at either end of the long dining table.

And then there was the fuss about who had forgotten the water.

And then where was the corkscrew?

And then – would people *please sit down* . . .

Where was Tippee?

Where was Piers?

Had anyone seen . . . ?

Where the bloody hell was Charlie?

(Gone for a pee.)

Should they start anyway?

Could everyone *please* sit down?

Where had Putin disappeared off to now? Didn't he know it was dinner time?

Nicola thought Putin was fetching Bunny.

Adele had nipped off to the ladies' to wash her hands.

Charlie had been sent to find Tippee.

Nicola had gone to fetch a sweater because she heard Bunny saying she was cold.

Esmé had gone upstairs to call his children.

The process took twenty minutes at least. By 9.18 p.m. (and 34 seconds) there were eleven people sat at the table, eyeing the pasta, working out how far they were from the parmesan.

Tippee Tysedale was still missing.

And so, of course, was Elizabetta.

But Adele had retrieved her gluten-free snack boxes from the fridge, warmed the food and laid it onto individual plates for her and Tippee's dindins. She'd also broken one of her strictest healthfulness rules this evening, and was at that moment already halfway through quite a large glass of pink wine. It presumably explained the flattering (symmetrical) spots of colour on her sunblock-smothered cheeks.

On Alice's advice, Lady Tode and Leonardo were keeping a low profile.

She had noticed that, unlike anyone else, Bunny Rostovsky could see and hear the ghosts quite clearly, and that their presence was making her jumpy.

Lady Tode might have ignored the advice. (What did she care if Bunny was jumpy?) But Leonardo persuaded her otherwise. He hated to see people frightened by him. It only exacerbated his sense of unending solitude, he said. Which comment, complained Lady Tode, left her feeling more than a little undervalued. In any case, the ghosts had taken themselves elsewhere, to a plane of existence unknown to us, and were at 'that moment' (inasmuch) attempting to resolve their differences in ways we must never presume to understand.

To *this* moment: 9.19 p.m.

Food, glorious food.

'What a beautiful night!' cried Egbert(Mr). 'Have you noticed, guys? It's a full moon. Make a wish!'

It was indeed a beautiful night. The garden looked spectacular, bathed in moonlight: bushes, trees, Roman pigsties and medieval altars stood out in silhouette, and here and there, water glistened.

'Stunning!' said Putin. 'Alice and Ecgbert, *thank you.* I should say I'm sorry to be gatecrashing your gorgeous honeymoon, but I have to say sorry-not-sorry!'

He and Bunny cracked up. 'By which I mean to say, I can't think of a place more lovely than this, and the smell of this pasta is killing me … and honestly, I don't think there is a place in the wide world I would want to be more than right here, right now. Even if—'

A whopping, blood-curdling scream filled the night air.

Tippee Tysedale emerged from the darkness, moving faster than his mother had thought possible. She thought: *Maybe athletics? Maybe that's where he can shine?* But she didn't think about it for long. His face, as he reached the terrace, indicated to her, to everyone present, that the lad was profoundly disturbed. Something had happened. Even his father sounded concerned.

'Tippee?' Charlie said. 'What's up? What's going on?' Even now, he couldn't quite keep the irritation out of his voice.

'The girl.' He stood at the edge of the terrace, leaning against a pillar, too puffed out to speak.

'What girl?' snapped his father. 'For fuck's sake, Tippee.'

Tippee panted.

Adele said: 'Tippee, love. Calm down. Catch your breath.' She patted the seat beside her. 'Come and sit down.'

Tippee said: 'The Italian one.' He looked at Frederica. 'Not that one. The other one, who was in Rome. She's floating.'

'*Where?*' – '*What?*' – '*Why?*' the people cried, looking this way, and looking that.

'At the bottom. I thought she was a grapefruit. But there's blood spurting.'

'BLOOD SPURTING!?' cried Lady Tode, emerging from her other plane. Leonardo stood beside her. He looked serious. He said to Lady Tode: 'How, in this light? You cannot see blood against water in the darkness. The boy is speaking lies.'

178

Adele said: 'Sweetheart, take a moment. Breathe. Remember? Breathe ... We don't understand. Who was a grapefruit?'

He breathed. He stopped panting. He stood up straight and seemed, at that point, somehow to have collected himself. He said: 'I don't know her name but she looks like that one ... The one we saw at the hotel last night.'

'*Elizabetta*,' murmured her sister.

Egbert(Mr) said, slightly irritably: 'I thought we'd established that was someone else?'

Tippee said: 'She's floating in the pool where you and your wife were nuddy-bathing this afternoon—'

'TIPPEE!' snapped Adele. 'Don't be silly.'

'I haven't touched her, but I prodded her with the stick and she's not moving and her eyes are open. I think she's dead.'

One by one, they stood up from the table. Egbert(Mr) asked India if she was sure she wouldn't prefer to stay behind. She ignored him.

Nicola paused to reprimand him for his sexist attitudes, but no one was listening.

And then Tippee led them through the moonlit garden.

'Don't just walk! *Run!*' Frederica ordered Tippee. 'Show me where!'

Tippee kept walking, but he pointed towards a corner of the garden.

The adults hurried past him.

Leading the pack was Frederica: then came Piers (not together, very much apart), then Egbert(Mr) and Esmé, and behind them Adele, Ecgbert(Sir), Alice, India and Bunny. Everyone ran, except for the trio at the back: Putin, Charlie and Nicola, who were either not fit enough, sober enough or (in Nicola's case) curious enough to keep up.

... Moonlight, the smell of jasmine, the singing cicadas ...

The party lumbered on down the hill to the spring pool where the floating grapefruits bobbed. At the pool, beneath the surface, water flowed: it flowed up from the ground and it flowed in from the stream that ran through the citrus orchard above.

But here, where Elizabetta's body now floated, the water was quiet. The surface of the water was so still you could see the perfect moon reflected.

Elizabetta's limbs were caught up in the long stems of a water hyacinth. She was floating, almost as Tippee had described her, dark hair splayed out around her, but – it's worth noting – she was floating face down, rather than up. Around her, the bobbing grapefruits shone, almost luminous in the moonlight, but Elizabetta's dark head was all but invisible. She wore a dark T-shirt; her shoulders, her face, her brown arms, were invisible below the water's surface.

Tippee stood by the bank and pointed. 'There,' he said. 'There she is.'

It wasn't obvious at first. Frederica said: '*Where?*'

Piers kept moving. He ran on, straight into the water. He took hold of Elizabetta's shoulders and carefully turned her over. The eyes were open. Blood was not spurting.

At first glance, yes, perhaps, *like this* – she might look like a grapefruit.

She was dead.

Alice put a comforting arm around Tippee, but he quickly shook her off, and quite vigorously. As her bare leg brushed against him, she noticed that his shorts were wet.

Nobody said anything at first. They were too shocked. They

stood and watched as Piers tugged at her body, disentangling her from the weeds.

Eventually Egbert(Mr) broke the silence. He said: 'Can you see, Piers? Is she dead?'

There was a choking noise from the back of Piers' throat: half laugh, half sob. He said: 'Of course she's fucking dead.' The others still said nothing. They just stood and watched. Piers tugged angrily at the body and lost his footing. For a second his head disappeared beneath the surface. This, at last, seemed to jolt the others into action. Ecgbert(Sir) leapt into the water. After that, a lot of them followed suit.

So much splashing.

Esmé, Egbert, Ecgbert, Frederica, Bunny and Adele were all in the water. Silently they pulled at the hyacinth stems. Tippee moved to join them, but Alice put her arm around him again, and held him back.

'Tippee, don't,' she said.

From the water, Adele said: 'Tippee, you've seen enough. Go back to the house.'

He didn't move.

'Right *now*.'

He ignored her. But nor, at least, did he jump into the pool. Alice held on to his bony shoulders and this time, he didn't shake her off.

They disentangled the body, and dragged it to the water's edge, where Putin stood ready to take her. With an almighty groan, he bent over, grasped Elizabetta from the armpits and dragged her onto the bank.

And there, in pink, standing above her, waiting, peering down, stood Leonardo.

'Sir Ecgbert, may I ask you, kindly. There is hair obscuring my observation of her neck. I need to see her neck. I think there is something ... Might I ask you or your wife – would you kindly move the hair from around her neck.'

Ecgbert(Sir) was still hauling himself out of the water. As was Bunny. She stared at Leonardo, muttered something to herself, but said nothing. Ecgbert(Sir) said to Alice: 'Alice, did you hear that? I think—'

'*Quickly! Please*,' Leonardo ordered, before checking himself. He glanced up at Alice. 'I apologise for my brusque tone, Alice. Would you mind very much?'

Gingerly, Alice stepped towards the body. Elizabetta's long hair hung loose around her face. First, Alice closed the eyes. She set about moving the hair.

Charlie said: 'What are you doing? Get off her!'

Egbert(Mr) said: 'I say, Alice – I think we really ought to leave her *as is* – you know? Out of respect.'

Alice ignored him.

Putin was stepping towards her, bending down to pull Alice away.

'*Hurry!*' Leonardo ordered.

She scraped back the hair.

Leonard inhaled. An inhalation that, just for one moment, seemed to stop the cicadas in the trees. A moment of pure silence. He bent over Elizabetta's body close enough that his nose and her collar bone merged.

'*Ma perché?*' he muttered. '*Perché ... ?*'

Bunny was still in the water. Her husband moved to offer her a hand.

'All right, Money-Bunny?' he said but she looked right through him. She couldn't take her eyes off Leonardo.

She said to Alice: 'Who *is* that guy?'

Alice said: 'What guy?'

Putin, worried that the others might think she was insane, said to the group: 'Bunny sees ghosts.'

'Ah!' said Ecgbert(Sir). 'You're one of us.' But then Alice sent her husband a warning look, and he shut up.

Bunny said to Ecgbert(Sir): 'Can *you* see him? The pink guy. Can you *see him*?'

Ecgbert(Sir) shook his head. 'No. Not at all.' He turned back to the body. '*Anyway*,' he said, '*What I meant to say is . . .* This is . . . This is very . . . ' He was unsure how to finish. Piers had pulled himself out of the pool and was standing beside him looking down at his wife's corpse, wiping the water from his face. 'This is a very nasty surprise,' Ecgbert(Sir) said at last.

'Bit more than that, Coz,' said Egbert(Mr). 'It's a tragedy.'

'Well put,' Ecgbert(Sir) agreed. 'That's actually what I meant.'

Piers remained where he was, wiping the water, staring at his dead wife. It was hard to know what he was thinking because his face was absolutely blank. Egbert(Mr) rested a hand on his shoulder. ' . . . Are you all right, mate?' he said.

Piers did not reply.

Frederica kneeled by her sister, took the limp body in her arms and began to weep.

Leonardo da Vinci stepped back from the body, towards Lady Tode. He whispered something into her ear. The cicadas stopped. Maybe even, for a second, the burbling stream stopped burbling. In any case, his whispered message whispered all through the garden, so that Ecgbert(Sir), Alice, and now, apparently, Bunny Rostovsky heard it perfectly.

'*M-U-R-D-E-R-!*' he declared. 'The poor dear lady was done in. Take note – at the base of the neck . . . '

Lady Tode, Alice and Ecgbert(Sir) craned forward to take

note of the neck base. But there was nothing to see. Or nothing they could see. Unlike Leo, they had never made much study of human anatomy. They didn't really know what they were meant to be looking for.

'Hmmm,' said Lady Tode, because she hated to disappoint him. 'I see . . .'

Alice said: 'We should call the police.'

Egbert(Mr) nodded. 'Let's hope they're a bit more responsive than the chaps at the taxi service.'

'What *is* your infatuation with the police?' Ecgbert(Sir) asked Alice. 'It's the only aspect of your character I utterly cannot understand.'

'I'm not infatuated with the police,' Alice replied irritably. 'I – just. We keep coming up against these murders. And normally – in the normal run of things – when there's a murder, people call the police.'

Frederica, still kneeling on the ground, cradling her sister, looked up at Alice. Her face was wet. 'Why you saying "murder"?'

'Well, I . . . I'm not sure. Maybe it *wasn't* murder. I'm just saying – suggesting – that if it *was* murder –'

'But there is no "if" about it!' cried Leonardo.

'– which it might have been,' continued Alice, 'we should probably call the police.'

Bunny spoke. 'The police are agents of the state,' she said to Alice.

'What?' Alice laughed. 'I'm aware of that.'

'The state *is not your friend.*'

'Here, here!' cried Ecgbert(Sir.) 'Excellent point, Bunny!'

Alice said: 'I'm not talking about – Bunny . . . This isn't a time for politics.'

Frederica looked up from cradling the body. 'Always, it is a time for politics. That Russian lady is right.'

'Anyone got a phone?' Egbert(Mr) said: 'Italianos being the madcaps we know and love, it's probably all the same number! Taxi – mafioso – polizio – whatnot. They're probably all the same people! Frederica – this is your country. Am I right? What do you think?'

'No police,' said Frederica.

Alice looked around at the group, bewildered. Apart from Egbert(Mr), nobody else seemed inclined to join the argument. Nor was anyone exactly leaping to support her call to inform the police. 'Well – we should at least call an ambulance . . .'

Frederica said: 'What's the point? Already she's dead.' She stood up. 'Piers, stay beside her. I go now to call Papa. He will organise everything. He will hold the *volante* – the wheel – now.' She looked at the guests. They stood in a limp circle around her sister's body, uncertain quite what to do next. She said: 'Nobody. Do. Nutting.'

She walked away, across the grass, and they did as they were told. A silence fell. They looked at the body. The cicadas sang.

Tippee sniggered.

'There wasn't any blood spurting,' he said.

It broke the spell. India, for lack of a more nuanced response, began to sob. Egbert(Mr) patted her on the shoulder and told her 'not to worry'.

But his mind was racing.

How could it be? This was meant to be their lovely romantic getaway and now, here they were again. Tangled up in another ruddy death scene! *Another* premature death on Tode property! Would this one reach the newspapers? The girl's death clearly had nothing whatsoever to do with the Todes. Nevertheless . . .

185

Nevertheless ... What he hoped – gosh, he wished his darling wife would stop crying – what he sincerely hoped was that Frederica's pa, whom he'd never met, while taking over the steering wheel, might be persuaded to jolly well leave the Todes' name out of this mess altogether ...

In the meantime –

Piers had taken Frederica's place beside Elizabetta's body. He was cradling her, hiding his face in the crook of her neck, rocking back and forth. It was an intense and painful and private moment, and it led everyone present to come to a similar conclusion. It was time to shuffle away.

Slowly and quietly, they filed back to the house.

Tippee said he wanted some pasta, but Adele told him not to be silly. This wasn't the time for pasta. She took him to bed. The others opened more wine, and waited for the arrival of Signor Ranaldini.

So ended the great honeymoon.

TODE HALL

YORKSHIRE
ENGLAND
FOUR MONTHS LATER

A NICE DAY IN OCTOBER

AFRICA FOLLY

2.18 P.M.

Mr Egbert Tode opened his eyes. Saw a dozen concerned faces peering down at him. He rubbed his head. *Yikes. What a bump.*

And there was something wet trickling into his ear.

Double yikes. Blood.

'Eggzie!' India cried. 'Eggzie! You're alive! What happened? Are you OK?'

He said: 'Golly ... I'm so sorry. I wanted to propose a toast ...' He frowned. 'And there was something else, too. What the hell was it?'

'Were you shot?' India asked. 'What was the noise?'

He was covered in tiny pieces of broken glass, India noticed: his hair, his face, his outer shooting jacket. Gently, she began to pick them out.

Mr Egbert Tode had not been shot.

The noise was the sound of a magnum bottle of champagne exploding in his hand. Esmé, having taken the bottle from his

189

cousin in an effort to prevent further spillage, was still holding on to its remnants – but the contents were undrinkable now, of course, due to the shattered glass.

Egbert(Mr), still lying on the floor, chuckled bravely. A bubble of blood at the side of his mouth popped and splattered. 'Papa always said magnums were a bit much,' he said. 'So it probably serves me right . . . '

'Your papa,' said Geraldine, Lady Tode, who was hovering close by, 'was absolutely right, of course. They're the height of vulgarity.' Egbert(Mr) couldn't hear her. Had he been able to, he might have been pleasantly surprised to note the relief in her voice. It turned out, despite everything – his lack of poetry, her haughtiness, the ghastly middle-classness of the daughter-in-law who birthed him – Lady Tode was fond of her grandson, Egbert(Mr). She was pleased to note that he was still alive.

Leonardo, standing beside her, felt a little foolish. Also, on behalf of his friend, Lady Tode, relieved and pleased. *Also* – eternity being pretty endless, and a frisson of drama to break it up from time to time never going amiss . . . quietly, a tiny bit disappointed. The killer had *not* struck again. On the contrary. Lady Tode was quite annoyed with Leonardo for having jumped to the conclusion so quickly, without thinking of the effect of his own words. She said to him: 'You scared the living daylights out of me' – before realising this was inaccurate and that he might choose to mock her for it. 'You, Leo [she corrected herself quickly] are what the young nowadays refer to as a "drama queen". My grandson is perfectly fine. He is in peak physical fitness. There is nothing dead about him. Except – his imagination. He lacks imagination. But he always has lacked imagination. And the world needs people without imagination, to keep the trains running on time.'

At this point, Egbert(Mr) had been picked up off the floor and placed in a seat at the head of the table. He was spattered in blood and apologising a good deal. Esmé had poured some water onto a corner of the tablecloth, and was urging him to use it, to clean the wounds.

'I'm fine. I'm absolutely *fine*,' Egbert(Mr) kept saying. 'I'm nothing but an idiot, that's all. I am just terribly, terribly sorry ... what a silly fuss. Please do, everyone, *sit down!* Lunch is running late enough as it is.'

He told India he still wanted to make a toast, but first he needed to go back to the Hall to fetch some more champagne. India insisted he stay put, of course. She called Mr Carfizzi, who was already in the car, transporting dirty dishes Hallward. Could he please return as soon as possible, she asked him, with more champagne. And no magnums this time. Just nice, normal-sized bottles. 'But not,' Egbert told India to tell Carfizzi, '*Not the ... Not the ...*' He noticed Charlie looking at him, listening in. So, instead of saying 'Not the really good stuff', which is what he meant, he took the phone from his wife, and described to Carfizzi in painstaking detail exactly which cellar shelf to take it from. He glanced at Charlie as he finished the call. Charlie smirked knowingly.

It was annoying. Charlie, with all his sneering and smirking, was actually a very annoying man, Egbert realised. Also, not much fun to have around. Also his wife was hell. All of these realisations strengthened Egbert's resolve vis-à-vis the announcement he was about to make. He had made a decision and it was not going to be popular. Almost everyone was going to be cross and it was just too bad. In light of what was happening *at this very moment* at the Rospo nel Buco stazione de polizias whatnot, it was really the only way

191

forward. At least for the time being. Needs must. Keep calm and carry on, etc.

... But first, he needed to have a quick word with Piers and Frederica. They needed to be updated on the situation. Somewhat urgently.

Half an hour later, Egbert pinged his fork on his glass and stood up.

Oops. Still a bit woozy.

'Eggzie darling, are you all right? For goodness' sake – do be careful.'

'Don't you worry, Munchie!' he said.

Everyone cheered (quite drunk by now, what with all the delays).

'Hail, the great survivor!' said Piers. He was in an excellent mood.

Egbert(Mr) smiled. 'Hardly,' he said. 'I survived opening a bottle of champagne, which is not a great feat. Let's face it. Unfortunately the bottle didn't survive quite as well as I did!'

Pretty lame. But Piers seemed to find it exorbitantly funny. Even Frederica cracked a tight little smile.

'Anyway, as you can see ...' Egbert indicated Carfizzi, behind him, who was fussing over glasses and duly delivered, normal-sized bottles. 'I have delegated that most dangerous of tasks – opening the champagne bottles, ha ha ha! – to the wonderful Mr Car Fizzy ...' Carfizzi acknowledged this with a most minimal of bows. 'And while he ... takes his life in his hands ...'

Piers laughed so hard his head almost fell off.

The others chuckled obligingly.

'... I actually wanted to propose a toast ... If I may?'

'Toast! Toast!' they all bawled.

Egbert(Mr) held up a hand. 'Four months ago,' he began, 'we barged in on their private honeymoon. And actually, looking back, I'm not at all sure what the hell we thought we were doing! It was their *honeymoon!*'

'Shame!' said Putin jovially. 'Shame on us!'

'We got our comeuppance, though, didn't we?' said Esmé. 'When we tried to stay for supper!' He glanced at Frederica and Piers. 'Sorry. *Sorry* – I didn't – I don't mean to be glib or insensitive.'

Magnanimous Piers smiled sweetly. He said: 'No need to apologise, Esmé. No offence taken. We understand!'

Egbert(Mr) cleared his throat. 'The point is, we interrupted a *very special* time for my wonderful cousin Ecgbert and his absolutely amazing wife, Alice, or, as we should henceforth refer to Tode Hall's fantastic Chief Organisation Officer, *The Lady* Tode!'

A smell of methane from the corner. And a wisp of green smoke. Geraldine, Lady Tode said to Egbert(Mr), who of course wouldn't have been able to hear her: 'Oh do *get on* with it, Egbert!' She turned to Leonardo. 'Why must people hold the floor like this? Nobody wants to hear what he has to say. Propose the ruddy toast, and *sit down.*'

Mr Carfizzi had quietly opened the champagne and was distributing glasses around the table. Tippee had asked for one. Adele was at the moment frowning symmetrically and taking the glass away from him.

'Honestly,' Egbert(Mr) said, 'India and I absolutely adore

you, Alice. In our wildest dreams we could not have wished for a better cousin-in-law! So, anyway, first things first: I want to apologise, on behalf of all of us, for barging in on your honeymoon. And I want to welcome you, once again, to the Tode family. Tode Hall would be half the place without you!'

India raised her glass, beamed at Alice, and said, 'Yay!'

'Wait, Munch,' Egbert said. 'One sec! You're jumping the gun!'

India giggled and apologised. She put the glass back onto the table without drinking from it, and mouthed to Alice, *I love you so much!*

Alice felt embarrassed.

Egbert lifted his glass a little higher. 'I've actually got two toasts to propose,' he said, 'and actually quite a big piece of news to announce. So – if you wouldn't mind giving me a few more moments of your time . . . However – Munch you're quite right: *first*, I want to propose a toast to Sir Ecgbert and Lady Tode! We are happy you found each other!'

'Sir Ecgbert and Lady Tode!' cried the guests, raising their glasses.

'And we are *sorry* we wrecked the honeymoon!' Egbert(Mr) said.

Again, the guests raised their glasses. 'Sorry for wrecking your honeymoon!' they agreed cheerfully.

A silence while they slurped.

And then Egbert(Mr) continued. 'In other news . . . ' He cleared his throat. 'I think, given the circumstances of the last time we were together, you will all be interested in this little piece of news . . . I'm telling this to you all, now – but rest assured, some people present,' he nodded at Frederica, 'are of course already up to speed with the situation . . . and have given me permission to fill you in. I got a call today. As we were about to tuck into our pud. Actually – not long before the ruddy champagne bottle exploded!'

Ha ha ha.

'As luck would have it, it was from the Polizia Superintendus in Rospo nel Buco. Frederica, please forgive my Italian.'

'*Il sergente di polizia.*' Frederica smiled as she corrected him. It looked strange. No one had seen her smiling before.

'Anyway, the chap who runs the little police station in Rospo nel Buco called me up just now ... and it turns out – well, it turns out all sorts of things, frankly. But the main point is – it turns out poor old Elizabetta seems to have got herself caught up in – again, forgive me, Frederica – but I think it would be fair to say she got herself caught up in all sorts of dodgy dealings. Would that be right?'

Frederica tipped her head. Yes. It would be right.

'And from what I understand, the situation vis-à-vis Elizabetta's, as it were, "business dealings" has been shunted up the chain of command, as it were. So the "murder", as it were, is no longer a matter for the local polizios. They've called in the big honchos ... *It turns out* that naughty Elizabetta was much, much cleverer than the rest of us, but not quite as clever as perhaps she thought she was. They've uncovered a lot of dodgy cash, a lot of activity which involved – well, I suppose, we have to call it what it was: the naughty girl had been laundering tonnes of illegal cash through our wonderful Rospo gardens.'

Gasps from the gallery. Frederica and Piers sat tight and looked smug.

' ... Which actually explains a lot of things,' Egbert continued. 'But the point is ... we have nothing to fear! Fear not, family

195

Tode! We, the Todes, are one hundred per cent in the clear. We have had, and continue to have, absolutely *nada niente* zero and zilch to do with all this! We haven't made a bean out of it. Quite the opposite, in fact. And the nice polizia chappie assures me, they haven't the slightest interest in coming after us . . . '

'Hurrah!' said Esmé.

'Phew!' said India.

'As I said to the polizia chappie, I suppose it does explain why one never actually saw any tourists at Rospo . . . or sort of ever met anyone who'd managed to actually buy a ticket to see our fabulous gardens . . . It transpires . . . Well, it doesn't matter too much. I won't bother you with the details. I only want to say that my dear cousin, Sir Egbert, has – as I am sure you are aware – been referring, somewhat cruelly, to this weekend house party as "the weekend of the suspects". Well . . . my dear friends . . . *not any more!* From what I understand, there are various friends of poor Elizabetta being carted off to the slammer for a bit of extended questioning as we speak. So. My next task is to propose a toast to this, the Weekend of the Innocents! And then—'

Ecgbert(Sir) interrupted him. 'Actually, Egbert. Just to be clear. I was very careful *not* to tell the guests they were all murder suspects. So I'm sorry you just said that.'

'Also,' piped up Nicola, 'I don't see how Elizabetta laundering money automatically puts everyone here in the clear. On the contrary. I still have my suspicions.' She glared at Putin. 'I can think of plenty of people around this table who would have liked to see Elizabetta dead. Let's not get complacent.'

'BE THAT AS IT MAY,' interrupted Egbert. 'And by the way, I apologise, Ecgbert. I didn't mean to offend you . . . The reason I'm telling you all this – aside from the fact that we're all off the hook, ha ha ha—'

'I repeat,' said Nicola. 'We are *not* all off the hook.'

'Good point, Nicola,' said Ecgbert(Sir). 'And very well put. Just because there are more suspects being added to the list, doesn't actually mean the original suspects are automatically innocent.'

Nicola said: 'That's not actually what I meant ...'

And all the Todes in the room, children included, uttered a groan.

Adele was offended: 'Actually, I don't imagine we are *all* "murder suspects", as you put it, Sir Ecgbert. I don't suppose, for example, that you suspect my Tippee of murder!' She tittered. Perhaps it was meant to be a joke. Unfortunately the idea that her Tippee might have done the dirty deed had occurred to everyone around the table, more than once. So the comment fell rather flat. Ecgbert(Sir) looked at her in mild bewilderment, and turned back to Egbert.

'Come on then,' he said. 'Get to the point. What are you trying to tell us?'

Egbert(Mr) shuffled around a bit. He looked at his feet. He looked as if he hoped something might occur to open up the lovely flagstones beneath them, so he could quietly disappear. He glanced at India, in search of reassurance. But she couldn't help. He'd not even told her, yet, what he was about to say. She was just sitting, waiting. She smiled at him encouragingly.

Still he didn't speak.

'Come on, Eggzie!' she said. 'Spit it out!'

'You may wonder why I'm telling you all this ...'

'Well, yes. We do. Although I'm seriously beginning to lose interest at this point,' drawled Charlie Tysedale.

Dreaded Adele tutted. He heard it, and twitched: his whole face, for one half of a second, contorted with the purest dislike.

197

Egbert(Mr) said: 'All right. Well. As some of you may be aware, *Rospo* . . . The villa at *Rospo* . . . There has been . . . Quite a few of you . . . Look, I'll level with you. This is very awkward. But I've made a decision, actually, having spoken to the polizia chappie, and also, consulted very seriously with my own sense of *fair play*. And it's jolly hard. Because I know that, frankly, until six months ago one was hardly even aware that the villa at Rospo belonged to the estate. I mean, *of course* one was aware of it. But not – But then suddenly it's become the hottest property in town! *Everyone* wants it! And here I am, and it's up to me to decide who should get it. Now,' Egbert(Mr) nodded at Esmé and Charlie, both of whom were now on full alert and ready to pounce. 'Esmé, Charlie . . . I know full well that we were – in fact, *are* – due to have a meeting on this very subject later on this afternoon, before dinner. Also,' he nodded to the newlyweds, 'Ecgbert and Alice . . . I'm aware . . . ' Egbert(Mr) couldn't quite bring himself to look at them. 'I'm aware that you, too, have expressed a strong interest in starting a new life out there . . . '

'WHAT?' said India. 'You told me they hadn't! Alice, you can't!'

Egbert(Mr) pressed on. 'And for heaven's sake, what a splendid idea! Why not? . . . Why shouldn't you? . . . And finally there's Piers and Frederica. Not family, obviously. But . . . '

'Hang on a mo.' Nicola was still munching on something as she stood up. Despite the ruckus about everyone still being a murder suspect, her presence was so peripheral, people had already more or less forgotten she was there. Her unexpected insistence that they all 'hang on a mo', and at such a critical moment, caused a bit of a stir.

'For God's *sake*,' snapped Esmé. 'What now?'

Everyone turned to look at her.

She swallowed whatever she'd been munching.

'What about *me*?' she said at last.

Egbert(Mr) said: 'Hmm? . . . Sorry, Coz. Non comprendio! What about you?'

'How do you know *I* don't want to live at Rospo?'

'I don't know that,' Egbert(Mr) said carefully. ' . . . But you don't, do you? Anyway, it's not really the point.'

'*Not really the point?*'

'What I mean is, actually, Nicola . . . really sorry . . . but you haven't mentioned you wanted to live at Rospo until now. It has literally never come up. For heaven's sake . . . '

'Well,' she said, 'I do want it. I'm saying it now. I want to start a new life at Rospo.'

Once again, there rose a collective groan. India, Ecgbert(Sir), Esmé, Egbert(Mr), Charlie Tysedale, Tippee Tysedale, Piers Slayer-Wilson-Tite, Frederica Ranaldini, Passion and Ludo Tode – even Alice – groaned.

'Come on, old girl,' Putin chuckled. 'You're just being difficult, aren't you?'

'Far from it. I'll have you know . . . ' began Nicola.

Who knew what Nicola really wanted? It was a safe bet, however, that until that moment, the idea of starting a new life at Villa Rospo had never once crossed her mind. The only thing Nicola ever seemed to want was an argument. For several minutes, she took on the room. When Charlie Tysedale and Esmé Tode joined forces to mock her – and it looked as though she might either cry or stab them with a carving knife – Alice, India and the E-berts pulled back.

'Enough!' Egbert(Mr) declared. 'Nicola, you're too late. Bad luck.'

Nicola muttered something about consulting her lawyers, and returned to her seat, ready for the next argument, and Egbert at last delivered his unpopular and surprising announcement. *For the next year or two,* he told everyone, *until everything settles down* – he and the polizia chappie, in conjunction with the kind and helpful Signor Ranaldini (father to Elizabetta and Frederica), had agreed that the simplest way forward, vis-à-vis Rospo, was to return the villa to the safekeeping of Piers and Frederica—

Uproar.

Esmé, Charlie, Ecgbert(Sir) and Nicola all started yelling at once.

Putin glanced at his watch. He glanced at Piers.

Piers sat at the far end of the table, long legs crossed, looking beautiful and serene, and outrageously smug. He slid his hand across the table top and rested it on Frederica's. Her stony expression did not change. She didn't look at Piers. She removed her hand from beneath his. Meanwhile, the shouting continued. Egbert(Mr) tried his best to restore order.

'Because . . . *because . . . Wait. PLEASE listen . . . PLEASE . . .* This is a good idea because – the *Ranaldinis* . . . and the polizias . . . '

He thought it was a good idea. Maybe it was. However, his reasoning wasn't tiptop.

Charlie told Egbert(Mr) that he was only doing what he was shouted at because he was a coward, and he was scared of the Italian police. He said Egbert had been a lily-liver at school, and he was a lily-liver today . . .

'That's right!' said Esmé, who was very, very angry. 'You can run as many triathlons as you want, dear cousin. You might achieve the body of a warrior . . . '

'The body of a warrior!' guffawed Geraldine, Lady Tode. 'What is he talking about?'

' ... but it won't make you a man!'

Double uproar. Nicola took massive offence, for obvious reasons. The ghost of Geraldine, Lady Tode laughed so hard it caused a very minor earthquake, which sent at least two wine glasses crashing to the floor. Leonardo da Vinci looked on in amazement. *Why was Geraldine laughing? Why was Nicola shouting? Also, underneath his shooting jacket, did Egbert(Mr) really have the body of a warrior?*

Egbert(Mr) said: 'There's no need to be silly, Charlie. I think what you just said was very sexist and offensive, and I think you should apologise to the ladies present, who probably, like me, do *not* believe that warrior-qualities belong exclusively to the male sex.'

Lady Tode laughed so hard she turned into a puff of smoke.

Piers said: 'Here, here.'

The dreaded Adele nodded. Her mind was working very fast indeed.

She'd been having second thoughts about Charlie's involvement in the Rospo project since the weekend began. Even more so, after her glasshouse chat with India. Adele, being Adele, had, already – just before lunch – whizzed off a little note to her financial advisers suggesting a pause ... Maybe this surprise setback was a blessing in disguise? Maybe this was the universe protecting her financial interests? Maybe, with negotiations hotting up in the US, it might anyway be preferable – better optics – to keep Charlie closer to home?

Putin looked at his watch again, and looked at the seat that was now empty, where Bunny had once been. Amid all the shouting, he sidled up to India. He didn't want to interrupt, he told her. But he was feeling a bit under the weather.

'Oh *no!*' said India, trying to listen to all the other stuff. 'I'm so sorry. That's dreadful. *Poor you!*'

'I think I'm going to skip the afternoon shooting, if you don't mind,' he said in his best Russian accent. 'I think I'll toddle off for a bit of a lie-down . . . Will you tell Egbert? Tell him I'm sorry. And I'll see you all at dinner. Is that all right?'

'Yes, yes,' she said, craning around his massive body, so as not to miss out.

Egbert(Mr) was trying to bring lunch to a close. He wanted to shepherd everyone up from the table and back outside for a last few drives before darkness descended. But it wasn't easy. The alcoholic merriment of not so long ago had turned sour.

Almost everyone was furious.

THE GARDENER'S HOUSE

3.48 P.M.

E cgbert(Sir) wasn't shooting. He'd never liked it, even as a
  boy. (It was just one of the many reasons his dead father
always considered him a dud.) Once lunch had broken up, he
and Alice walked back to the Gardener's House together.

Egbert(Mr)'s surprise Rospo announcement had infuriated
him, but he'd contained it well. In another life, the one before
he married Alice, he might have made a fool of himself. He
might have turned the table upside down and fired a nearby
shotgun at the ceiling. He was different now. Everything
was different now. The two of them had exchanged glances
across the table. Alice had smiled and rolled her eyes. And
Ecgbert(Sir), most untactical of men, thought to himself: *No
point yelling and screaming. We need to think.*

They didn't say much as they tramped across the fields
towards home. Alice felt deflated, and a bit silly. Also, guilty
about India. She'd avoided talking to her after lunch, but she
couldn't avoid her for ever. She deserved an explanation.

203

Ecgbert didn't feel either of those things. He was furious and flummoxed. It was one thing, giving the house to Esmé (as he said to Alice). Esmé, after all, had had a bad run with the Australian experience. Plus, he was family. But to give it to Piers and his horrible, truculent, yoga teacher girlfriend whose dead sister now turned out to be a money launderer – *why?*

But Alice wasn't used to getting houses on whims. The idea that she and Ecgbert might, by a stroke of weird good fortune, have been permitted to build some kind of life at Villa Rospo seemed already like a mad, silly dream. By the time they had reached the Gardener's House her thoughts had moved on.

As they pulled off their boots, she said to Ecgbert: 'So – what do you reckon? On the murder . . . Do you believe they're all off the hook, like Egbert says?'

'Top question, Trudy. And no, I am not convinced. Are you?'

Alice said: 'I'm not sure . . . No . . . No, not really.'

'It seems a bit convenient, doesn't it? Just as all the suspects are congregated here for the weekend, and we're finally about to find out which one of them did the dirty deed—'

'Were we, though?' interrupted Alice. 'I'm no wiser than I was four months ago – are you? I still think any one of them might have done it . . . Though I suppose I'm veering towards the Russians . . . '

Ecgbert(Sir) said: 'You're being a bit argumentative, Trudy. If you don't mind me saying . . . '

'Seriously,' Alice said. 'The Russians are very odd – and I still think Piers may have had something to do with it frankly. With or without Frederica . . . Or possibly Adele . . . there's something uncomfortable about her . . . all of them, really. I'm even beginning to suspect E—'

'Bingo!' continued Ecgbert(Sir), who wasn't listening. 'And

204

then out of the blue, who should suddenly call, but the Italian polizias, gabbling away in Italian about money laundering. How did Egbert understand what they were saying, anyway?'

'Well, maybe—'

'Can the polizias in Rospo speak English? I doubt it very much ... And we know Egbert can't speak Italian. I tell you what, I smell a rat, Trudy. Do you?'

Alice didn't answer at once. She put the kettle on, and reached for her tobacco tin. No, she wanted to say, she didn't *exactly* smell a rat. On the other hand ... she didn't exactly *not* smell a rat, either ... 'It is a bit odd,' she conceded.

Ecgbert(Sir) plopped himself down at the kitchen table. 'Dead right, Trudy,' he said. '"Odd" is the exact word I was looking for. Something highly fishy is going on. And, by the way, something fishy which we now have a very serious interest in getting to the bottom of. Otherwise, we'll never get our hands on Rospo.'

She smiled, surprised he was still talking about it ... On the other hand – maybe he had a point? Maybe, if they could get to the bottom of what was going on with Rospo, the crazy dream was not lost after all? She sat down beside him, ready-rolled spliff and lighter in hand.

Then the ghosts barged in. There was an air of self-importance about the way they did it which, after quite a difficult day, grated slightly on Alice's nerves. She'd been looking forward to a peaceful smoke. She didn't show it, of course. (Not that it would have bothered them much anyway.)

Lady Tode shimmered into her usual spot at the head of the table, bringing with her the usual displacement of air, the smell of methane, the slight drop in temperature. Even before her form was fully realised, her loud, drawling voice was berating them for 'glugging tea and smoking', *while family heirlooms were being looted, under their noses.*

'Your ghastly father spent a small fortune on the sort of burglar alarms they probably use at Fort Knox,' she said to Ecgbert(Sir). 'Why doesn't your cousin *use* them? It's almost as if he *wants* the Todes to be destitute ... Actually,' she added, perking up, 'one shouldn't be surprised if that were true. After the way your father treated poor Albert* I wouldn't blame Egbert one bit if he had a secret vendetta against us. Your father was *vile* to poor Albert.'

'Yes,' said Ecgbert, 'but Father was vile to everyone. It doesn't count.'

'Don't be ridiculous, no he wasn't,' replied Lady Tode, shifting position but keeping her back straight at all times. 'Also. Please don't talk about my darling son in that way.'

'Oh *piffle!*' said Ecgbert(Sir), stretching for biscuits. (Ecgbert didn't smoke.) 'Granny, seriously ... ' Nobody had referred to his father as a 'darling'. Not ever. Not in any circumstances. It was embarrassing. 'Now you're being ridiculous.'

A fresh cloud of methane. Quite disagreeable. Alice had to open the window.

Alice said: 'The problem with the alarm system Ecgbert's father installed is it's too good for its own good. When there are guests staying they have to switch it off. And actually, more and more, even when the public are in. Otherwise life just becomes impossible. The wretched things go off every time someone sneezes. Like those fire alarms that go off every time

---

* Lady Tode's other son, Egbert(Mr)'s father. Please see family tree on page x.

anyone cooks sausages ... You have to disconnect them, or they send you crazy.'

'What *are* you talking about?' asked Lady Tode, although she knew perfectly well what Alice was talking about. She'd been present here at Gardener's House, only a couple of months ago, when Alice had disconnected her own fire alarm, after grilling sausages. And she'd had a great deal to say about it at the time. But that was then. This was now.

Leonardo da Vinci was sitting quietly in the window seat, scribbling words (upside down and backwards, as was his wont) into a tiny notebook. Now he joined the conversation: 'What Alice means,' he said, 'is that the alarms in the Hall are super-sensitive. The slightest movement triggers them, consequenting in an invasion of law enforcement officers and other pigs, barging in from the nearby cop-shop. You understand? These alarms might well be triggered each time a person belches.'

Lady Tode moved swiftly on. 'The point is – while you're sitting here rolling yourselves cigarettes, or whatever it is you're smoking there, Alice; and while you're slopping about sipping tea, Ecgbert dear – two things are happening in the Hall. The Russian woman, if Russian she really is, is floating about the place as if butter wouldn't melt in her mouth, while her suitcases are crammed with sack-loads of priceless *objets* filched from every corner of the house. Despite our reporting this to you this morning, Alice, nothing appears to have been done. Or not that I am aware. Meanwhile – *as I speak* – the Russian woman's fat Russian husband, if Russian he is, is downstairs in Egbert's study, rifling through poor Egbert's desk. Leo and I have come directly from Egbert's study to alert you; but I begin to wonder if there's any point. My question is: *Alice*, as Tode Hall's Organisational Manager, are you going to sit there smoking all afternoon, or are you actually going to do something about it?'

Alice was slightly irritated. Lady Tode assumed the worst, as always. Alice was accustomed to this; also to her rudeness. These things washed off her. It so happened, however, that she and Mr Carfizzi had already resolved the matter of Bunny's excess-luggage. Or they thought they had. The stolen objects had been discretely removed from her suitcase by Mr Carfizzi while Bunny was at lunch, and returned to the display cabinets where they belonged. Alice and Carfizzi had calculated that Bunny, seeing the artefacts gone, would feel ashamed of her thieving efforts and touched by the tactful way those efforts had been thwarted. Both, after the lives they had led, were great believers in second chances. They assumed she would not be tempted to try pulling the same trick again.

The update on Putin's current activities, therefore, which Alice assumed could only be connected, came as quite a shock.

There followed an intense confab, during which the four of them disagreed on how best to proceed. Lady Tode wanted to call in the 'village thugs to bash some sense into the pair of them'. Alice wanted to know what 'village thugs' Lady Tode was referring to, and on examination it transpired she was referring to a group of young men who'd used to hang about Todeister bashing sense into people shortly after the War. So that was no use. Leonardo was initially inclined to call the police, but Lady Tode and Ecgbert(Sir) would not entertain it. Even Alice thought a slower and slyer approach might be preferable. She and Ecgbert wanted to know if there was a connection between the thieving here in Yorkshire and the murdering and the money laundering at Rospo. They wanted the Russians to stay for dinner so they could observe them more closely.

So. Between them, in a few minutes – the situation being quite urgent – they came up with the following action plan:

- Stop Putin from rifling through Egbert(Mr)'s desk.
- Take care not to arouse his suspicions.
- Find out what the hell he and Bunny were up to.

Step 1.

Alice telephoned India on Ecgbert(Sir)'s mobile phone. She said: 'India, I know we have to talk about Rospo, and I'm looking forward to explaining everything at dinner. But this is a bit urgent. I'm so sorry. I've been so stupid. I can't find my mobile phone anywhere and I'm almost certain the last time I saw it was in Egbert's study . . . '

India had forgotten about Alice's Rospo plans from the moment she heard they were thwarted. She was in her bedroom, watching an episode of *Selling Sunset*, and about to get in the bath.

Her house was very large. Egbert's study was a good seven-minute walk away; plus, she needed to put on some shoes. Nevertheless, India, forever sweet natured, said she'd pop over to the study at once. She said she'd call Alice back on Ecgbert(Sir)'s phone the moment she found Alice's phone, or the moment she didn't.

'Fingers crossed!' she said. 'Give me half a sec!'

EGBERT(MR)'S STUDY

4.16 P.M.

As expected, India did not find Alice's phone. She found Putin sitting at Egbert's desk, tapping away at Egbert's keyboard, staring at Egbert's computer screen. She pushed back the big, mahogany door – and stopped in her tracks. She was a bit shocked.

'Oh!' she said. 'Hello, Putin . . . What are you doing in here?'

Putin barely missed a beat. Sherlock Holmes, had he been in India's shoes, might have noticed a millisecond of disquiet in Putin's moon-sized face. Sherlock Holmes' laser vision might have noted the teeniest bead of sweat breaking out around the hairline of Putin's enormous head. But India was no Sherlock.

Putin smiled at her: a big, warm smile. Putin had taken a shine to India, in any case. He thought she was adorable. 'Hullo, hullo, India! Now *there's* a sight for sore eyes!' he exclaimed, in his Russian accent. 'Am I pleased to see *you*!'

India, feeling quite embarrassed, said: 'I was actually looking for Alice's mobile. I don't suppose you've seen it, have you? She thought she might have left it in here ... '

Putin was on his feet to help, right away. He looked under the chair, under the desk, under the keyboard ... But no! No, he couldn't see Alice's mobile anywhere.

'This is most mysterious,' he said. 'Where can it be? Is Alice absolutely certain she left it here in the study? Perhaps she is mistaken? Perhaps she left it – oh, how inconvenient it would be, but *maybe* she left it up in that enchanting little folly where we all had lunch ...? Perhaps – do you have her husband's telephone number? Perhaps we can call her on his number and speak to her. We can ask her – or perhaps she left her phone in the bathroom? Or – has she been in her car today?'

There were so many possibilities. India's head spun.

At some point, she asked him again what he was doing in her husband's study. But he never really answered. Instead, he asked about the provenance of three of the paintings on her husband's study walls. India didn't know their provenance. She thought one of them was a Sargent but she wasn't certain. She might be confusing it with something else. He asked her how she managed to run such an enormous and important house, and still manage to stay looking so gorgeous, and she seemed to think that it was a question which merited a considered answer. He asked her if she'd ever been to Russia. In any case – she didn't stand a chance. He swept her up and wouldn't let her go until they had left the study far behind them, and were at the very opposite end of the house. By which time India had forgotten why or even whether she'd dropped in on her husband's study, and certainly she didn't remember to call back Alice to report on the failure of her forgotten mission.

She'd left the bath running. Not that it much mattered.

There was a system thingy at the top which stopped it from overflowing. She found herself telling Putin about a recently uncovered stash of 'old sketches and stuff', found under a lot of cobwebs, on the floor at the back of the silver safe. It had caused a lot of excitement among 'the art people'. So far as she knew, she said, nobody had yet done anything about them.

Putin said: 'But how amazing! How romantic! Where are these sketches now?'

She replied: 'I know! Amazing! They were just sitting there, in one of those big old leathery foldery thingummies ... ' She said they were in a storeroom on the top floor now, far away in the East Wing, waiting to be archived.

Putin said to India: 'Will you show them to me?'

And India said: 'Ha Ha HA HA! That's so funny, Putin! Why don't you come up and see my etchings!'

He didn't know what she was talking about, but he laughed along.

And then, because she was quite bored and the children had gone off with Kveta the au pair, and it was going to be ages until supper, and she'd forgotten about the bath, she said: 'But yeah! Why not? Follow me!'

GRAINSFORD HILLOCK WOODS

4.28 P.M.

Charlie Tysedale stood at his peg, waiting for the birds to fly overhead so he could pepper their little bodies with lead ball bearings, or whatever they put in cartridges these days, and watch them fall from the sky. He thought it might improve his mood. He was fuming. Too angry to speak to Esmé, but looking forward to bullying him when the chance presented itself, later today, and for the rest of his time on earth. How the hell had Esmé allowed this to happen? And how had Charlie been fooled into thinking Esmé was somebody worth going into business with? It had all been a monumental waste of time and money. Perhaps he could sue Esmé for – what could he sue him for? Giving him hope of a route out of his matrimonial misery?

Esmé had sworn to Charlie they could get Rospo, and Charlie had sworn to Esmé he could provide the capital needed to transform it into the wellness centre of their dreams. Now – what? *What?* Adele – the dreaded Adele – had initially been quite taken with the idea. She was impressed by the family:

the size of Tode Hall, the title – and so on. She approved of the project. She had agreed to make £8 million available. Every penny of it conditional, of course, and scoured over by her own lawyers. Nevertheless. It was a decent sum of money, and Charlie had it there, waiting. (Or he thought he did.) Now, he needed Rospo. And bloody, fucking, stupid, fucking *Esmé* . . . had let him down.

He stood there, still waiting. Where the hell were the stupid birds anyway?

Tap tap.

Getting cold.

He needed a slug of something . . . Adele must have taken the whisky flask out of his jacket pocket. Bossy bitch. She was standing with Egbert(Mr) at the other side of the clearing, in plain view. From the looks of things, Egbert was showing her something: giving her a little lesson in how to hold a gun. Charlie could tell from her body language that she was flirting. *Bitch.* Just because Egbert was rich and he had a big house. God, she was pathetic. God, he loathed her.

'Hullo, hullo . . . looking for this?'

At the sound of his voice, Charlie turned. Piers was approaching, gun over one shoulder, smirk on the vampire chops. He was holding aloft Charlie's great-grandfather's silver whisky flask.

'Oh,' Charlie said. Pleased enough by the sight of the flask to forget, very briefly, how much he now also loathed Slayer-Wilson-Tite. 'Where d'you find it? I thought my wife had confiscated it.' He took the flask, slurped on it. Offered it back to Piers. Piers said he'd already had some, thanks.

They stood together in silence. A heavy silence. There was a lot to be said.

Piers spoke first – which, in itself, was annoying to Charlie, who had been four years ahead of him at school. Piers said, with a snigger: 'She's got you by the balls, mate, am I right?'

Charlie laughed. It was quite funny. In a way. Given how Frederica had slapped Piers at the yoga class this morning, in front of everyone, and not even apologised afterwards. Charlie said: 'You can talk!'

A breath.

And the battle began.

They stood side by side, looking out over the clearing, not looking at each other. Charlie said: 'By the way, this is my peg. I hope you're not planning to shoot.'

Piers said: 'No, no. You go ahead . . . I'll be honest with you, Charlie. Don't tell Egbert. I find shooting quite dull.'

Again, Charlie chuckled. Some things were never meant to be said. In truth, he didn't disagree. The only reason he'd come out today was because of Rospo. This entire weekend was all about Rospo.

Which reminded him. Which reminded them both.

Piers experienced a flicker then: a flicker of glee. A flash of Charlie, back at school. How vile he'd been to all of them – all the younger boys. Charlie probably couldn't even remember. He probably thought it was normal, and maybe it was. But Piers remembered it very well. He remembered it especially at this instant, as they stood together in the field, one of them a winner, the other a loser. For Piers, this was a good moment.

'You must be disappointed,' Piers said.

'Disappointed?' replied Charlie, with a little chuckle.

At that point, thankfully, there came a shout from the beaters. The birds were up! They were flying right over Charlie's head.

POW. POW.

PLOP.

Got one of them, anyway. Not so bad! Charlie was out of shape and drunk, mostly, but he'd been shooting all of his life.

'Nice shot,' said Piers.

Charlie popped open the shotgun and reloaded. A smell of gunpowder. Both men's ears were ringing. Piers was too vain, Charlie too sloppy to use the earmuffs.

Charlie said: ' . . . Disappointed in what way?'

Piers giggled. 'Well now. Let me think—'

'Actually, Piers, I'm not remotely disappointed. Far from it. Esmé and I have a meeting scheduled with Egbert this evening, before dinner. I don't imagine we'll have much difficulty changing his mind.'

Again, Piers giggled. 'Are you sure?'

Charlie blinked. In his arms, the newly loaded shotgun tickled. His trigger finger itched. 'Piers—'

Piers said: 'I was thinking we might be able to work out something *together* . . . If you were willing to consider it . . . ?'

This was not what Charlie was expecting. He waited.

Piers edged a step or two closer. It wasn't natural. Charlie might have stepped back. Put a bit of space between them. But – perhaps there was something about the two of them *together* which had yet to be explored. Maybe. In any case, whatever it was – they stood very close indeed. Charlie did not step back. He lowered his gun.

'What are you suggesting, Piers?' he muttered. The nape of Piers' neck was within sniffing distance. A delicious smell! Charlie felt very slightly dizzy. 'Spit it out, Piers,' he said. It was meant to sound brisk, but there was a frog in there . . . Charlie had to clear his throat.

It made Piers smirk.

'I'm saying – exactly what I just said. Maybe we could work something out. Maybe we could do something with Rospo together. If we wanted.'

'Why?'

Piers looked disappointed. He shrugged. 'Well – *I don't know!*' he said.

'Seriously,' Charlie said. 'Why? Why are you saying this?'

Piers laughed. 'I remember you at school, Charlie ... You used to be – seriously – you were *the coolest guy* in the house. By far. Always. Fearless and funny and ... Everybody loved you ... What's happened to you?'

Charlie swallowed. The words had taken him by surprise. They had left him slightly winded. The last few years had been – very difficult. And nobody asked him things like this any more. Not ever.

'What happened, Tysedale?' Piers asked him again. His voice was soft and sensuous and, above all, vampire-like. One hundred per cent irresistible.

'What's that?'

'You heard me. What happened?'

'Well – I ... ' Charlie laughed. He regrouped. 'I've no idea, Piers, "what happened". Rather a lot has happened, frankly. It's been almost twenty-five years ... '

Piers edged closer still, their manly thighs a hair's breadth from touching. 'You know what I think?' he murmured. 'I think *Adele* happened.'

Charlie said: 'Ha! Well, *yes.* Among other things. Adele happened ... '

'The dreaded Adele,' Piers said.

It's unlikely, but Charlie might have been about to defend

his dreaded wife at that moment. As it turned out, he didn't get a chance. Another shout from the beaters. Birds above. BANG BANG. Charlie missed both shots. Popped the gun, ears ringing.

'Bad luck,' Piers said. 'Well, I should get back to my peg ... Just ... Let me know how things go with you and Egbert, yeah? It would be fun to have you at Rospo. We could do amazing things together.'

Pause. Vampire lips, smiling.

When it came to it, Charlie was less interested in the lips. Much more interested in the business opportunities at Rospo. But both – could be fine. Could be better than fine. *YOLO, as the kids put it*, he thought to himself. *Try anything once.*

He said: 'Have you discussed this with Frederica? I presume she has an opinion?'

'Frederica is very much on board,' Piers said, still wearing the smirk. 'But even if she weren't ...' He shrugged. 'She and I have a very fluid approach to all sorts of things, Charlie.'

'That's not really what I meant,' Charlie said. But it was, in a way.

Piers said: 'We can do this without Esmé. We can do this without Adele ...'

'Adele is my wife.' He might have said, *Adele has all the money*. But he didn't say that. Certainly not. Too much of a gent.

Again, Piers shrugged. He glanced across to where Adele was still standing, without Tippee by her side, for once. It so happened she was just then looking back in their direction. Piers sent her a little wave. 'So. Divorce her,' he said. 'You, me and Frederica – I think, between us, we could have a lot of fun. Make a lot of money ...'

Charlie stared at him. He didn't believe it, not really. Not for a second. It was the divorce that had caught him. *Divorce her, indeed* ... Piers made it sound so simple.

'Have a think about it,' Piers said. 'Let me know. Only hurry up, yeah? We're looking for a UK-based partner. Someone just like you, Charlie. We can't wait for ever.'

And with that, he turned and left Charlie standing there.

A shout from the beaters. Birds overhead. Too bad, Charlie had forgotten to reload his gun.

LONG ACRE CLEARING

5.15 P.M.

H ome time. Piers was trundling Hall-ward, alone, his gun half-cocked and unloaded, resting in the crook of his arm. An observer would not have seen it, but inwardly, he was on the point of combusting with glee. He was joyous. He was in an excellent mood. He'd walked ahead of the others, taken a long way home, specifically so he could spend some time alone, exulting in his triumph.

After the last few months, he felt he'd more than earned it.

Frederica was hell. He hardly even found her attractive any more. For the moment, however, their lives were welded together. Developments regarding Rospo, on this day of days, meant any plans he may previously have been fostering to get rid of her were now very much on the backburner, at least for the moment.

He missed Rospo nel Buco.

Actually – he missed Elizabetta. Of course he did. Despite so many things. He missed Elizabetta.

He was sorry for the way things had worked out between them.

There were a lot of things he was sorry for.

He missed her. He tramped on, trying not to think about the things he was sorry for; trying to cling to the jubilation. It wasn't easy. And then he was distracted – thankfully – by the sound of a woman's voice behind him.

'Coo-ee! Hellooo! Piers! Wait for me!'

Piers turned around. *Oh, God. What did she want?*

He cocked his head appealingly and waited until she'd caught up. 'Hello, hello,' he said, with a sexy smile. 'I was just thinking about you, Adele!'

Adele said: 'That's nice . . . '

Actually he'd been too wrapped up in his own regrets to notice it, but Adele had been playing a sprinter's game of grandmother's footsteps with him for the last ten minutes. When she spotted him in the distance, disappearing over the brow of the hill, she'd quickly handed her gun to Egbert(Mr) saying it was too heavy for her to carry, and jogged off to catch up with him.

In any case here she was, dressed in however many layers of clothes for shooting-in-Yorkshire, having jogged and ducked and ducked and jogged for at least a mile, and she wasn't even panting. She'd barely broken a sweat.

The thing about Adele – one of the many things about Adele: she had a fitness regime, and she stuck to it. Strong as a carthorse, she was: inexhaustible.

'What sort of things were you thinking about me?' she asked him coquettishly. The thing about Piers – one of the few things about Piers: everybody flirted with him. It was impossible not to. '*Nice* things, I hope?!'

'Absolutely nice!' he exclaimed. 'Very nice indeed!' One of the other things about Piers: he always flirted back.

In the meantime, his mind was working fast. *What did she want from him? What might he want from her? What was to be gained? What was at risk? Why was she following him?*

' ... I was thinking,' he continued, 'about what a lucky man your husband is. If you want to know. That's what I was thinking ... How in the hell did Tysedale manage to snare an amazing woman like you?'

Adele thought this was a good question. One she found she asked herself more and more. Nevertheless, she was not a fool. Also – much more importantly – she was a professional. Always. Multi-million-selling relationship experts like Adele Tysedale would not remain multi-million-selling relationship experts for long if they dropped their guard so easily. She smiled – super symmetrically – and said, 'Ah! But the thing about my gorgeous husband, Piers, as with all husbands and all wives ... he has hidden depths. He's an amazing man.'

'*Is that so?*' (Vampire sex-fuzz.)

Adele couldn't smell him, but even so she felt *slightly* dizzy. 'Yes, he is, I'll have you know!'

Piers offered up an understated sigh. 'Plus, I suppose he's loaded, is he? The rest of us wouldn't stand a chance.'

That annoyed her. 'Thanks to me,' she snapped. 'That is ... ' She smiled. 'We help each other! I've been very fortunate, with the money that I make. In fact – ha! – my agent told me this morning, I'm actually year-on-year the fourth highest-earning UK mainland-based self-help-slash-relationships author in the whole of the US! Which chuffed me to bits, I must admit! Little me! I couldn't quite believe it!'

'How amazing ... '

'Mm. Thank you, Piers! But that's how marriages work, isn't it? It's all about sharing . . . I'm sure you remember.'

She didn't seem to notice his lack of a reply; it didn't appear to strike her that the last was an odd, perhaps, even, an unkind thing to say to a man whose money-laundering wife had recently been found dead, floating in spring water and surrounded by grapefruits. It seemed that Adele was more concerned with getting the message across that Charlie relied on her for money, and not the other way round.

After a while Adele said: ' . . . Anyway – I'll send you a copy of my book. If you haven't already read it. It explains a lot about Charlie and my relationship. How we worked together in the early days, and, in the revised, updated editions, there are several chapters explaining how we still make it work today.'

'I'd love that,' said Piers. 'Thank you.'

She was insane, clearly. Nevertheless . . . Piers' brain continued to whir . . . So *she* was the one with the money, was she? Not Charlie . . . Piers thought he might do a little research when he got home. In the meantime, he never liked to let an opportunity slip by. Not an opportunity for pleasure. Not for malicious fun. Not for self-interest. And not for revenge. Driven by all of the above, he heard himself saying: 'I was actually just trying to lure Charlie away with me to come and help with the relaunch at Rospo.' He gave her a smile. 'You probably saw us talking.'

'I did,' Adele replied. 'It's why I was—'

'I was hoping I could steal him from you for a couple of years. Take him out to Rospo . . . Exploit him viciously, body, bank and brain. Get the new Rospo Wellness Centre up and running . . . and then return him to you. What's left of him. Et cetera. I thought I might be giving you a well-deserved break!'

'A break? From what?'

'I'll be honest. He seemed keen.'

Adele laughed uncertainly. Unsymmetrically. Beneath the beige foundation, her cheeks burned red. *What was he saying?* She said: 'K-keen on what?'

He smiled again, and there was not meant to be any ambiguity in it. Its loucheness sent shockwaves to her steely core. All the symmetry left her. For a moment, even walking in a straight line seemed impossible. She wobbled. Piers caught her. He smiled again, and, honestly, there might have been a dribble of blood slipping down one side of his chin; and honestly, when he caught her arm, to stop her from falling over, she could feel the burn of his touch through all the layers of waterproof outer clothing. *Maybe*, she thought, *maybe he really was a vampire.*

(He wasn't, of course.)

He said: 'Now I'm wishing I'd asked *you* to come with me, instead, Adele.'

Adele replied: 'Charlie doesn't go anywhere without me. We don't go anywhere without each other. That's – I saw the way you two were chatting. You looked so intense – I wanted to ask you what you'd been chatting about. That's all. Well, I can tell you now – Charlie and I are a team. Buy one of us, you get the other one free! So. That's a "No, thank you", Piers. A "No, thank you" from both of us.'

Piers looked unconvinced. He said: 'Well ... Have a think about it. Let me know ... Only hurry up, yeah? We're looking for a UK partner. Someone just like you, Adele ... We can't wait for ever.'

THE LOG ROOM BEHIND
THE PANTRY

5.15 P.M.

Yet again. The new boy responsible for delivering kindling to the log room didn't appear to understand the basic elements of his task. Mr Carfizzi was grumbling to himself about this, making a note to lodge a complaint with the Estate Ranger, who was meant to oversee these things. Because of course it was no good, Mr Carfizzi thought to himself, using titchy kindling in the Great Hall. And it was equally no good using massive kindling in the bedrooms. And it was no good using titchy or massive kindling in the Chinese Drawing Room ... In truth, this was a long-running battle. The last boy hadn't understood the importance of medium-size kindling either.

Mr Carfizzi, hammer and hatchet in hand, was expertly chopping – large kindling into medium – when Tippee Tysedale, appearing from nowhere, sloped into the room.

225

He stood behind Mr Carfizzi and watched him work for a while.

'What are you doing?' he said at last. It was the first conversation Tippee had initiated in several years, but Mr Carfizzi wasn't to know that. Also, Mr Carfizzi had been so wrapped up in his negative thoughts, he'd not noticed Tippee coming in. The sound of Tippee's voice made him jump. Made him almost cut off his own finger.

Carfizzi was too irritated to reply.

Tippee continued to watch him in silence. After a while, he said: 'Are you turning large kindling into medium-size kindling, so it fits in the correct fire grate?'

Carfizzi paused. He turned to the boy in astonishment. 'That is exactly what I'm doing, young man,' he said. 'How is it you can understand this and yet they cannot? They continue to deliver kindling that is utterly useless to me. Or, I should say, useless for medium-sized grates.'

'But it's obvious,' Tippee said. 'With so many different-sized grates in a house like this. Of course. You can't use titchy kindling in the Great Hall. And it's no good using massive kindling in the bedrooms.'

Carfizzi nodded. *What an excellent boy!* he thought. *Alert and sensible.* 'Every week, I ask them to supply medium-size kindling for the drawing rooms, and every week, they fail me . . .' He kept chopping. Hammering and chopping.

Tippee said: 'You're very good at it.'

Carfizzi grunted.

Tippee said: 'Can I have a go?'

Carfizzi kept chopping.

' . . . Please?' said Tippee. 'You must be tired, being so old. I can help you, if you show me how. If it's not annoying?'

Who knew what came over Tippee at that instant? Albeit, the bar was low, but it was the most considerate, most chivalrous speech the boy had put together in his lifetime.

Carfizzi couldn't have known this. Nevertheless, he was touched. He handed Tippee the hatchet. 'Be careful,' he said.

Tippee took hold of the hatchet. With his other hand, he picked up the large kindling.

Chop. Oops. Missed. Chop. It wasn't as easy as Mr Carfizzi made it look.

Mr Carfizzi chortled. 'Watch out!' he said. 'Don't do it like that . . . Use the hammer, too. Don't hold on to the log or you'll cut your own hand off.'

There were times – not many, but this was certainly one – when Mr Carfizzi regretted never having had a son of his own. He would have liked to share a moment like this, teaching the boy how to turn large kindling into medium size. It would have been . . . joyful. Mr Carfizzi's heart ached, as it often did, these days.

Too bad.

'First,' Carfizzi said, 'you need to wedge the blade into the timber . . . like this! . . . And then . . . *crack* . . . There. That's it! Little taps. You don't need big taps . . . Very good. *Very good* . . . A hammer and hatchet, used correctly, could chop anything, did you know? It could fell a three-hundred-year-old oak tree.'

'Really?' asked Tippee politely, chopping and whacking. 'How fat is a three-hundred-year-old oak tree?'

'Well. It's . . . anything between this . . . and this . . . ' said Mr Carfizzi, stretching out his little arms. '. . . Fatter than this, even. Three metres or so. They can grow to forty metres tall . . . '

'Wow!' said Tippee. *Chop, Whack. Chop. Oops.*

'Watch it!' chuckled Mr Carfizzi. 'I don't want to have to tell your mama you've chopped your own hand off.'

'Don't worry!' said Tippee. He laughed. It was a merry laugh. His parents would have been amazed. 'She thinks I'm in a Classical Studies lesson but me and my tutor are going to pretend the wifi wasn't working.'

Mr Carfizzi beamed indulgently. 'So, so naughty.'

Tippee said: 'You won't tell her, will you?'

Mr Carfizzi made the sign of the cross. 'On my dead body,' he said seriously.

It was a nice moment. A rare moment of trust, for the boy.

And then – out of nowhere, there was Piers, leaning against the doorframe, smirking, looking irritating. Piers said: 'What was that, Mr Carfizzi? What aren't you telling Tippee's mother?'

Carfizzi's face clouded. He didn't like Piers. 'Never you mind,' he snapped.

It infuriated Piers, the way Carfizzi didn't even attempt to hide his disdain. So Mr Carfizzi could suck on this: 'I wanted you to tell Mrs Carfizzi that Frederica and I have decided we're *not* going to be vegetarian for dinner this evening. We're celebrating ... Could you be sweet and let Mrs Carfizzi know?'

Carfizzi scowled. 'Why don't you tell her yourself?'

Piers smiled. 'Because, dear Mr Carfizzi, I am asking you.' And with that he wandered off, to spread his sweetness and light elsewhere.

Tippee studied Carfizzi's angry face. After a while, once Piers' footsteps had faded, he said: 'Why do you hate him?'

Carfizzi laughed. 'Of course I don't hate him! I think he is a lazy, stupid man ... Also ... ' Carfizzi leaned in. He

228

lowered his voice. 'You know, he murdered his wife. I'm quite sure of it.'

Tippee stepped back. He gave Carfizzi a very strange look. Something had wrecked the vibe.

QUEEN CHARLOTTE'S BEDROOM

5.36 P.M.

Outside, the light was dimming. The sunniest day in the history of late Octobers was fast losing its sheen, and the pheasant shooters were mostly in their baths. Bunny Rostovsky never did rejoin them. She slid away from the table just as Egbert(Mr) had collapsed to the ground, covered in champagne and scratches, and she never returned. She had spent the afternoon, busy and secretive as ever, furthering her own mysterious interests; communicating with her mysterious contacts via end-to-end PFS encrypted networks, and then, at some point, she had stumbled upon an idle moment. She had thought maybe it would be nice to get a cup of tea, but that would have involved making polite conversation with the kitchen staff. She thought it would probably be easier to drive into Todeister and buy a cup of tea at the petrol station – but did she really want a cup of tea that much?

She was in her bedroom, trying not to think about the ghosts. To distract herself from that, not to mention the tea drought, and since no one was around, she thought it might be enjoyable to spend a moment revelling in her weekend booty ... She was particularly pleased with the nineteenth-century malachite crucifix, lifted last night from a glass-covered cabinet in the Yellow Saloon.

Bunny pulled her suitcase from its hiding place beneath the four-poster bed. Maybe, she thought, as she turned the lock, pulled back the lid and began to rummage for the hidden goodies, maybe, considering the little crucifix was so beautiful, and this had been such a successful weekend, she might just this once allow herself not to sell it but to keep ... to keep the ...

Her rummaging picked up pace. It became more frantic. Finally, in a rage, Bunny tipped the suitcase's full contents onto the floor.

Gone. *Everything*. It was all gone! Someone had got in there. They had unlocked the case – it was easy enough, of course. They had rifled around among her belongings, her silky under-wear – they had taken her stuff! She had been robbed!

White hot rage. *White hot.*

Who would dare?

Did they not realise who they were dealing with?

Bunny sat back on her heels.

Now what?

THE YELLOW SALOON

5.49 P.M.

Piers found her in the Yellow Saloon, without the lights on. She was bent over a glass-covered display cabinet, and she didn't move when he stopped at the doorway.

'Hullo,' he said.

She didn't hear him.

She'd spotted the malachite crucifix. Right there in the cabinet, exactly where it was before she stole it.

'Hullo hullo,' said Piers, again.

Again, she didn't hear him.

Had she not taken this, only yesterday? Had she not opened this very cabinet, lifted that very cross, taken it upstairs, wrapped it in a cashmere sock and hidden it in her suitcase?

Was she going mad? She peered a little closer. *The ghosts*, she thought.

Piers settled against the doorframe and watched her. The windows of the Yellow Saloon were vast. They stretched 30 foot, from floor to cornicing, and there was enough light beyond them for Piers to admire Bunny's magnificent, porn-star silhouette, while also wondering at the intense craning of her neck over said display cabinet. The intensity piqued his curiosity as much as the porn-star silhouette. He flicked a switch beside him, and the display cabinet lit up. That made her jump. She spun round, expecting to see the ghosts again. She was quite relieved when it was only Piers.

'Oh,' she said, 'it's you. What are you doing?'

'What am I doing? Well – I'm switching on the light for you, so you can see better. What are you doing?'

'What am *I* doing? Well – I'm – What does it look like I'm doing, Piers? I was just admiring this . . . this . . .' She waved at the display cabinet, taking care to encompass everything, not just the malachite crucifix.

Piers stepped into the room. As per usual, he ignored the normal rules of personal space, and stepped right up to her. But unlike his usual targets, Bunny remained unruffled. She allowed him to do this and did not by one inch retreat, even when his body was touching hers, his stomach to her chest. She waited.

'Seriously,' he said, glancing down at the cabinet. 'What were you looking at? With so much concentration?' With a little laugh, he put his lips to her ear. She could feel his breath on her neck. 'Bunny,' he murmured, 'you look like you've seen a ghost.'

She was unimpressed. Actually – to his dismay – it seemed that his normally fail-safe vampire-sex-fizz approach had landed a bit flat. Perhaps, he thought, she used similar tricks herself.

Nevertheless, he kept trying. In truth, he didn't have many other tricks. He inhaled through the nostrils, and pushed his pelvis into her stomach.

Bunny smiled.

Oops. Stiffy alert. *Who was in charge here?* Piers suddenly felt less sure of himself. He took a step back.

She said: 'No. No ghost.'

'What then?'

She said: 'Something I stole earlier. Seems to have been returned to its place.'

The vampire inhaled. *Was she joking? Was she not joking? Of course she was joking – or wasn't joking?* She eyeballed him, watched his confusion with some amusement. It didn't clarify things.

He laughed. 'You're *good*,' he said.

She didn't care.

He said (a slight change of tone): 'You disappeared in the middle of lunch. I was looking for you . . . I suppose you're up to date with all the gossip?'

She claimed not to be, so he filled her in: arrests had been made at Rospo over the murder of Elizabetta, which meant the guests were off the hook. And he (and Frederica) had been given run of the villa for the foreseeable future. Beaten Esmé, Charlie, Ecgbert and Alice to the prize . . .

She acted surprised. Piers could not work out if this was genuine. Everything about her was confusing. He said again: 'You're good.'

She still didn't care.

He asked her if she and Putin had been hatching any plans regarding Rospo, 'since everyone else seems to have been', to which Bunny replied: 'That reminds me. Have you seen him anywhere? I haven't seen him since lunch, and he's not picking up his phone . . . I was actually just looking for him . . .'

'In the display cabinet?'

'Yep.' Still, she didn't care.

He thought she was the sexiest woman he had ever met. Ever. It was amazing. He said: 'Your husband's not really Russian, though, is he? Elizabetta – my wife . . . ' A pause. 'My late wife, Elizabetta,' he said again. The smallest of falters. He continued. 'She told me she recognised him from *EastEnders* . . . She told me the name of the guy he played . . . He played a guy called Mick, apparently. After she died, I looked it up. I was very curious. You can imagine.'

Bunny said nothing.

'It took a while because "Mick" didn't have a massive role. Three episodes or so. Nothing. But I found him . . . And sure enough, there he was . . . Derek Hunter, born in Stevenage in 1959. And I remember that because it was the same year as my mother . . . '

Bunny said nothing.

Piers said: 'You're good,' for the third time. And then, when still she didn't respond: 'So what are you really up to?'

'I told you. I am looking for Putin.'

Piers laughed '"Putin!" . . . Haile Selassie . . . Ra-Ra Rasputin. Whatever. I think we've already established the guy's name is actually Derek. So . . . ' An idea occurred to him. *Why not?* He'd proposed it to everyone else this afternoon. Just to fuck with them. But this time – he thought he almost meant it. 'How about you dump your failed actor boyfriend, called Derek Hunter, and come live with me at Rospo instead? How about it? We could build the business together . . . We could clean up, Bunny. What do you say?'

Bunny, true to character, said nothing at all. She stepped away from Piers; she glanced over his shoulder, nodded coldly at whoever she saw standing there, and slowly walked away.

Piers turned to look.

Oops. And double oops. It was Frederica, and she had been standing there for the last five minutes, listening in on every word.

EGBERT(MR)'S STUDY

6.19 P.M.

Dinner had been scheduled late because of the much-vaunted business meeting between Egbert(Mr), Esmé and Charlie. The meeting was meant to have started at 6 p.m., but it was 6.19 p.m. now and Egbert(Mr) still hadn't appeared. Esmé and Charlie were sitting, waiting, in Egbert's study – not long vacated by Putin and India. A rather grim silence hung between them. Charlie kept tapping his hand on his knee. It was annoying.

Esmé said: 'What's the matter with you? Stop it. Why are you fidgeting? Are you nervous?'

Charlie didn't reply. For a moment, he stopped tapping.

The silence grew heavier. There was a fire in the grate, at least. They listened to the logs popping. And then – Charlie started tapping again.

'It's very irritating,' Esmé said.

Charlie said: '*You're* irritating.'

More silence.

Esmé pulled out his mobile for the first time in forty-five seconds. 'Do you think he may have forgotten? Shall I call him?'

'No.'

An unusually loud pop from the logs. They both jumped.

It lifted the mood, at least for a moment. They looked at each other and laughed. *Had it come to this?* Logs making them jump, Little Tode squirts keeping them waiting in their private studies?

'We can rescue this,' Esmé said. 'Of course we can. We've just got to get him to realise he's making a massive mistake. And I believe he is. Really, I do. Wilson-Tite is a joke. I mean – I can't believe we're even having to say this. They've been using Rospo to launder money, right under his nose. And he didn't even notice! Well. Either that, or he did notice, and he's in on it ...' Esmé laughed. 'What kind of a manager does that make him?'

Charlie smiled non-committally. His tapping grew more frantic.

'I'm pretty sure,' he burst out, 'that Adele and I are calling it quits.'

'Hmm?'

'I think we're splitting up. Me and Adele.'

(And what the hell, Esmé wondered, did *that* have to do with the price of chutney? At a time like this!) 'Oh. Are you? Well ... I'm sorry to hear it.' He thought for a moment. 'When did you decide that? Or should I say, when did Adele decide? I presume it's her decision, is it? Has she had enough of you, Charlie?' He smiled, almost kindly. After all, he was still fresh from his own divorce battlefield. 'Well – you can't really blame them, can you ...?' He was already thinking about himself. 'Ah well. Sorry, mate.'

Charlie said: 'Actually – no. It's not really Adele. She doesn't believe I'll do it . . . Maybe I won't. She's got me tied up in so many legal tangles.'

'That stinks,' observed Esmé. He wasn't really listening.

'I'm part of the brand, Esmé. You can't write multi-million-selling self-help books about how to stay married to someone if you're actually getting divorced from them. Can you? I'm her USP . . . Without me . . . KABOOM! . . . Know what I mean? It's game over.'

'Oh,' said Esmé, wondering how long they had to talk about this before he could politely dial Egbert and find out if the meeting was still on. 'Well – kaboom! Anyway. Sorry. I suppose financially, you're fairly separate entities, are you? That's a plus, I can tell you. Might make things a bit simpler. Chelsea-Reine pretty much . . . ' He was going to say, 'cleaned me out', but then he remembered he was talking to a future business partner. Assuming things could be put back on track. ' . . . Chelsea-Reine was very keen on getting her grubbers on my cash. Bless her. *Anyway* . . . Where the bloody hell is Egbert? Little *fuck*. How dare he keep us waiting like this?'

The door opened and in he walked, fresh from the bath. Esmé jumped to his feet, noisy and gushing, praying his cousin hadn't overheard him, which Egbert(Mr) had not, because he was already apologising before he turned the doorknob.

Middle age and social status don't bring out the best in the male sex. Makes them windy. Sadly Mr Egbert Tode, though brimming with admirable qualities, was no exception to that rule. In recent years he had grown a bit too fond of the sound of his own voice. There weren't enough people in his life to tell him to shut up.

'I'll come clean,' Egbert began, once they'd all settled down, and he was safely ensconced on his throne. 'I was absolutely dreading this meeting.'

'Oh no!' cried Esmé, in full suck-up mode now. 'But that's awful! Surely *not!*'

'I was dreading it because there's literally nothing I hate more than disappointing people. And I know – I *really do know*,' he said (although of course he didn't), 'how important this project is to you both, how much *effort* you've both put into it, and how absolutely *passionately* you feel about it ... And frankly,' Egbert(Mr) furrowed his brow and smiled at his hands, which were spread out importantly on either side of his keyboard, 'I can't think of anything I'd like more than for Villa Rospo to be transformed into a viable, eco-friendly, high-end super-deluxe lifestyle membership club as you describe ... I presume India and I would have life membership?' He was joking. He laughed. Nobody else did. 'I mean – what more could we want? And I can't think of two people I would prefer to hand that project to, as it were. *However* ... ' He sighed. He shrugged his shoulders. Windy, he might have grown. But it was true, he hated to disappoint people. ' ... I was just now observing to Munch, as I was making my way down here to see you both,' he continued, '"Munch, it just seems so *cruel*" – and Munch agreed. "Life *is* cruel," she said. "Especially ... "'

Egbert(Mr) looked at Esmé, who was leaning forward, not listening, waiting for his cousin to stop talking so he could set to work on changing his mind. Esmé had flowcharts and budget projections and architectural mock-ups all cued up on the iPad ready to go, and his hands were sweating.

' ... "Especially",' Egbert(Mr) repeated miserably, 'Esmé, I know you've had some rotten luck, what with Australia turning so vile and all that ... And also I'm fully aware, having done

240

such amazing stuff with your Sydney-based luxury gym brand, that you've got some really serious experience in this area. Running membership clubs. And so on. And Charlie – gosh! I mean – name a man who doesn't have at least one item from Mark of Marylebone in their wardrobe! I know I can't! Such an amazing success ... All I can say is I *really am sorry. I wish we could run with this. I really, really do. But in the circumstances I just cannot*—'

Charlie ran out of patience. 'Cannot what?' he said. 'You don't even really know what we're proposing. We've given you the sketchiest outline—'

'Well, *no*, Charlie,' Egbert(Mr) said, bridling a bit. 'I don't think that's entirely fair—'

'It's more than fair. So why this sudden change of heart? You led us to believe—'

'I know. I know I did ...' Egbert(Mr) looked utterly wretched.

'So what changed? I mean – it's one thing, your cousin Ecgbert – *Sir* Ecgbert – suddenly this morning declaring an interest in the villa, just because he's found a bird to marry him ... *That* we could deal with. We can buy them another house nearby. Whatever. I'm sure we can sort something out. But to hand the place to Wilson-Tite ... Of all *useless* people. *Why?*'

Quite a long pause.

Esmé and Charlie waited.

And Egbert writhed. 'It's complicated,' he said eventually.

'In what way, complicated?' Charlie persisted.

Egbert(Mr) didn't want to explain. He'd not been intending to explain it, either. India had strongly advised him to say as little as possible. She said it would only make them really angry.

But – they were already really angry, and with good reason. And under their blazing interrogation (see above) Egbert found himself unable to resist. Munch was wrong, he said to himself. The poor chaps deserved some sort of an explanation.

He said: 'Honestly it's not really about Piers ...' He stopped. And started again. 'By which I mean ... it's absolutely about Piers. He is a very clever, very talented guy. It turns out. At least ...' He tried again. Changed tack. 'The fact is, it was his *wife* who was murdered!' he said. 'After all. In case you hadn't realised.'

'Yes. We're aware of that,' Charlie said patiently.

'Well. All right. I know you are. Aware of that. I'm just saying that one can't simply sweep that aspect of the situation aside. As if it weren't a very real factor ...'

'For heaven's sake, Egbert,' snapped Esmé. 'What changed? Piers' wife has been murdered since we ever started discussing this wretched thing with you. She was murdered when we arranged this meeting, last week. She was murdered this morning, when I was telling you how excited Charlie and I were about our plans. What are you *talking* about?'

Egbert(Mr) took a breath and settled down. He dug deep. Put on his most pious expression. 'What I'm trying to get across to you,' he said, 'is that this isn't just *any old* sort of "business deal". And it's only fair to *highlight* the fact that we have not only a grieving *widower* in the mix. Also – *also* – guys, listen. *Also* that we have a grieving *family* ...'

'Hmm?' Charlie looked confused.

'Back in Italy. We have a grieving *family*.'

'Egbert, what are you talking about?' snapped Esmé.

'Also, of course, we have poor Frederica, here in the UK, longing – literally *longing* – to return to her homeland. We have to appreciate that the Ranaldinis lost a much-loved daughter and/or sister. And when you guys come at me, insisting I hand over Rospo, right now, this minute, I don't feel you're really taking their grief into account ... '

Esmé and Charlie were silenced. (What the fuck was Egbert talking about?)

And then, finally, Egbert(Mr) took a deep breath and spat it out. Almost. He almost spat it out. 'I don't want to upset the Ranaldinis. They called me this afternoon. And as you know there's been a lot of activity ... vis-à-vis criminality at Rospo and so on and forth and laundering money and mountains of cash discovered on the premises, and the fact is, *as things are ...* we ... ' Egbert looked at Esmé. 'By which I mean the Todes – the Tode family name – is in the clear. The Ranaldinis are in the clear. More or less. They've arrested Frederica's uncle, I think, and those charges ... It's very hard to understand quite what's going on. The salient points are ... ' Egbert, attempting to restore dignity, took a deep breath and listed the salient points, one on each finger: '*Firstly*, that we are all entirely innocent, obviously, and in the clear. Clearly. I'm sure I don't need to tell you that. *Secondly*, and this is the most important point, that Signor Ranaldini has very kindly agreed to keep our names out of everything, and to testify to that ... But what I'm trying to say is ... ' Egbert lost count. He put his fingers back down. 'It's the Ranaldinis that one has to ... err ... The Ranaldinis are very sort of *thick*, as it were, with local law enforcement, and also from what I can gather ... The point is they're on top of it all. Which is wonderful news. And the last thing *any of us* wants is to drag the Tode family name through the mud.'

A long silence. The penny dropped. At last Esmé and Charlie understood.

'The Ranaldinis are very keen for their only surviving daughter to return to Rospo as soon as possible, so she can look after her poor ma and pa while the uncle is doing his bird time ... and they also want for her and Piers to take up the management reins, as before, of villa and garden. More or less. That's the gist of it. Except, obviously, without poor Elizabetta. And so on. And the fact is ... you know ... this being "Italy", as it were, one is slightly out of one's depth ... After all, who is one to argue?'

Esmé was outraged. He said: 'You don't mean you're going to let them carry on doing it?'

Egbert was outraged. 'What? *No!* Certainly not! The Italiano polizias have done their bit, so far as I can tell. Absolutely splendid work. And we should respect them for that. In the meantime, as I keep explaining, the Ranaldinis have very kindly agreed to keep our name out of it all, as long as I allow Piers and Frederica back to the Villa Rospo, where they can continue managing villa and gardens as before. Without Elizabetta, and indeed, the wicked uncle's shenanigans vis-à-vis muddying the water ... For pity's sake, Mrs Ranaldini has lost one daughter; the other one's miles away, here in the UK. Uncle's been carted off to the slammer for a year or two. What's the poor woman to do?'

Charlie said: 'And Piers?'

Egbert shrugged. 'It's a mystery. I agree. But yes. Signor and Mrs Ranaldini are pretty adamant that they miss him. They say they want Piers ... I suppose we should be pleased that somebody does.'

THE CHINESE DRAWING ROOM

8.00 P.M.

Nobody was looking forward to the evening ahead. Except possibly Tippee Tysedale, who always enjoyed watching adult discomfort, and also (for not dissimilar reasons) Lady Tode and Leonardo. The guests had been advised by Mr Carfizzi, as was the tradition, to gather for drinks in the Chinese Drawing Room, bathed and changed, from 7.30 p.m. onwards. Oddly, by 8 p.m., there was still no one there. This was unusual.

India arrived first, looking elegant and fresh in an under-stated get-up (trousers and silky turtleneck discovered, brilliantly, *hidden away* in the Armani sale). She was annoyed to find the room empty. She could have spent more time on her luxury divan bed, watching TV with the children. She considered retreating back upstairs – but decided against. It was unfair on Mrs Carfizzi when everyone was late for dinner. On top of which, her bedroom was miles away.

She asked Mr Carfizzi to bring her a glass of champagne, settled down with the November issue of *Vogue*, and waited.

245

Next came Egbert(Mr), rubbing his hands together, preparing to be host. He too was surprised to see the room so empty, and pleasantly surprised to find the only person present was his wife.

He told her a bit about the meeting with Esmé and Charlie, and how very awkward it had been. He said: 'But we patched things up in the end. I'm fairly certain ... I mean – it's business, isn't it? One cannot take these things too personally ...'

Carfizzi came in, bearing Egbert's usual gin and tonic.

'Ah, *thank you*, Mr Carfizzi. Gosh. Marvellous. Absolutely *just* what the doctor ordered. Thank you so, so much.'

Slurp.

India hadn't been listening. She was trying to concentrate on an article about how to get the sun-kissed freckled look without the harmful UV rays, and she slightly wished he would stop talking.

Next came Frederica, looking jubilant. Radiant. Joyful. Looking as beautiful as anyone had ever seen her. Which was interesting. Or it would have been, if Egbert(Mr) and India, like Alice and Sir Ecgbert, had been bothered to remember their detective hats.

But India had long ago forgotten the point of the weekend. She was actually checking Frederica for freckles, and finding none, and wondering what the secret was. She said: 'Wow, Frederica! I've just had a really good look, and I can't see a single freckle or blemish. How do you do it?'

Frederica said she didn't know. Then, in a most uncharacteristic move, she crossed the big room to where India was seated on the sofa, bent down and gave her a hug.

'Gosh!' said India, slightly embarrassed. 'What was *that* for?'

Frederica said: 'I wanna say jus' *tank* you.' She turned to

Egbert(Mr). 'Tank you both. I am too happy. Tank you for allowing me to go home.'

Egbert laughed, even more embarrassed than India. 'Well, my dear Frederica,' he said. 'But we weren't keeping you hostage! You could have gone home any time!'

She smiled politely – again, this was uncharacteristic. 'I am happy,' she said. 'Tank you.'

When she turned away to give her drinks request to Mr Carfizzi (in Italian: he replied in English), Egbert(Mr) and India exchanged bewildered glances. India had been more in favour of giving the place to Esmé and Charlie, so they could turn it into a place she wanted to go – but Egbert(Mr) had given her a long spiel about keeping the Tode name out of the press . . . Plus, there was the added drama of the uncle Ranaldini having been arrested, and naughty Elizabetta using the place to store money . . . Egbert insisted he was acting on the advice of the police, but he kept on and on referring to the Ranaldinis, and what they thought and felt about the matter in a way that India found strange, not to say *suspicious*. She said: 'I bet it's all tied up with the mafia and Mexican cartels and stuff!' She was quite shocked by the way Egbert had snapped back at her. Truth was . . . she didn't really care who got Rospo (as long as Alice stayed with her at Tode Hall). She much preferred Greece and/or Ibiza anyway. She felt sorry for Esmé. But on the plus side, it would be a relief to get rid of Frederica.

India felt a little bad, remembering that Alice and Ecgbert had also put in a late bid for Rospo. This was quite hurtful, considering how much she loved having them around at Tode Hall. Nevertheless – luckily the police or the Ranaldinis or both or whoever had decreed that it wasn't to be. So that was that.

And now here they both were. Sir Ecgbert and Alice: late for dinner and looking adorably scruffy, as usual.

Ecgbert(Sir) cut straight the point.

He said: 'Ah. Car-Fizzy. Good to see you. I'm on the Coca Cola tonight. Got to stay sharp.' He tapped the end of his long nose and winked at the butler. Obligingly, the butler winked back. 'Not sure about Alice . . . Trudy? What do you want? Are you on the sauce tonight? Or are you staying sharp?' Tap. Wink.

Alice, according to habit, had smoked a small spliff before coming out. What with so many potential murderers and actual thieves in the house tonight, and – worse still – the conversation she knew she had to have with India about her and Ecgbert's failed bid for Rospo, there wasn't much about the evening that Alice was looking forward to.

'I'm on the sauce,' she said with a smile. 'Definitely.'

She sat down on the sofa beside India – better to get the conversation over and done with – and waited for Mr Carfizzi to bring her some gin.

Alice said: 'I'm really sorry. I would've mentioned it but we only thought of it this morning . . . '

India gazed back at her blankly. 'Thought of what?' she said.

Alice hesitated. 'Well . . . Italy . . . '

A beat. And another.

'*Ohhh*. You mean about Rospo? Yes, I was quite miffed about that, Alice, tbh. But anyway, apparently it's impossible so let's forget about it . . . ' She laughed. 'I thought you were talking about your phone! I'm so sorry, I completely forgot to call you back. It wasn't there.'

Alice gazed back at her. 'What phone? . . . Oh! Yes, of course. So stupid of me! I *found* it!'

They laughed a lot. Alice, because she was slightly stoned

and mightily relieved not to have hurt India's feelings; India, because laughter always came easily to her, and because it was funny, them talking at cross purposes about Rospo and telephones.

It was growing late. Dinner at Tode Hall was normally served at 8 p.m. sharp. It had been postponed by half an hour (amid some grumbling from Mrs Carfizzi, who was getting old, and liked to be in bed by ten) to allow time for the Esmé–Charlie– Egbert meeting. Now it was 8.35 p.m., and still most of the guests were missing.

Mr Carfizzi muttered as much to India when he delivered Alice's gin. India said, 'I know, I *know* ... *where are they?!* Mega-apols to Mrs Carfizzi ... Shall we give them another ten mins? And then – I think we should probably just start without them. Don't you think?'

Esmé came in next, dressed nicely but looking very sullen. Trained from babyhood never to keep Mrs Carfizzi waiting, it was a sign of quite how badly he felt, that he should have arrived to dinner so late. He apologised to Mr Carfizzi, but didn't acknowledge anyone else. He glanced around the room, picked up a copy of the *Economist* which was lying boringly on a side table, settled himself down into a quiet corner, and pretended to read.

India, Egbert, Ecgbert, Alice and Mr Carfizzi all felt bad for him, so they left him to it.

Nicola also had been raised to arrive promptly for dinner. She came in just then, in her smartest dinner-party leggings, having – most remarkably – abandoned the usual visor and gloves. Her eyes were shining, and there was a wonderful sense of purpose in her step as she crossed the room towards India. She was carrying an envelope.

India tore it open at once. But not quite fast enough for Nicola. 'It's from Bunny,' Nicola said. Shouted, actually. All the room stopped to listen. 'Well, it's from both of them. But Bunny gave it to me. She found out which my bedroom was – I suppose Car Fizzy, you told her, did you? Someone did. Anyway – there she was, standing outside my door! She delivered the letter direct to my door . . . '

A short pause. They were all quite curious. India frowned, focused on the page. The letter had been written on Tode Hall writing paper, and sealed in a Tode Hall envelope.

'She's gone!' Nicola said joyfully. Joyful, not because she was joyful to see Bunny go (far from it), but joyful because she, Nicola, was the one in possession of the news. 'She and the husband are very, very sorry, but they had to rush back to London. I just dropped them off at the station. That's why I'm so late.'

' . . . *Wily*,' observed Ecgbert(Sir). '*Extremely* wily . . . Did they give a reason . . . India? Do they give a reason in the letter? . . . By the way, Egbert, I seriously advise you to check out the display cabinets in the Yellow Saloon. Also – various objects that may have gone missing from the chapel and various other places. Trudy, can you remember?'

India didn't reply. She was scowling at the letter. 'But that's *so rude!*' she said. 'They're expected for dinner! . . . I can't believe they'd just leave like that . . . '

'They were very, very sorry,' Nicola said again, beaming with pride. 'They sent a special message to everyone, saying how sorry they were. Anyway.' She shrugged. 'They're gone now, so there's not much point in fussing.'

Ecgbert(Sir) said: 'I agree with Nicola. No point in fussing. However – as I say, somebody really ought to check out what they've carted off in the way of swag ... I don't suppose you noticed anything special about their suitcases, Nicola? Did your friends appear to be struggling much, getting them into the car?'

Nicola said: 'You're being typically silly, Ecgbert. As usual. And no. I did not notice anything special. Just because they're Russian, you don't have to be racist. Not all Russians are thieves. In case you didn't know ... '

'*Russian?*' repeated Ecgbert(Sir). 'What are you talking about? Since when were they Russian? Trudy, am I missing something? Why did no one tell me they were Russian? I've never met any Russians. I would have had so many questions.'

Alice giggled. Partly because she was a little stoned. She had no idea if he was being serious.

'You are mistaken. Those guys, they are not Russian,' Frederica said. 'Ecgbert is correct. "Putin" is an actor. From UK. Of course. My sister tell me before she die. She know this as soon as she see him.'

'Whaaaaaat?' India was flabbergasted.

Egbert(Mr), too, could hardly believe his ears.

Esmé abandoned any pretence at being interested in his magazine. 'Frederica,' he said, 'thank you for this. I had suspected as much. I must say they never did strike me as very Russian.'

'Of course they're *Russian*,' said Nicola furiously. 'You're all just being racist. As usual. Bunny Rostovsky is as Russian as ... ' She couldn't think of anything Russian to compare her with. 'Those furry hats,' she muttered uncertainly.

251

Luckily, no one was listening. Egbert(Mr) was finally waking up to what his cousin had said about the display cabinet. Had the Todes been robbed? Under their own noses? How did Ecgbert(Sir) know this?

'It doesn't matter, does it, *how* I know,' Ecgbert(Sir) said – cleverly. He winked at Alice. 'All I'm saying is, someone ought to check it out. Don't you think, Trudy?'

Alice nodded.

'Also,' continued Sir Ecgbert, 'Nicola, did you happen to notice what train they got on? Are they on the train to London, because if they are, and they've run off with lots of our kit, then we should . . . ' He paused. Ecgbert(Sir) couldn't bring himself to finish the thought.

'. . . Call the police?' said Alice. She chortled. And then snorted.

He rolled his eyes. 'Actually I was thinking the station-master – or better yet, the ticket collector. If we can get a mobile for the ticket collector, that would be ideal. He's bound to have one.'

Egbert(Mr) held up a hand. 'Let's just take a moment to assess the situation first, shall we?' he said. 'Before we get anyone else involved.'

Esmé agreed. They should try to find out what, if anything, had been taken.

It was decided that Egbert should check out the chapel and the Yellow Saloon; India, the Chinese Dining Room, the Knights' Parlour, and the East Ballroom; Alice, the glass cabinets in the Octagonal morning room, the Library, the Sing-Song Room and the Jade Drawing Room; Ecgbert(Sir) the Long Gallery, where there were many treasures on display, and Nicola the Great Hall. If any obvious gaps were discovered in the cabinets, then action would have to be taken. Egbert(Mr) reminded everyone not to panic. He was mindful of numerous insurance clauses and sub-clauses. Depending on quantity and quality of stolen goods – if indeed there were any – it might, he said, be simpler to 'manage the situation in-house'.

'Good thinking,' said Ecgbert(Sir), standing up. 'Also, frankly, we've got a hell of a lot of kit. We probably wouldn't miss it, anyway. We could probably go for years, not missing whatever junk they've made off with. Whereas – I don't know about you, but I am already concerned about missing dinner. I'm starving.' He looked around him. Still no sign of any Tysedales. No sign of Piers. 'Where is everyone anyway?'

Talk of the Devil.

Enter the dreaded Adele, smiling symmetrically, wearing a wrap dress, neatly fitted over her muscular body, and on her feet, some perfectly matching shoes with quite high heels but not very. Not a hair out of place on that smiling head of hers. Not an unruly piece of flesh anywhere on her body. The dress was from Reiss. She was carrying a copy of the most recent version of her book about Apes and Unicorns, which she handed to Egbert(Mr). Everyone had to stand around and listen while Egbert flicked through it, feebly, and assured her how much he was looking forward to reading it.

'Come on!' said Ecgbert(Sir). 'Are we going to find out what's been stolen or aren't we? Seriously I'd much rather we found out after dinner.'

THE CHINESE DRAWING ROOM

9.07 P.M.

They reconvened, post investigation. So far as anyone could tell, the 'Russians' had not stolen anything. All the things that Alice and Carfizzi had removed from Bunny's suitcase and returned to their rightful place remained in their rightful place.

Nicola, especially, felt vindicated.

'I told you they were Russian,' she said.

'*Obviously*, Nicola, that doesn't follow,' said Ecgbert(Sir).

'And I hope,' she continued, 'that you're all feeling silly for jumping to your racist conclusions. Just because they're quote-unquote "foreign" and/or diverse, doesn't *automatically* make them robbers.'

It was definitely time for dinner. Charlie Tysedale had made an appearance at last, overdressed in a dinner jacket, apologising for his lateness and claiming to have fallen asleep in the bath. And then, at last, in sidled Tippee: present in body, if not in spirit or mind. He tucked himself and his iPad into a surly corner of the room, and sat there, very still, looking even more wretched than usual.

Alice felt sorry for him. She said: 'Hello there, Tippee! I was wondering where you'd got to. I thought you might have got lost in this massive house. Very easy to do. I still get lost in it. What have you been up to?' He didn't appear to hear her. Or at any rate, he didn't reply. She tried again. She asked him how his online tutorial in Classical history had gone, and he said: 'Can't remember,' but he didn't look up.

India watched this exchange (if that's what it was) with half a mind. There was plenty going on in the other half – why was Charlie wearing a dinner jacket? Was Adele's body made of metal? Why wasn't Nicola wearing her face-visor? Putin was a funny name. Where was Piers? Should they go into dinner without him? Why hadn't Adele allowed Tippee to eat dinner earlier, with Passion and Ludo? . . . And then, from nowhere in that busy mind, there came an arrow, tipped with horror. The most appalling realisation.

Putin had seemed awfully taken by the sketches she'd shown him earlier. She'd got a bit bored, watching him stare at them. After about half an hour – or maybe ten minutes. After a couple of minutes, she'd left him to stare at the wretched sketches alone, and gone off to have the bath.

Should she mention this to anyone?

Maybe not.

Maybe she'd pop up to the East Wing later. Just sort of check everything was still in place.

She said, vaguely, to the room: 'Does anyone know where the Rostovskys live, or anything? Do we know where they've actually gone?'

It turned out nobody did. Egbert(Mr) thought they lived

in Primrose Hill. Nicola was adamant that they didn't live in London at all, but failed to come up with an alternative location. Alice said she thought Bunny had mentioned living in France, but she couldn't swear to it. Charlie Tysedale said: 'Pentonville', which – out of nowhere – made his miserable son snigger.

Adele said: '*Tippee!*'

He returned to his iPad.

'Well, anyway,' India said brightly, 'they're gone now! We may never know where! Very rude of them to rush off like that, just before dinner. Let's not think about them any more. Let's *eat*! I don't know where Piers has got to, he'll just have to catch up.'

THE RED DINING ROOM

9.17 P.M.

t was outrageously late for dinner. They couldn't wait any longer. Those guests that had bothered to turn up followed India into the Red Dining Room, where Mr Carfizzi had, unusually, already put out the first course, it seemed. Or maybe the main course. India noticed this – the salver and cloche on the side, the empty soup bowls on the table – and felt vaguely confused.

You didn't serve soup on a salver. Obviously. And yet there were clearly soup plates on the table ... Maybe they weren't having soup? Carfizzi was obviously in a terrible bait, due to the lateness of dinner. And with good reason. India assumed, inasmuch as she assumed anything, that the food, as arranged, had been laid out in unspoken protest at the chaotic dinner hour. No doubt all would become clear.

She urged everyone to sit down. 'Mr Carfizzi's obviously furious,' she said. 'Please, everyone, hurry up and sit down.'

Frederica, beaming and beautiful, rubbed her hands

257

together in anticipation. 'I wonder what's for dinner,' she said. 'I am *starving!*'

'You're in a very good mood,' observed Charlie Tysedale sourly. 'Wonder why?'

Adele said: 'Charlie, there's no need for that.'

His face distorted. He seemed almost to gag with dislike. Adele readjusted the bow that fastened dress to metallic body, and asked Tippee if he'd washed his hands. Esmé noted all this, and thought to himself that, even if his ex-wife had been a money-grubbing bitch – it could be worse. He could have been married to Adele.

Egbert(Mr) stood at the head of the table and pinged his glass. He said: 'When you've all sat down, I'd like to make a little announcement ... '

'Oh Eggzie, not *again*,' India groaned. 'You made a very long announcement at lunch, and it didn't go down terribly well. Let's just eat, for heaven's sake.'

Egbert(Mr) frowned apologetically: 'All right, but I just wanted to say – what with all the fuss about Piers getting Rospo, I didn't think we made enough of the good news about – Elizabetta ... '

'What good news? She was murdered, Egbert,' Alice said. 'I didn't think there was any good news?'

'I mean,' Egbert(Mr) clarified, 'that now we know they've arrested someone ... it must mean everyone here is innocent! I don't know about you, but I think the weekend has been a teeny bit *tinged*, as it were ... by none of us being quite sure who to trust, but now here we are. The Russians have split ... All we have left are the good guys! Personally, I think that's something to celebrate. No?'

Ecgbert(Sir), waiting to take his seat, said: 'Egbert you're turning into one of those bores who have to keep making announcements. That last announcement, if you actually think about it, was completely unnecessary ... ' As he spoke, and since he was standing beside it, wondering what was for supper, Sir Ecgbert lifted the silver cloche – only slightly, because lifting silver cloches prematurely was, in his experience, the sort of thing that tended to land a Tode in trouble.

So he bent down and peered inside.

Stayed very, very still.

Whispered: 'Trudy ... Psst, *Trudy* ... '

She didn't hear him. She was saying something to Tippee, trying to get him to smile.

Slowly, carefully, Ecgbert(Sir) replaced the cloche. Still with his back to the room, he breathed in. And out. Felt the earth's energy travelling up, through his brogues, his legs, stomach and so on. He looked up at the Gainsborough hanging above the sideboard: a painting of the 5th Bart, with a shotgun hanging from one arm, and a dead rabbit from the other. In all these years, Ecgbert(Sir) had never really looked at the painting. Now – he saw the dead rabbit, floppy and murdered, and the killer 5th Bart, with his gloating face. Ecgbert couldn't take his eyes off the wretched thing. What was *wrong* with people? What was *wrong* with his family? Why were they always on killing sprees?

'Nicola,' he said, with his face still to the wall. 'Nicola, you *cannot* keep doing this. It's not fair on people. You've got to get a grip.'

THE KITCHEN

9.23 P.M.

M r Carfizzi had reminded India that dinner was served well over an hour ago. If she couldn't persuade her guests to turn up in time to eat it, then so be it. The food was already ruined. And now Mrs Carfizzi had gone on strike. He was a little afraid of her nowadays, at the best of times. When she was angry (as she never used to be) there was no knowing what she would do, or whom she might run off with. Mr Carfizzi never did find out any details from the last time she did it, but the day she returned to him was without doubt the happiest of his life.

The point being, he didn't want to lose her again. These days, he tiptoed around her. If Mrs Carfizzi was angry about something, Mr Carfizzi looked sharp. Things had changed.

And already, at 8.07 p.m., Mrs Carfizzi was angry. At 8.15, when there were still no guests in the dining room, Mrs Carfizzi had taken off her apron and left the kitchen. She was currently lying in bed in the downstairs flat she shared with her husband, watching *Selling Sunset.*

Mr Carfizzi had done his best to cover for her. He had laid the table and kept the soup simmering. At 8.30 p.m. he'd snuck down to the flat and tried to lure her back upstairs to the kitchen again.

At that point, Mrs Carfizzi was in the bath. For ages, he sat on the carpet outside the bathroom, speaking in wheedling Italian, pleading with her to advise him what to do about the pudding. She'd refused to answer. At 9.03 she'd unlocked the bathroom door, dressed in a navy blue flannel nightdress he'd never seen before, swept past him to her separate bedroom and locked the door on him once again.

'OK, my poppet,' he said to her. '*Sei stanca, cara mia. Non ti preoccupare.* I will take care of everything. *Sogni d'oro!*'

She didn't even reply.

And so here he was at 9.23, back in the kitchen, taking care of everything. The soup was warm. The venison – was it over-cooked? He would leave it to stand on the side. First he should take in the soup.

The guests must be hungry, he thought. He could hear them in the dining room, still in the process of sitting them-selves down.

Nicola sounded angry . . . Well, *didn't she always?* (He smiled affectionately.)

He placed the silver tureen beside the stove, and slowly, carefully, poured in the soup. He put the lid on the tureen and the tureen onto a trolley, being too old, these days, to carry it himself. He wheeled the trolley to the door of the dining room. A swing door. He continued wheeling.

Most of the guests still hadn't sat down. Annoying of them.

He stopped wheeling. To his right was the side table, the Gainsborough painting with the dead rabbit, and Sir Ecgbert

261

and Nicola, facing one another, blocking his path. He lifted the tureen from the trolley, and waited for the path to clear. Nicola, he noted, looked even more outraged than usual.

'I RESENT THAT IMPLICATION, ECGBERT,' she was saying. She was very angry indeed. 'HOW DARE YOU?'

For some reason Nicola was holding a silver cloche. It confused Carfizzi. Had the guests already skipped to the main course? Impossible! The venison was still in the kitchen.

Nicola's extraordinary rage, also the large silver cloche, also Sir Ecgbert's long body combined to prevent Carfizzi, or indeed anyone else, from noticing what was behind her on the sideboard. Only Ecgbert had seen it, and he, unlike his sister, looked quite white: as if – indeed –

Sir Ecgbert swooned.

His long, thin body collapsed into a heap on the dining-room carpet.

A beat.

Quietly, carefully, Nicola returned the cloche to its place on the salver.

A beat.

Tippee Tysedale stepped forward. He stepped over Ecgbert's long body, and quietly, carefully, lifted the cloche from the salver once again.

And then the following people screamed:

Charlie Tysedale
Adele Tysedale
Frederica Ranaldini
Egbert(Mr) Tode
India Tode
Alice Tode

262

Esmé Tode
Mr Carfizzi

Tippee Tysedale did not scream. He was mesmerised.

A smell of methane.

Lady Tode appeared, dressed in flamenco dress (Balenciaga). 'Oh my good Lord! Leo! Do look! *Leo!*' she cried. '*You must have a look at this!*'

An expulsion of dismay: of wild, ghostly frustration. The table shook. Leonardo da Vinci swept through the dining room, faster than sound but slower than light.

What had he missed? How could he not have seen this coming?

'The killer!' he cried. 'The killer has struck *again*. It's a cert. Make a path, Ecgbert! Alice, please to remove the fruit and vegetable garnishings. I MUST SEE THE NECK!'

On the silver salver, where Carfizzi might have been about to put the venison, there balanced the severed head of Piers Slayer-Wilson-Tite. Someone had tried to decorate the dish. There were slices of apple and a few lettuce leaves wedged beneath his chin, and a thick slice of orange stuck to one of his open eyes. And somehow, in spite everything, he was smirking.

THE RED DINING ROOM

9.37 P.M.

Another meal abandoned before anyone had a chance to eat it. Mr Carfizzi managed not to drop the soup on the carpet, at least. He did, however, in the initial shock, rest it directly onto the polished mahogany dining table, and now there would be a mark on the wood for ever: a memorial, or so the butler would come to look at it, to his lack of professionalism in a time of crisis.

In the meantime, he rescued the situation as soon as he could, scooped up the tureen and scuttled back into the kitchen to empty it and wash up. They would not be wanting soup for supper now.

Tippee, holding the cloche aloft, looked around the room at each of the horrified faces.

He said: 'He was already dead. I didn't kill him.' But nobody heard him.

'Piers, oh my Piers!' sobbed Frederica.

'The Russians!' cried Esmé.

'Is he *dead*?' asked India.

Alice dropped to her knees. She bent over Ecgbert(Sir)'s long body, slapped his cheeks and pumped his heart. He opened his eyes.

'I didn't do it,' Tippee said again, in a small voice.

Charlie stepped over Ecgbert(Sir), and took the cloche from his son's hand. In a rare moment of paternal engagement, he patted Tippee's shoulder. He bent down and muttered into his son's ear: 'Tippee, I wouldn't say any more. Don't say any more. Don't say a word . . . ' Tippee looked at his father, his face expressionless. 'Darling boy,' Charlie said in a louder voice, so everyone could hear, 'this is all a bit horrid. I think you should go to bed.'

Tippee didn't move. Charlie cast around for Adele, normally on top of situations. At that moment she was looking a long way from on top of anything. No symmetry anywhere. *Terror* on her face. She looked, Charlie thought, even uglier than usual.

'Adele!' he barked at her. 'For Christ's sake. Can't we do something about the boy?'

She nodded. The features snapped back into place. She stepped over Ecgbert(Sir), still causing an obstruction, and took hold of Tippee's upper arm. He wasn't much shorter than she was, but he allowed himself to be yanked away. She led him to the door.

Leonardo cried out in frustration. 'For pity's sake, would *somebody* please remove this silver hood? How am I to examine his injuries when the man's head is all under cover?' His fury caused the crystal chandelier above the dining table to rattle.

Alice, normally so careful not to speak to the ghosts when others were present, forgot herself, briefly. She resented Leo's insensitivity. His obsession with the facts obscured his understanding, she felt, of the myriad emotions in the room. She, personally, had never liked or trusted Piers. Nevertheless, there were people who did care about him – possibly. In any case, only a monster wouldn't feel sorry to see a person they once knew reduced to such a state.

'It's pretty obvious what the injuries are,' she snapped. 'Nobody wants to keep looking at him ... except you.'

'Except who?' asked Egbert(Mr), finding his voice at last. He thought Alice was looking at him, albeit with slightly crossed eyes. He and Leo were standing on the same spot. 'I certainly don't want to keep looking at him. And actually ... much as I hate to say this, I really do think we should call the police ...'

The dreaded Adele had dragged Tippee as far as the open door. But for once, it seemed Tippee was fighting back. He stamped his foot. She shoved him. He refused to leave. 'TIPPEE TYSEDALE!' bellowed Charlie, from the other side of the room. 'DO AS YOUR MOTHER TELLS YOU, AND GO TO BED!'

Tippee jumped. Terrified. He scampered into the outer hallway, more frightened of his father, it seemed, than of a big old house hiding a headless corpse.

'You still need to brush your teeth, Tippee,' Adele shouted after him. 'I'll come up and see you in a second.'

When the door was closed, Charlie turned to Egbert(Mr). 'Before you call the police,' he said, 'we need to get Tippee away from here.'

Egbert(Mr) said: 'That's going to be rather difficult.'

'I don't want him talking to the police,' Charlie said. 'He absolutely must not speak with the police.'

Geraldine, Lady Tode, until this moment, uncharacteristically, too astonished by proceedings to take any part, gave one of her disagreeable laughs: as if she knew all the answers, which she did not. 'The boy's virtually admitted to doing it. Was no one listening? Of course you must call the police.'

Ecgbert(Sir), still on the floor but fully conscious now, said: 'No, he didn't, Granny. He explicitly said he *didn't* do it. *You* obviously weren't listening. Don't be so horrid.'

Methane.

Sir Ecgbert sat up. He turned to Nicola. 'Nicola – I think we need to find the Russians.'

'On the subject of the Russians . . . ' India said, looking uncomfortable. She cleared her throat. ' . . . I think I may have made a boob . . . '

('A "*BOOB*"?' said Lady Tode.)

' . . . Before supper, I found Putin in your study, Egbert. I don't know what he was doing in there. But for some reason I ended up showing him the silver safe sketches . . . And now I think about it he was obviously super blown away by them. So I think he may have stolen them . . . '

'Whaaat?' Egbert(Mr) replied, clasping his hair. 'Darling, Munchie . . . You mean the da Vinci sketches . . . ?'

'No. The ones they found in the silver safe – They weren't – I would have remembered if they were da Vinci . . . They weren't, were they? Why didn't you say?'

Egbert noted her dismay. He said: 'Well – look – never mind. They hadn't been verified, anyway. Never mind. You mustn't worry, Munch.'

'Phew. Well. I'm jolly glad I got it off my chest, anyway ...
I suppose if Putin had thought they were da Vinci he would
have been super determined to take them. But how would he
have known?'

Egbert(Mr) didn't reply. He held his hair and shook his head.

'And I suppose,' she continued, 'seeing how things have
turned out, poor Piers must have caught him and Bunny on
their escape ... So in a way it's partly my fault ... '

'Nonsense, Munchie!' said Egbert(Mr) emphatically.

India turned to Nicola. 'Please, Nicola, don't take this as
racist ... Just ... Did you – by any chance – make a note of
which train they got on?'

Nicola appeared to be as shaken as the next person by the
turn of events. She told India, in a perfectly normal and inform-
ative manner, that – in fact she hadn't dropped the Rostovskys
quite as far as the train station, after all. They had insisted on
being left on the ring road on the way in to Todeister. Nicola
said she had put this down to their excellent manners, because
they didn't want to cause her unnecessary bother, and they
were aware she risked being late for dinner. But now – what
with Piers, and the stolen da Vinci etchings – she had to admit
that maybe they were not being as straightforward as it had
appeared. She was almost apologetic.

Esmé said: 'We need to call the police.'

A silence fell. Or it fell for most of the room. Alice and
Ecgbert were forced to listen to Leonardo, whining. The stolen
sketches had not distracted him one iota. (There was always
someone in the world claiming to have found something of his
in their attic/silver safe.) He wanted someone to lift the cloche.
If they would only let him examine the head, he would be able
to tell them how long Piers had been dead.

This might have been useful if, in fact, almost everyone in the party had not seen Piers alive in the last few hours. It wasn't yet known – clearly – which among them had seen him last, but they'd all seen him at around 4ish, towards the end of the shoot.

Leo said: 'I beg you, grant me a deco at once. Alice? Sir Ecgbert? I want to examine for any puncture around the jugular, if the bombsite is not too matted in blood and guts. Above the jugular, indeed. Elizabetta was punctured beneath the jawline. Thus.' Leonardo pointed to a corresponding spot, somewhere in the midst of his massive beard.

'Was she?' Ecgbert(Sir) asked. 'You never said so before.'

'I did,' Leo replied. 'Geraldine, tell your grandson how many times I said it before. Sir Ecgbert, Alice – one of you, lift the lid! Do it!'

Alice wasn't easily freaked out. But she didn't much fancy seeing that head ever again. She said to Ecgbert, 'You do it.'

Egbert(Mr) said: 'Who are you two talking to? Do what? Said what before? ... *Ecgbert! What are you doing? Don't do that! Put that thing down! Leave it down!*'

But Trudy's wish was Sir Ecgbert's command. He had lifted the lid. Leo released a huge sigh of satisfaction, and once again, the chandelier shook. His pleasure was slightly disgusting. Even Lady Tode thought so. 'Would you contain yourself, Leo darling? Curiosity is an admirable quality. I'm not suggesting it isn't. Nevertheless – the man was supposed to be joining them for dinner. Perhaps a little sensitivity ... '

Leo ignored her. He said to Ecgbert(Sir): 'I can't see everything. You need to move the apple slices. Move them!'

'Say please,' Ecgbert said, irritably.

Egbert(Mr) said, 'Please!'

Ecgbert(Sir) ignored his cousin. He gagged a little as he lifted the nearest apple slice. Everyone in the room, except Alice, yelled at him. He was tampering with evidence, they said – or words to that effect. And yet still, none of them stopped him. Still, no one called the police.

'Move the greenery. Do it!'

He moved the lettuce leaf.

Frederica said: 'What the fack, Ecgbert? Wat are you doin'?'

Ecgbert, not enjoying himself, said to Leo: 'Have you seen enough yet?'

'YES!' shouted Egbert(Mr). 'For heaven's sake, Ecgbert. We've all seen more than enough.'

Leo gave another gusty sigh. The lettuce leaf rippled in Sir Ecgbert's hand, and the thick orange slice plopped from Piers' eye, onto the silver platter.

India screamed.

Egbert(Mr) cried: 'Oh, Munchie!'

Leo said: 'I have seen enough. It is the same killer. The same system of the killing – you see the puncture? You see it?' Leo pointed, Ecgbert(Sir) peered, but saw nothing.

'I need my specs,' he said. 'Alice, can you see it? . . . Can you bear to look?'

Alice's specs were hanging around her neck. She took them off and passed them to Ecgbert(Sir).

'There!' said Leo, pointing.

Lady Tode stood beside them. 'Yes, I see it,' she said. 'A tiny puncture. Needle puncture. See it? Slightly swollen. Do look.'

Ecgbert(Sir) bent a little closer. 'Ah-HA!' he said. 'I see it!' It was just in time. Egbert(Mr) had come up behind him, taken the cloche from his cousin's hand and replaced it firmly onto the tray. Piers' head and punctured neck were hidden again.

'I'm sorry,' Egbert(Mr) said. 'I don't mean to be bossy. But we can't just stand around doing nothing. Plus, the Russians are getting away. Every moment we do nothing, they get further away. It's not ideal. Charlie, I do appreciate ... But I'm going to have to call the police.' He was already patting his pocket, reaching for his phone.

The following people asked/yelled at him to wait:

Charlie Tysedale
Frederica Ranaldini
Esmé Tode
Sir Ecgbert Tode
India Tode
And – most forcefully of all (though most people couldn't hear him) – Leonardo da Vinci, who wanted more time to solve the crime himself.

Egbert(Mr) looked at the Tode faction in bewilderment. He understood, he thought better than anyone, the desire to keep their family name out of the public eye. But the situation was extreme. He looked at his wife. '... Munchie? ... Not you, either?'

India shrugged. Of course they would have to call the police eventually. Just, maybe they could put it off for a bit? 'It's just they always seem to be barging in,' she said, 'taking over the house, wrecking the vibe ...'

'I think the vibe,' said her husband, 'has already been pretty wrecked.'

'I'm with India!' cried Ecgbert(Sir). 'They'll barge in, make an enormous fuss, get the wrong end of the stick, as always, fail to find the Russians ... make us all feel like we're the killers ...'

'We must *never* trust the police!' cried Esmé, punching the air, remembering his years in Australia.

Ecgbert(Sir) nodded. 'Plus – if young Tippee is mixed up in it – which sadly he may be – we may want to tamper with the evidence before they get here.'

Adele said: 'Tippee has nothing whatsoever to do with all this. How dare you?'

Lady Tode gave another of her disagreeable hoot-laughs. Ecgbert(Sir) shot her a look and she quietened down.

'Tell them we need to take stock of the situation,' Leonardo prompted.

'We need to take stock of the situation,' Ecgbert(Sir) repeated. 'See what we can straighten out between ourselves first – Trudy? I know you love bringing in the police any chance you can . . . What do you think? Are you on board with putting them off, just for a while?'

Alice nodded: 'Ecgbert's right. We need . . .' she said, 'First and foremost, we need to look out for Tippee.' She glanced at Adele, whose face was getting red. 'Just in case,' she added quickly.

'So,' said Leonardo. 'Question Numero Uno: Where is the rest of the body? Ecgbert, Alice. Ask them, where is the body?'

It was a good question. And not one to which anyone present was likely to admit knowing the answer. Lady Tode knew the house better than anyone, and she moved faster than any of the mortals present. She said she would investigate. A puff of green, and off she went.

'Look in the larder,' Ecgbert(Sir) called after her. 'That's where we found the last one.'

'Ecgbert, for the millionth time,' said Egbert, 'who are you talking to?'

'We need,' explained Alice, 'to find the rest of the body.'

And already – Lady Tode was back in the room.

'As I thought,' she said, 'his body is, of course, exactly where one would expect it to be.'

And then came Leo. Faster than sound, but slower than light. They had travelled and returned together – or separately. It was hard to tell. The headless body was in the bathtub, he reported, in the bathroom that adjoined Queen Charlotte's Bedroom – which, until recently, of course, had been Bunny and Putin's bedroom.

'But this is almost too obvious,' said Leo, rubbing his chin.

'Good point, Alice,' Esmé said. 'Where's the rest of the body? Also. I think the weapons – we need to find whatever weapons were used.'

Leonardo rolled his eyes. 'Tell them about the puncture! Why haven't you told them about the puncture already?'

Ecgbert said: 'We haven't had time.'

'Darling, tell them!' said Lady Tode. 'They're gawping at you. You must try to keep the idiots in the loop.'

Ecgbert(Sir) said: 'Turns out the body is in Bunny and Putin's bathtub.'

Frederica gasped.

Ecgbert(Sir) glanced at her. 'Sorry,' he said. 'Also ... Alice and I have noticed ... there are some similarities in the, er, *neck* area of both murder victims, Elizabetta and Piers. They both have – had – have ... had ... Anyway, teeny little puncture marks at the neck. As if they had been injected with some-thing ... *However* ...' Leonardo stood beside him, short arms crossed over portly belly, nodding approvingly. Ecgbert(Sir) glanced at him resentfully. '... *However*, as we all know, noth-ing was found in Elizabetta's body. So it's probably nothing.'

Leo said: 'It is most certainly not nothing!'

Frederica said: 'How do you know this?'

'What?' Ecgbert(Sir) replied. 'Well, go and see for yourself, if you don't believe me. His head's under there. You can see the puncture quite clearly. And his body's in the Russians' bathtub ... However, I don't actually know ...' He turned to his grandmother. 'What is the situation up there, roughly? Is it a horrible mess? Blood and everything?'

'Fortunately,' replied Lady Tode, 'most of the blood has drained down the plughole ... There's a teeny axe, also in the tub. It's resting on top of the body, isn't it, Leo? Just a miniature axe –' She held her elegant hands less than a foot apart. The diamonds on her fingers caught the light. 'I'm assuming it's the one Car Fizzy keeps in the log room for chopping kindling ... But obviously one doesn't *know* ...'

'I think Ecgbert's losing the plot,' said Esmé. 'And by the way, I'm not blaming you, Ecgbert. In the circs any one of us might go a bit doolally ... Even so, the Russian bathtub makes a lot of sense. It's not a bad suggestion. Someone should go up and check.'

Lady Tode continued. 'In any case, Car Fizzy would recognise it, I'm sure. Alice, you might recognise it. As I say, it's just a teeny little axe ...'

Egbert(Mr) said he would check out the Russians' bathroom. He turned to Esmé, hesitated. He turned to Charlie, hesitated. He turned to Ecgbert(Sir). Finally he turned to the dreaded Adele. 'Adele,' he said, 'maybe you could hold the fort, as it were? I'll be back in half a tick.'

Actually, for mortals, the journey from Red Dining Room to Queen Charlotte's Bedroom and back again took more than half a tick. At a brisk walking pace, it took a minimum of ten minutes. Egbert only broke into a run when wearing the correct breathable quick-dri sportswear, and only when there was a clearly defined sporting prize or target in the offing. So – he stalked off at a brisk walking pace, looking more middle aged than he realised; dreading what might lie ahead.

The room fell silent for a moment. Perhaps, for a moment, the tragedy was allowed to sink in. Piers, after all, had been a youngish man – at any rate, not an old one; and he'd been in a phenomenally good mood that afternoon. Now – *this*. Struck down in his prime, and more than likely by Russians, to boot.

'He didn't have much luck, did he?' India said. 'First his wife gets murdered ... And I'm guessing a lot of us couldn't help wondering if he'd played a part in that ... which he obviously didn't,' she added quickly. '*Obviously*. We know that now. And then, just as things were turning around for him ... *this*. It's amazing anyone could do anything so cruel ...'

'So true,' said Adele.

'Heartbreaking,' said Esmé.

'It's a wicked old world,' said Charlie.

Nicola perked up. 'Can I just remind everyone not to jump to conclusions regarding the Russians and/or Russians in general? Just because the body's likely to be in their bathroom—'

'And just because they've done a runner,' said Esmé, rolling his eyes.

Alice cleared her throat. 'I probably should have mentioned it before,' she said. 'Earlier today Mr Carfizzi and I did find a few bits and bobs in Bunny's suitcase—'

'Alice, don't!' interrupted Lady Tode. 'There is no need. You'll only complicate matters.'

'You what?' Nicola glared at Alice. 'What were you doing, looking in Bunny's suitcase in the first place?'

Alice stared at her dumbly. With so much else going on, she'd not prepared an answer for that. What possible excuse could she have for rifling through a guest's suitcase? 'Well, I ...'

Lady Tode sighed. 'I told you.'

Leonardo said: 'Tell her the suitcase fell open.'

'The suitcase fell open ...'

Leonardo nodded. '... While Mr Carfizzi was lugging said cargo to the bitch's flophouse.'

'While Mr Carfizzi ... was ... taking Bunny's cases up to the bedroom,' Alice said. 'The suitcase fell open. He and I agreed that the best thing to do would be to replace the items, and sort of pretend it never happened ... I realise now,' she added, 'that that was probably a mistake ...'

'Alice, you twit!' cried India, delightedly. It appeared she wasn't the only one to have aided and abetted the Rostovskys on their robbing spree. 'Are you crazy?! You should have reported them! Never mind! They're gone now. The damage is done.' She sighed. '... I wonder what Egbert's up to? He's taking ages.'

'*You* say "never mind",' said Nicola. 'I think the police may have something more to say about it. Frankly. Just because they were diverse you assumed they were robbers and you went through their private luggage. That's racist assault. That's hate crime ... I, for one, am not OK with that, Alice ... I thought better from you.'

'Number One,' said Esmé, 'you're an idiot. Number Two ... they've just murdered poor old Piers. Also – possibly – Elizabetta. And you just helped them to escape.'

'*Possibly* Elizabetta?' exploded Leo. 'Of course they killed Elizabetta!'

'So – basically, Nicola ... [Esmé was still talking] I'll thank

276

you to put a sock in it. Just this once. Wind your trunk in. We've got enough on our plate as it is.' He turned to Alice. 'However . . . Alice – maybe . . . I dunno . . . perhaps you might prefer to keep that piece of info to yourself? . . . It just might be easier for you and Car Fizzy . . . '

Adele said: 'With respect, Esmé, I actually think that information might be useful to the police. It's added evidence, isn't it?'

Until this point Frederica had been sitting quite quietly, dabbing a tissue to her eyes and saying very little. For some reason this last comment from Adele made her explode with rage. Why were they sitting around, doing nothing, waiting for Egbert, discussing suitcases, while every moment Piers' killers were getting further away? Why was no one calling the police? Why had the Rostovskys not already been arrested?'

Of course it was convenient for everyone to talk as if they were quite certain of the culprit. But in actual fact, in the back of everyone's minds, there remained many unspoken, uncomfortable questions. Why, for example, would the Rostovskys bother to kill Piers when they could just as easily have escaped the house and grounds with their booty, leaving Piers intact? He wouldn't have tried to stop them. He wouldn't have cared two hoots. Anyone who ever spent five minutes with Piers would know, for certain, that there was nothing selfless or heroic about him. So why would they have killed him?

That was one question hovering in people's minds.

Not to mention several other lingering suspicions.

For example: Esmé couldn't help wondering about Nicola. Given her unusual lateness to dinner, her inexplicable decision to drop the Rostovskys on the Todeister ring road just before dinner (if it was even true), her fury with poor Piers at lunchtime regarding his 'jumping the queue' in being given Rospo ... Also it was hard for Esmé to completely dismiss his sister's track record in the field of killing people. She seemed to like it.

Nicola, on the other hand, suspected everyone, and, above all, Tippee. She had been brooding bitterly, post Adele's comment regarding 'added evidence' against the Russians. She said suddenly, after quite a long silence, 'Seeing as how your son is so obviously tangled up in all this, it makes perfect sense, you wanting "added evidence" to deflect suspicions away from him.'

Adele was mortified. Her cheeks burned. Her chin dropped. 'How *dare* you?'

'... I'm just saying,' continued Nicola, quite unabashed. 'Everyone's so keen to say it was the Russians. What if it wasn't? What if it was Tippee? And actually the more I think about it the more I think it probably was.'

The genie had been released. An explosion of accusations followed.

Adele waved a muscular arm, fully outraged now: 'It was probably *you*, Nicola. Frankly. That was my first thought, even in Rospo, when they found Elizabetta. I thought it was bound to be you.'

Esmé said: 'It probably *was* you, Nicola. Tbh. I'm not saying that's what I'll be telling the police ... But seriously, I don't think you should be throwing accusations around the place. Given your history. Everyone knows about – *you know what* – they're just being polite about it. But let's face it, you're the only person here who has actually killed before.'

Ecgbert(Sir) thought this was offensive (despite harbouring a few unspoken suspicions himself). Also, after the life he'd lived being a lanky, mostly unloved misfit, any kind of bullying made him see red. He snapped at his brother: 'Leave her out of it, Esmé. It was probably you, anyway!'

Charlie laughed.

Ecgbert(Sir) said, 'Or *you*, Charlie. Most likely it was probably *you*. Both of you, together. Trying to get your grubbers on Rospo.'

'Ecgbert, you are ridiculous!' Esmé smirked.

'Idiotic,' said Charlie. 'Utterly idiotic, and quite insulting.'

But Charlie and Esmé didn't look at each other. They both looked at the ground.

'At any rate,' Ecgbert(Sir) continued, quite surprised by their obvious shiftiness: perhaps he'd hit on something? 'It's more likely to be you two than Nicola. Leave her alone.'

A moment of silence. Charlie Tysedale was behaving oddly. Plus, there was no doubt he was a nasty piece of work.

Lady Tode voiced a roomful of thoughts when she said: 'Ecgbert is quite right. The Tysedale man has plenty of motive, after all.'

Alice nodded. She said to Charlie: 'Actually, it's not that idiotic, Charlie. There's no need to sneer.'

And then a light-bulb moment for India: a vivid flash of Charlie at the Hotel de Russie in Rome, passing Elizabetta that envelope of cash ... She said, 'Was Elizabetta blackmailing you, Charlie? Is that why you killed her? I saw you, in Rome. Giving her the cash. I'm not stupid, you know.'

Again, Charlie laughed.

They waited.

'Nothing to say?' asked Alice.

Charlie said: 'Absolutely not.'

Everyone looked at Charlie. Esmé said: 'Bloody hell, Charlie ...'

Charlie turned on him. 'Don't you "bloody hell" me, you useless prick. You know exactly what the cash was for. We discussed it at length.'

Esmé said: 'No, we didn't.'

Charlie said: 'Yes, we did.'

Esmé said: 'Did you kill Piers, too?'

Charlie said: 'Of course I bloody didn't. Did you?'

Esmé said: 'Don't be absurd!' And then, because everyone was still looking at him: '*No*. Of course I didn't.'

Ahhh, who to believe?

Frederica didn't appear to be interested in any of their theories. She was more exercised about the Rostovskys. 'Fack Charlie and his cash. It's not important. We know why he gave it to Elizabetta. He thinks to pay my family – Elizabetta trick him. Also she trick her family. Esmé and Charlie are wicked, like each other. It is more important, we find the—'

'Pardon me, but I think you're jumping to a few conclusions, Frederica,' said the dreaded Adele, cheeks burning bright. 'Please don't implicate my husband in your filthy family dealings. Thank you so much.'

Frederica laughed *in her face.*

Adele, cheeks scorching now, pulled out a mobile phone and waved it gently (symmetrically), at shoulder height. 'Before *any of you* says another word, attempting to implicate my family in this mess, you should all know, *all of you*, I have my lawyer on speed-dial.'

'PAH!' Frederica dismissed it. 'We are wasting time. All the time our so call "Rostovskys" are escaping. Why are you wasting time calling your lawyer? My phone is upstairs. Someone! Why aren't you calling the police?'

Nicola said, 'Actually *sorry*. Sorry to burst your bubble, Frederica. His name *was* Rostovsky. And by the way, in case you were wondering, no it hasn't escaped anyone's notice that you were having extra-marital sexual intercourse with Elizabetta's husband when Elizabetta suddenly turned up dead in the water. And also by the way, we all noticed you this morning, when you were literally punching Piers in the face, and now *he's* dead in the bath. So – whatever. Go figure. Just saying. I think *you* probably did it.'

Frederica lunged at Nicola. Esmé and Charlie tried to pull them apart, but then somehow, in the scrum, one of the men jabbed the other one, accidentally on purpose, and immediately they forgot about Frederica and Nicola and started punching each other instead. Ecgbert(Sir) yanked at Esmé, and pulled him back. Charlie used the moment to land his fist on Esmé's nose. Ecgbert(Sir) tall but not a natural wrestler, leapt ineptly to his brother's defence. Alice and India stood on the periphery, shouting at everyone to stop. Adele did nothing: paralysed by the anarchy.

Hearing the shouts, Mr Carfizzi ran in from the kitchen to see what he could do. Nothing. He could do nothing. The situation was out of control. Any moment now, someone would knock the salver and cloche, and Piers' head would roll onto the floor. Nobody wanted that. He decided he would transport it to the kitchen until everyone calmed down. So he tottered across to the sideboard, passing the scrum *en route*. But he was an old man. His balance wasn't what it was. His physical strength had never been up to much, and he'd aged significantly since the crisis with his wife a few years ago. He reached for the salver. Somebody's limb got caught up in the move. Carfizzi lost his balance. The cloche, the tray, the butler and Piers' head all fell to the floor.

Silence. Everyone stopped fighting. They watched the head rolling to a halt. And then the room shook, because Leonardo and Lady Tode were laughing so much, and so loudly. On the eastern wall, a nail popped out of the plasterwork, and a painting of a horse slipped its position 90 degrees and hung, sideways, horse's bottom to the carpet, nose towards heaven.

Very frightening. Very disturbing.

Lady Tode noticed and stopped laughing. 'Ecgbert! The Stubbs!' she cried.

But the painting hung and didn't fall. Piers' head stopped rolling. The crisis passed.

Nobody knew quite what to do.

It was a relief when the far door burst open and Egbert(Mr) walked in. He was looking pale and grim, and carrying, in one hand, a very small axe – or a hatchet – covered in blood. In the other hand, by the scruff of his neck, he was holding Tippee.

Adele said: 'Tippee!'

Tippee sent her a look of pure and perfect hatred.

Adele said: 'You are meant to be in *bed*!'

Egbert held up the hatchet: 'I'm afraid I've just taken this little axe off young Tippee,' he said.

'Oh *Tippee*,' said Carfizzi, his voice full of regret. 'What have you done?'

Tippee said: 'It wasn't me. I haven't done anything.'

'I found him on the landing. Unfortunately his bedroom is next to the Russians'. So – anyway – the poor chap was prob-ably just curious. Nevertheless, I thought it better he joined us downstairs. Keep him out of any more mischief . . . On the other matter ... *yes*. I popped into the Queen Charlotte bathroom. And unfortunately, Ecgbert, you were absolutely right, God knows how. Piers is indeed in the bathtub. But there's not a great deal of mess ... Most of the blood appears to have gone down the plughole. Which is a great plus ... '

Egbert(Mr) didn't want to incriminate the boy any more than he needed to. In fact, he'd not found Tippee on the landing. He'd found him in the Queen Charlotte bathroom, bent over the bathtub, in the process of cleaning the hatchet under the hot tap. When Egbert asked him what he was doing, Tippee had jumped out of his skin. Dropped the hatchet onto Piers' headless body. *Thunk*. All he could reply to Egbert's gentle questioning was: 'I didn't do it.'

Just then, Egbert(Mr) noticed Piers' head lying on the floor. His first instinct was a concern for the carpet: three-hundred-year-old silk, Chinese, itself as large as the ground floor of a decent-sized suburban house. He said: 'Oh God ... could someone ... ?' He stopped himself. Of course they couldn't. A man should never ask another man to do something he wasn't willing to do himself. Gentlemen's Code.

He laid the hatchet on the dining table. He released his hold on Tippee, and went, solemnly, to pick up the head.

The others stood and watched as he laid it back on the silver salver and covered it, yet again, with the cloche.

Tippee sidled closer to the hatchet. He seemed to be quite fascinated by it. Adele said: 'Tippee, leave the little axe alone. I don't know why Egbert brought you down here, or why you were out of bed. This is very unsuitable. Go back to bed at once.'

He ignored her.

Charlie said: 'Tippee, do as your mother says.'

Tippee looked at his father. He said, defiantly: 'I'm not going to bed next to that body. It's disgusting. I'm staying here.'

Egbert(Mr) turned to the parents. 'He has a point,' he said. 'It's probably a bit scary up there, all on his ownsome ... Maybe he could go into the kitchen with Mr Carfizzi and watch some telly, or something?'

Mr Carfizzi, his face full of regret, crossed the room. He reached out to put a hand on Tippee's shoulder. He said: 'Young man, why don't you come with me?'

But Tippee, the little axe clasped tight in his hand, leapt away from him.

'Tippee!' said his mother.

'I told you,' said Lady Tode. 'That boy is *awful*. He should be in an asylum.'

Leonardo da Vinci thought his friend was being unnecessarily spiteful. 'Silence!' he snapped, and immediately regretted it ... Lady Tode had quadrupled in size, and her mouth was gaping open. ' ... If it pleases you, Madam,' he amended. 'Please, to hush up, my friendliest. Geraldine, honey ... Let us hear the boy speak. He's a darling boy. I believe this.'

Tippee was already speaking. He was brandishing the hatchet, waving it this way and that, ordering everyone to stand back.

'I didn't do it!' he kept saying. 'I know you all think I did it, but I didn't. I didn't do it ... '

'Nobody thinks you did it, Tippee,' said his mother, edging towards him.

'LIAR!' he yelled. 'She's a LIAR!' He turned back to the others, directing his words mostly at Alice, whom he seemed to have identified as an ally, at last. 'Yes ... I did the last bit, with the little axe.'

Mr Carfizzi held his head in his hands, and groaned.

Tippee noticed this. 'But I didn't kill him,' he said.

Charlie had had enough. 'Tippee, you're talking drivel and you need to shut up. Of course you didn't kill him. And, my dear fellow, nor did you chop his head off.'

'I did! I axed it off with this axe. There's chips in the bath, where I hit the bathtub. You can see for yourself.'

'You didn't do anything of the kind,' said his father. 'Now put the axe down and *shut up.*'

'It's been a long day,' said the dreaded Adele. 'He's upset.'

'We're all upset,' pointed out Esmé. 'The point is ... Tippee – you admit to cutting off the poor guy's head, do you?'

'No, he doesn't,' Adele said. 'He misspoke.'

'Yes, I do,' said Tippee. 'I cut off his head. But Mummy killed him.'

'TIPPEE!' bellowed Charlie.

'She's *always killing people! I'm sick of it. She's got to stop!*'

'How *dare* you?' cried the dreaded Adele. She looked around the room, a hand to her heart. 'My own son! How could you, Tippee?' Her pretty face crumpled.

Frederica, exasperated, said: 'Why you all talkin' crap? It wasn't Tippee. He's just a boy. Of course it was the "Russians"! Always, it's the Russians. Why don't we go after them and not waste our time with this stupid boy?'

Tippee dropped the hatchet and ran.

They waited for either Charlie or Adele to follow him, but oddly, neither did. Charlie put an arm around his wife. She rested her head on his shoulder. They huddled and muttered, their backs to the room, as the slap-slap of Tippee's feet against the Great Hall's marble floor slowly faded.

'Now what?' Egbert(Mr) said. He didn't usually need to ask. But on this occasion – there was so much going on, and so little of it was clear. 'We can't just let the boy run off, can we? Shouldn't someone be going after him? Poor little thing . . .'

Lady Tode said: 'I'm telling you. The boy did it. Why is no one calling the police?'

Leonardo said: 'You are wrong, girlfriend. WRONG. By chance, the little fellow performed his decapitation – if he says so, we must believe him. And yet nobody mentions the puncture in the neck. Riddle-me-that, slinky hips. If you will.'

Lady Tode tittered: confused, delighted, above all unable to come up with a satisfactory answer.

Ecgbert(Sir) turned to Alice. 'Leo makes a good point. What about the puncture . . . Did the Russians have any syringes in their luggage? Do we know? I mean to say – Trudy, Leo, Granny, Car Fizzy – you all had a pretty good rifle through their stuff. Did you see any syringes? Any peculiar-looking poisons or whatever? Did you?'

Nicola said: 'Pay no attention to Ecgbert. He's insane.'

'That's not very nice, Nicola,' said Alice. 'Especially when he was just sticking up for you. And no, he isn't insane – not even remotely. And no, Ecgbert, since you ask. As far as I'm concerned, there were not . . . any syringes or funny-looking poisons in the Rostovsky luggage . . . I'm not sure where that leaves us . . . Are we certain about the puncture?' She glanced at Leonardo da Vinci, famous for the painting whose name she couldn't remember, and for designing helicopters that were never built, and for writing backwards in little books, and also, of course, for having made the first anatomical drawings known to humankind. He was a man with a fine track record when it

286

came to looking at things thoroughly ... If he said he noticed punctures on both corpses, then there were punctures. 'Sorry,' she said. 'Of course there were punctures.'

'Correct,' said Leonardo.

And then Mr Carfizzi cleared his throat. 'While I was in the kitchen, washing the soup tureen,' he said, 'I took the liberty—'

The door opened again. Tippee, looking quite mad now, stalked into the room. Clutched in his hand he carried what looked like a small powder-blue washbag.

Not a washbag, in fact.

His mother saw it first. 'TIPPEE!' she cried.

Without a word, he slapped the bag onto the dining-room table.

His mother lunged forward to retrieve it – but Charlie's arm was still around her shoulders. She was, as previously mentioned, a woman of enormous strength, whose body might even have been made of metal; even so, Charlie's arm held her back just long enough for the dreaded Adele, finally, to show her symmetrical teeth. She bit him.

Lady Tode laughed.

As Tippee unzipped the little bag and emptied its contents onto the polished table, Charlie and Egbert(Mr), and then Ecgbert(Sir), Alice and Frederica all had to work together to hold her back. Adele hissed and kicked and spat. She fought like a wild cat. It was a most unsymmetrical scuffle.

There wasn't much in the bag. Some ultra-slim, deodorising panty-pads for people-who-menstruate ... And rolled inside the sweet-smelling panty-pads –

A plastic case containing a syringe, and four symmetrical vials.

'Ha!' cried Leo. 'I told you! You see?'

287

Adele stopped fighting. She stared at the vials. Symmetrical eyes a-goggle.

'What is it?' Charlie asked. 'Tippee, what are you doing? What's going on?'

Tippee said: 'It's insulin.'

'Because I'm *diabetic*,' whimpered Adele.

'Easy to get on the internet,' Tippee continued, 'lethal in sudden, large doses, and untraceable in a post-mortem. The perfect murder weapon. She takes it with her everywhere, don't you, Mummy? Just in case you feel like killing someone ... '

'Don't be ridiculous!' she said, regrouping a tiny bit. 'How *dare* you?'

'She's always killing people,' he continued. 'Anyone who threatens the perfect image she puts out to the world. That's right, isn't it, Mummy? It's amazing you haven't already murdered Charlie and me, seeing as how we keep messing up ... Charlie and his prostitutes –'

'Tippee!' (This from both parents.)

'– me and my hyper-activity, or whatever it is you've got me on the meds for. I don't even fucking know –'

'**TIPPEE!**' (This from Adele.)

'– but you can't get rid of us. Because without me and him, you wouldn't even have a brand to protect. One murdered "ape" and one "baby mouse" who topped itself ... '

'*TIPPEE!*' (This from everyone in the room; even Frederica, who hated children.)

Tippee ignored them all. 'If people knew the truth about you, they'd throw your stupid books in the bin ... They'd probably burn them.' His voice wavered. It was possible, just for a moment, that he was about to cry. He swallowed. *Breathed.* Turned to the room. 'She killed Piers and I saw her doing it.'

288

'No, you didn't,' she said.

'Yes. I did! You took him into the Russians' bedroom, because I saw you doing it. And you knew the room was empty, because we had just seen them leaving it, hadn't we, Mummy? And before you answer and start lying to everyone, I know what you were doing in there because I saw you.'

'Don't be silly.'

'I was there! I *spied* on you, Mummy.'

'No, you didn't.'

'You pretended it was *your* bedroom. You asked him in because you said you had a business proposition and you said you didn't want anyone to hear it . . . I heard you tell him to stay far away from Charlie.'

'Don't be ridiculous!'

'And he laughed at you. And he turned to go, because he didn't know what you're really like – nobody does – and you went up behind him and stabbed him in the neck with the syringe. *I saw it!*'

'. . . Crikey . . .' said Egbert(Mr).

'She killed that Italian girl . . . Elizabetta. In Rospo. I didn't see her doing it, but I know – I knew it then, because she's always killing people, and I was there when Elizabetta suddenly gave Charlie a kiss in the garden – Remember that, Charlie?'

Charlie said: 'Yes. No. I'm not sure . . . I'm not sure if I do. Don't call me Charlie.'

'. . . And Mummy was looking out the window, weren't you, Mummy?' He laughed. '. . . And then in the bar in Rome. *I* saw it when Charlie gave her the money. I *saw* him give her the money, so Mummy, *you did too*, even though you pretended not to.' Tippee shuddered in disgust. 'It was all *so* obvious.'

289

'Don't be so silly,' said the dreaded Adele. 'How dare you rifle through my belongings? Put that washbag back at once, and go to bed!'

But somewhere along the line, perhaps when he watched her sticking a needle into Piers' neck, she'd lost her authority over him. Tippee didn't pause. He barely heard her.

'She's *always* killing people!' he said again. 'She killed my first nanny. And I think she killed both my grannies. And I don't know who else she killed, but I'm pretty sure she killed my teacher, Mrs Rawlins, because Mrs Rawlins never came back after they had the fight about me and the medications, and then I found out she was dead . . . ' He turned to his mother. 'Did you?' he said. 'Did you kill Mrs Rawlins?'

'You're talking nonsense,' Adele replied.

He stared at her. 'I was there, Mummy. I *saw you killing Piers.*'

Alice listened to all this. *Poor, poor boy,* she thought. *What's to become of the poor lad, with that wicked mother and that vile, selfish father?* Nevertheless, one question remained. She said: 'I believe you, Tippee . . . '

'*E anche io!*' cried Leonardo, clapping his hands.

A wisp of green stink from Lady Tode. She hated to be wrong.

'Me too,' said Mad Sir Ecgbert. 'I believe you, Tippee. Well done for speaking up.'

' . . . But Tippee,' continued Alice, 'what made you think it was a good idea to cut off his head?'

Tippee inhaled. He seemed to think it was a stupid question. 'Well, I had to do something, didn't I?' he told her patiently. 'To get people to notice. No one ever listens to me. She keeps killing people, and they don't even realise it's murder. Except Charlie . . . maybe . . . Did you know? Did you know your wife was a killer?' He turned back to Alice. 'But he's never going to do anything about it. Even if he hates her, which he does. He likes the money. Right, Charlie?'

'Fuck you, Tippee,' Charlie said. 'And don't call me Charlie.'

Adele shuffled a little closer to her husband. He put the arm she'd just bitten around her shoulder. 'You need help, Tippee,' she said. 'You need locking up.'

Tippee shrugged. He said: 'Someone's got to stop her.' And that was it. He stopped speaking. He'd run out of things to say. He looked around the room.

The adults stared back at him dumbly.

'Hmmmm,' Egbert(Mr) said at last.

Silence.

And then, far off, faint at first but growing clearer and closer, the sound of sirens: lots of sirens. They were coming off the slip road and turning up the long drive.

Mr Carfizzi cleared his throat for a second time. 'While I was in the kitchen, washing the soup tureen,' he said again, 'I took the liberty of calling the police ... I am sorry. I felt that somebody needed to.' He looked at Tippee. 'We have about three minutes, young man, to get you out of the way ...'

'Mr Carfizzi!' Alice cried. 'What were you *thinking*? You should have warned us! Ecgbert, where can we hide him?'

'Holy cow!' cried India. 'Think, everyone! Think! Have we got a priest hole, Eggzie?'

'Unfortunately not,' replied Eggzie. 'Priest holes had gone out of fashion by the time Tode Hall was constructed. Surprisingly, construction on the house didn't actually begin until 1701. And of course the Gunpowder Plot of 1605 was at the centre of—'

'I know just the place,' said Ecgbert(Sir). 'They'll never find us. Give me the hatchet, Tippee . . . *Give it to me!*' Tippee didn't want to give it up. Ecgbert grabbed it from him, wiped it on his shirt and in a sudden, unexpected move, tossed it hard and fast at Adele.

Adele screamed. She caught it with both hands.

'Oh, I say, bravo!' cried Leonardo da Vinci, clapping in delight. 'Behold, Sir Ecgbert! *What a move!*'

Sir Ecgbert turned back to Tippee. 'Hurry up!' he said. 'Alice and Car Fizzy will take care of everything. Come with me.'

Alium Dime in Jukebox Pone

From: India Tode

To: AlgieB, Antonia(family), Arabella, Alex, Alexandra&Heck, ArchieC-S, Archie Roper, Archie Swan, Aiden McR, Avery S, Bella, Boo, and 419 more ...

Subject: Happy Christmas!!!!

Greetings, Superstars!

293

Hello!! I can hardly believe it's Christmas again already, it feels like summer was only last week but here we are! And *yes*, as you all probably heard (or have you been living under a rock?!) yet again it's been quite a year *chez* the Family Tode!

FIRST, though, our big news is that Ludo – brilliant, brilliant Ludo – passed his Grade 5 (yes, five!!!) in Cycling Proficiency and Road User Awareness in September. This is such an achievement and he has a super-proud Mummy and Daddy!!! He's also turning into a super little rider, as evidenced by the amazing array of rosettes he has pinned all over the tack-room walls! You read it here first!!! Meanwhile, much to our surprise, Passion has decided she wants to be a *fashion designer*!!! She marches about the place wearing all her mummy's clothes, and I must say, she has quite a talent for putting a 'look' together! Attagirl! Watch out, Stella McCartney!!!!

The other fab news is about Eggzie's gorgeous coz, Ecgbert, who most of you know, got himself hitched to an absolute 'top bird', in the form of our amazing Chief Organisational Officer, aka the lovely gorgeous Alice, who was his childhood sweetheart! SOOO romantic! Lucky for us, Alice and Ecgbert are deciding to stick around at Tode Hall, thank goodness, so nothing much has changed except now they have found each other! We had a super fun wedding party in the summer (one of our 'Highs!') but we kept it small, so sorry not to have invited most of you!!

On the subject of 'Highs', I think I can safely say we have had a 'highs-and-lows' year here at Tode Hall (or should I say, Tode Mad House!). A lot of 'highs', as you can see, and also a couple of 'lows', e.g. with the terrible passing of our dear friend and an old school chum of Eggzie, Piers Slayer-Wilson-Tite, who lots of you knew of course. I won't go into it too much, since it was all over the media outlets at the time.

I'm happy to say, however, that after all the gory headlines, at least justice has been done. It turns out Adele Tysedale is one very brave lady. As her legal-eagle team said, she was a victim of 'co-ersieve control', and I think we can all agree that despite outer appearance, what we learned from the court case was that Adele badly needed some TLC. Instead, what she got was a terrible childhood which involved a bullying father and a distant mother, and latterly also a terrible marriage. Luckily, the jury saw this and agreed she was basically innocent, despite having done it, so anyway they let her off, thereby leaving more space in our jails for the *real* baddies!!

Adele is going from strength to strength, so I understand, still living in Australia, where they have welcomed her with open arms, although with all the palava of her getting the correct 'health certificates' for Oz, as they are so pernickety about health certificates these days, she unfortunately forgot to take Tippee! All in all, we Todes think this is probably for the best.

Adele is busy writing a fab new book, so I understand, based on her childhood, her terrible marriage and so on, about surviving 'co-erseive control'. I read in the *Mail* that the book is called *SURVIVING*, which is more than poor old Piers managed to do, or the Italian girl at Rospo who she also probably killed though this is not proven (please don't sue me!!!!), also quite a few other people, if you believe her son, Tippee, and I must admit, personally speaking, I do lean that way, but never mind! 'Everything happens for a reason', as they say, and I am sure the book will be fab, and a real tearjerker.

In the meantime, her husband has gone seriously AWOL (unless any of you are hiding him in your attic?!!! Along with

Lord Lucan!!!! Sorry – I couldn't resist! Not that anyone's saying Charlie killed anyone obviously). Anyway, for the time being he is lying low, as everybody verbally abuses him on social media now they know what a 'co-erseive' hubby he was. Last seen a few months ago, as I read on my trusty Mail-on-Line he was fishing for fish in the Falkland Islands! Probably 'co-erseing' them too!! Anyway, good luck to the fish, is all I can say!!!!!!

A further piece of good news is about our friends 'the Russians'! I'm afraid we somewhat badmouthed them having misunderstood their intentions, after they disappeared with our sketches before the fateful dinner, and this, sadly, was reported in gory detail in that dirty rag, 'The Mail-on-Line', along with all the stuff about Piers' head being chopped off. However, the Rostovskys have since that time been in contact with us directly vis-à-vis said sketches, which they of course did not run off with intending to steal, as they knew they would not 'get away' with it in this day and age, what with DNA and micro technology and so on! They are actually very nice people, and very apologetic about the misunderstanding. They have returned the sketches, which they had on loan, in order to impress some very important guests they were having to stay at their palazzo in Lake Como – and yes, we are looking forward to an invite!! As I said to Putin when he called. Honestly, we have so much stuff to impress our guests here at Tode Hall, it would be rather mingy to refuse to lend them a few sketches, which incidentally Egbert took direct to Christie's, as soon as they were returned and they are not the orig, after all! And yes, I know what you are thinking! Egbert agrees with me they are exactly the same sketches as the ones they borrowed and not, as has been suggested, 'clever copies'!!! So – it was a storm in a teacup, thanks to the Mail-on-Lies! (LOL – I love it really!!!) Once again, all's well that ends well.

I don't want to dwell on the 'lows' but as you know poor little Tippee Tysedale has been 'through the mill' this year. Fortunately we Todes have all thrown our support behind him, along with Mr Carfizzi, also even his father, who stuck up for him during the trial, despite some very nasty accusations made by his mama, who was suffering from PTSD. As you probably heard, due to it being on the news, when Tippee finally came out of hiding, he was able to deny everything, as regards everything she said about him, which I certainly won't repeat on a Christmas round-robin!!!!

Literally *hundreds* of busy-bodies have been round, with their little clipboards, trying to drag him off to one of their dreadful orphanages or whatever, but so far, we Todes – mostly Ecgbert and Alice tbh – have kept them all at bay! Apparently – this is hilarious – they don't like coming out here any more because they say the place is 'haunted'!! You couldn't make it up!

Anyway, the best thing to have come out of all this is that Passion and Ludo have gained a new cousin! We are calling him a 'cousin' even though he isn't really a cousin, but he is a *fab* addition to the family, and after all he has been through, we love him dearly and more every day! Ecgbert and Alice are too old to have kids of their own, and also Alice already has three gorgeous triplets. But now that they have more or less adopted young Tippee, it's as if they have a bit of a 'family' situation going all of their own! Happy days!

So it's 'Happy Families' all round, here at Tode Hall!!

Wishing you and your gorgeous families the most sublime and utterly amazeballs Christmas!

PS Come and visit us in boring old rainy Yorkshire soon! We MISS YOU ALL!

Love from

Egbert, India, Passion, Ludo, Pepper the dog and not forgetting 'Cousin' Tippee!!!

XOXOXOXOXOXOXOXOXOXOXOXOXOXOXOXOXO

ACKNOWLEDGEMENTS

A million thanks to Anna Boatman and to everyone at Piatkus, especially Alison Tulett, Rebecca Sheppard and Kate Byrne. Thank you too, as always, to my agent, supportive through thick and thin, Clare Alexander. Thank you to all the people at the Gardens of Ninfa for their help and enthusiasm and for allowing me such generous access to the gardens while researching this novel. Thank you to Paola Frankopan in her official capacity as Ninfa's artistic promoter, and also for her friendship, generosity of spirit and all-round brilliance. Thank you to my incredible family and thank you, as always, to my old friend Immie, who always keeps it light, even when I'm muttering about blowing up newspapers and parliaments. Thank you!! And thank you to darling McLovin. Gone but never forgotten. And that's it. I was pretty gloomy while I was writing this book. I had to dig quite deep to find the funny side. (I did. Rest assured.) So, from this tiny corner, on behalf of the many millions around the world who felt the same way, I want to thank Novak Djokovic. Yep. He has been a beacon of courage (and humour) and grace – and hope – in some quite disappointing times. He's also the GOAT. Amen.